Salt and Silver

Salt and Silver

ANNA KATHERINE

TOR®

paranormal romance

A TOM DOHERTY ASSOCIATES BOOK
NEW YORK

SALT AND SILVER

Edited by Jozelle Khadine Gonzales Dyer

A Tor Book
Published by Tom Doherty Associates, LLC
175 Fifth Avenue
New York, NY 10010

www.tor-forge.com

Tor® is a registered trademark of Tom Doherty Associates, LLC.

ISBN-13: 978-0-7653-6304-6
ISBN-10: 0-7653-6304-6

First Edition: May 2009

Printed in the United States of America

0 9 8 7 6 5 4 3 2 1

Acknowledgments

The author would like to thank her resolutely fearless editor, Jozelle Dyer, for being resolutely fearless, and her agent, Diana Fox, for being a classy broad and a killer shark. However, the author's most pure and true love is for Tor's mass market art director, Seth Lerner (and the Seal of Solomon).

For more information on the myths, legends, folklore, and magics found in the book, as well as some of the famous recipes from Sally's Diner, please visit www.annakatherine.com.

après moi, le déluge

"Rocks, Caves, Lakes, Fens, Bogs, Dens, and shades of
death, a Universe of death."
—MILTON

Salt and Silver

1

This is not a long or a complicated story. There's a Door to Hell in the basement of my diner, right next to where we stack the boxes from food deliveries. It's really annoying; there's always mystical crap coming out, and then Ryan smashes everything up trying to get rid of said mystical crap. Blood gets everywhere, lots of demon guts, lots of salt circles and painted sigils. *And* I put all the replacement food and equipment on my credit card, so you can see how this gets tedious.

Not that I necessarily mind having Ryan around—he's a demon hunter. A guy with big, weird weapons, dark eyes, and stubble. Leather pants, leather duster, beat-up black T-shirt, and a big black cowboy hat he has very carefully explained is a Stetson and not, *ahem,* "a cowboy hat." In a word: *hot.*

In daylight, on the street, he looks like a poker player coming out of an all-night game, where the stakes were high and the players were rough and he doesn't quite remember that normal people don't generally try to hide their thoughts behind a blank face and lowered hat brim.

I don't usually see him on the street, though. It's always under the fluorescents in the diner kitchen, or under the bare lightbulbs of the basement. Ryan and sunshine and me don't seem to mix. Forget the poker player thing; to me, he always looks like he's just finished fighting a war. He hasn't, though—finished fighting, I mean. I guess he can't.

Ryan's got a cot in the basement—he has had for the last six years, ever since the Door was opened. (Okay, true confession time: Ever since *I* opened the Door, me and my two best friends. And yes, it was really, really dumb. We have gotten the lecture, read the pamphlet, and sat through the after-school special. We know.)

Anyway. Ryan's almost *always* near the Door. Sometimes, if a demon gets past him, he'll leave to hunt it down. And sometimes he just goes out to, I don't know, pick up his mail or something. I get kind of nervous those times, though—worried that one day I'm going to go into the basement to get, like, more rice or something, when he isn't guarding the Door, and end up vamped. Or eaten by a zombie. Or slimed on by a sludge demon.

Look, you never know.

And it's not as if I'm getting any perks by Ryan being around (aside from not being dead, I mean). I tried that once—okay, more than once; it was late, I was drunk, and we'd just met over the corpse of something that bled yellow—and he wasn't interested. Which was fine. Probably better, come to think of it. Ryan, for all that he's hot, is also a jerk.

And I'm not just saying that because he turned me down. Much.

I'm not much to look at, I guess. I can see that every day, when I look at Amanda. She's been my friend since before Mom ran off with her tennis instructor and, coincidentally, with the contents of the family coffers. It was Amanda who actually stuck around and let my father and me sleep in her family's pool house, got me out of bed in the mornings, and bullied the hell out of me until I got a job at Sally's Diner. She was even supportive when I *kept* working at Sally's, even though Amanda and I are from Long Island and Sally's is in Brooklyn. (If you're not from New York, stuff like that doesn't matter, but New Yorkers know it is a fight to the death between Long Island and Brooklyn.)

On the other hand, the problem with Amanda is— well, she has a lot of problems. Her biggest one, I guess, is that she's a crazy alcoholic who spends a lot of time having sex with inappropriate men to make up for whatever emotional problems come along with having too much money and not enough hobbies. Ryan probably falls into the realm of inappropriate men, and he wouldn't be the first to pass over me to settle on her. Even when she looks like trash, she looks classy. If she had perfect bow lips, she'd actually look a little like Greta Garbo, because she's very pointy; she doesn't, though. She's pointy and her lips are wide and plump. I kind of envy her lips. She doesn't appreciate them.

I don't actually know if Amanda's slept with Ryan. Now, if Stan had gotten down with Ryan, *that* I would have known about. He's the only other one who stuck around through the Great Depression of Me. The big problem with Stan, aside from how almost everyone he knows calls him Stan even though his name is Charles, is that he went from being a cute, nerdy, skateboarding geek to being a club kid. Like, he realized he was gay and bam! Or maybe he just watched too much *Queer as Folk* and thought that was really how gay men were supposed to be because he didn't know any better. So he spends a lot of time, like Amanda, having too much sex with people—except with Stan, I guess it's because he's making up for lost time. And also to find people who won't call him Stan, which makes sense. The club guys who give him blowjobs in alleys call him Dish.

That doesn't really bother me except for, you know, AIDS, and also that maybe one of those guys is Ryan. Except Stan swears not, and Stan wouldn't lie about that. So that leaves Ryan: tall, dark, handsome, leather-wearing Ryan, apparently surrounded by people who'd happily jump him, and *still* finding the Door to Hell a lot more interesting.

Here are some important facts about the Door. One: It was Amanda's idea to open it, not mine. Two: It was a joke. We didn't even realize we were opening a Door into Hell, because we were super-drunk at the time, and, seriously, joking around. Now that I know what Doors do and how they work . . . well, I never wanted something so bad that I'd open a Door for it. Because three: The reason anyone would *want* to open a Door to Hell in the first place—with the death, and the blood, and the bioluminescent goo that you can't actually ever clean off the floor no matter how harsh the chemicals or how many black cats you drive across the stain (and that's a fun story)—the reason you *do* it is because the Door . . . gives you things.

I don't know what Amanda gets, or Stan. I barely know what I get. I just know I'm happier now than I was before the Door and Ryan showed up in my life. It doesn't say much about my life before the Door that probable death is a step up.

Not that I'd open one again, or would have the first time, if I actually knew then what I know now. Ryan says that Doors, like the one in the basement, lead to nine hells—or hell dimensions, or just dimensions, it depends on who's talking and how much they've had to drink, and did I mention that there might be more than nine, or less, or maybe pi?—and when a Door is opened, demons try to get through them.

Hunters wait on the other side.

Sometimes not, though. They're there when a demon goes through a Door they're watching, but they can't be everywhere.

What this means *now* is that when someone pounds on the diner's metal grate, I wake up. Usually it's someone pounding at four or five in the morning—either right after I go to sleep, or right before I am supposed to wake up. I always think, for a brief second, that it's demons knocking down my bedroom door—but it's usually Stan wanting to sleep off a good time, or Amanda wanting to steal my pillows and ice cream and bitch about her parents. It's never someone telling me I've won a million dollars.

Tonight it's—Ryan? Last I saw him, he was waving goodnight as he headed into the basement. Now Ryan is waving his Stetson at me from the street below. I open the window and lean out.

"What are you doing? It's four in the morning!" I holler, with no regard for the neighbors.

"There's an animal problem!" he hollers back. He's got a nice twang in his voice, which gives me a nice twang in my belly. I sigh. Animal problem is code for werewolf.

"Then fix it!" I tell him.

"Lemme in, Allie!"

"Not if there's still an animal problem!"

"Now!" He hits his Stetson against his thigh. I can't really see his face—the moon isn't quite full and he's standing in the one tiny bit of shadow between the floodlights—but if I had to bet, I'd say he looks annoyed. And frankly, if he's going to keep yelling shit, the neighbors are going to call the cops. Again. So I pull on a robe and trudge downstairs to let him in through the side door.

"Ry." I greet him with a yawn. "What happened to your key?"

He ignores me. "The Door must've opened, because I ran into a werewolf on my way here," he says to me, and strides right past me into the back of the diner, coat flapping and everything.

"Sure it did," I say to the door as I close it. "And I'm happy to make a pot of coffee and stay up for the rest of the night and get no sleep and do everything and go everywhere and—"

"Stop bitching. I thought I trained you better than to let a werewolf get out of the Door." When I catch up to him, he's staring down at the line of table salt running in front of the basement door. He won't find any breaks in it, though—I handle foodstuffs for a living in a litigious society, I am *careful*.

Wait a sec. "How was I supposed to know you'd gone off?" I cross my arms over my chest. "Aren't you the one who's supposed to let me know when I have to guard the Door? When the mighty hunter has to go wander the fecund plains for shaving gel—"

"Quiet," he says, and pulls out his sawed-off shotgun from whatever magic pockets exist in his coat. The shotgun's shiny, and about a million years old. He doesn't shoot regular shells with it—just rock salt and iron buckshot. About a month ago we spent an entire afternoon sitting in a booth in the front reloading shotgun shells and telling bad jokes. He looked happy, and I guess that made me happy too. You know. If I cared.

He doesn't look happy now.

He pushes open the basement door slowly, and steps over the salt, gun barrel first. He goes past the door and into the dark and then—I hear a sharp intake of breath. Followed by a load of quiet speech in a language I can't even *identify*.

"Allie," Ryan says from inside. "What the hell did you do."

It's not a question, which is not even remotely reassuring. I squint hard and scoot over the salt, prepping for the sound of the Door.

"It can't talk to you." Ryan's leaning against the wall, his shotgun dangling from one hand. I guess this means I'm not likely to die from demons just this second. And wow, he looks good leaning there.

While my sleep-deprived brain is thinking things it shouldn't, he finishes: "Because it's not here."

It takes me a second to focus on what he's saying, and then—

No. No way. I look around. There's this week's food, and there's the big stain, and there are the scratches in the shape of Italy. There are the wire racks and the crates of bottled drinks and the rubber mat with all the soda water canisters for the machine upstairs. There's Ryan's camping cot pushed against the cement block wall. And right beside the cot, outlined in another half-circle of salt and with the weirdest stains splashed around it . . . there is just the basement wall.

Ryan exits behind me, though I don't notice it right away. I think for a second he's gone out the front grate, for wherever demon hunters go when they suddenly don't have a Door to guard anymore, and then I can't breathe—but he's sitting in the booth closest to the kitchen, with his feet up on one of the green vinyl chairs he's pulled over. His eyes are closed and there's a smudge of something on one of his cheeks. It looks like a bruise, but when I get closer, I realize it's blood. Dark, dried blood.

"Hey," I say softly, and he doesn't acknowledge me. He's either sleeping or thinking. Should he be asleep with the Door gone? I hope he's sleeping, anyway, because he looks exhausted. His eyelids are black spots in his face, and his stubble is stubblier than usual, almost a beard already, and he smells like blood—but not human blood. Not all of it anyway.

Human blood has a certain scent. It smells the way pennies taste when you put them in your mouth. When you've got a Door in your basement, you learn pretty quickly what human blood smells like, because there's usually a lot of it all over the floor. Sally's—that's the name of the diner, after the little old lady who actually owns the place—has been lucky so far. No one who has died here has caused any kind of ruckus, so no cops have ever come looking.

So far.

I start some coffee. When it's ready, I fix myself a cup, set it on the counter, and bring a cup and the carafe out for him. I go to put it down in front of him, but, I mean, should I? Will that wake him? Damn. I step back, but before I can get too far his hand snaps out, grabs the cup, and then sets it down to go for the carafe too—all with his eyes closed. I am impressed, even though I almost poured the thing all over him. Which is what he deserves for being *startling*. I guess this means I don't have to worry about waking him, then. I head back to the counter to pick up my cup, and sit across from him with it to wait.

In the light streaming out from the kitchen, he looks young; like he's heading toward thirty, a little older than me (okay, shh, I *am* almost thirty). Ryan doesn't say it, but I've got to wonder if that's getting up there for a demon hunter. I've seen him do things that would tax a triathlete, let alone some grizzled old-timer.

I've met a lot of demon hunters. They're usually in their early twenties. Demon hunting isn't a profession with a health insurance plan or a 401K, if you know what I mean. These guys don't last very long—most of them. I've seen older ones and I've seen younger ones. Ryan's getting up to the age of some of the older ones.

Most of the older ones are retired; most of them sit around and tell stories about their glory days, and they're founts of knowledge about obscure bullshit, but they don't fight anymore. They're missing eyes, hands, legs. One is missing his heart, literally, and he's kept alive by some crazy voodoo magic that I don't understand and he won't talk about.

His name is Dougal, and he always takes a seat by the front door; he says he likes the bell I've put up there. Some of the hunters who come in like to sit in one of the four booths next to the front windows, and they always have their Stetsons off and their faces toward the sun. I've got one guy who sits at the counter and doesn't say anything at all. The only reason I know he's a hunter at all is because of the hat—I thought he was a homeless guy for the longest time, before I clued in to the dress code.

I asked Ryan about Homeless Guy once—Ryan always sits in the booth by the swinging kitchen door

when he sits out front at all, and he watches the crowd—
and all Ryan would say is that if Homeless Guy ever
actually came out and told any of us his story, it'd be
time to cut our losses and run.

2

I'm asleep. In my dreams I'm being chased by a werewolf. Whatever you've read, they're not sexy. They're not seductive. They are scary as Hell—literally. They are demons that come out of their Hell dimension and into our Earth dimension, and take over the body of their victim through a bite. They start out huge, and then make themselves so small that they can wriggle in through the skin. They are like ticks, and they get so buried inside you that you can't get them out. Ever.

The only cure for being bitten by a werewolf is death. If you're lucky, someone will kill you quickly, before you start to feast on your younger sister or your boyfriend. If you're not lucky, by the time you're dead, you've gone on a killing spree and you're being hailed as a particularly hairy, strange-looking serial killer.

I'm trapped in a corner, and there's no way out, and then—then there's Ryan, saying my name and touching my shoulder. We could be fighting back to back and pushing the werewolves away, but really he's just waking me up.

"Allie," he says again, and this time he doesn't sound like he's saving me from the werewolves. He sounds like he smoked two packs of cigarettes last night, and is annoyed. "Allie, you need to tell me what you did to the Door."

I blink at him. He's sideways, because my head is on the table. Whoops. "I'm awake?"

"You're awake," he confirms. "Tell me. And make me more coffee."

"Some women might think the jackass thing is pretty sexy, because it makes you seem like a mysterious enigma with a murky past, but I know better." I lever myself up and step into the kitchen.

He's not a jackass, though, because he cleaned all the blood and crap off the chair he'd had his feet on, *and* he pulled all the chairs off the tables in the middle of the diner, setting everything up for opening. Even the blinds are opened, and dawn's beginning to stain the streets outside that weird shaded blue that I've only seen in New York City.

"The Door. What did you do to it?" He's standing right behind me. In my head, he comes up and slides his arms around my waist. Damn the demon blood, damn the human blood—he's got nice arms.

Anyway, it doesn't matter, because he's only behind

me to try to intimidate me, not because he really wants to get into my worn-out Winnie the Pooh sleep shorts.

The coffee machine isn't that complicated. I just dump in the grounds and turn it on. I lean against the counter and peer sideways at the clock on the wall. Six AM. It's actually time to start prepping for the breakfast crowd.

"I didn't do anything," I say as the water gurgles. I don't like the silence behind me. To fill the silence, I open the cold hold and pull out onions and peppers to dice. The breakfast potatoes have already been parboiled, and are waiting in one of the giant industrial fridges to be dumped onto the grill with the peppers and onions. "I don't know what happened."

His breath huffs out. I want to scrub at my neck to stop the tingling but instead I pick up one of my knives. It's the really nice one, with the hollow blade. It's a bit much for dicing, but I need the comfort of the expensive grip in my hand. Sally gave it to me as a going-away present when she moved to Florida; that and management of the diner.

"It didn't go away on its own," he says.

"Yeah? How do you know?"

He doesn't say anything. It is a heavy sort of not saying anything, the kind that sounds more like *I don't know* instead of the usual *My hunter secrets are too awesome for your comprehension.* I almost feel smug for scoring one off him, but . . .

Ryan usually knows *everything*—just as much as the old-timers, if not more. He can talk easily of ancient Sumerian demons, quote the Christian Bible, quote the Demonic Bible, and explain the origins of the vampire myths all in one breath. He's amazing, and impressive, and that he might possibly not know what's going on? That scares the shit out of me.

"I've got to go," he finally says.

I'm almost done dicing; the potatoes can be ready in minutes. So can pancakes, eggs, waffles—just about anything. "I think breakfast would be a better idea." I turn around to face him, knife in hand. "Waffles? Pancakes? Eggs?"

"I don't have time for breakfast."

"Then I don't have time to pour you more coffee."

"Brat," he says, and sounds almost affectionate.

"Shut up," I reply, but I'm only pretending to be affronted. Affection is one step closer to pure and true lust. Okay, maybe not, but I worry a lot that Ryan finds me incredibly annoying, because I am so helpless when it comes to so much of the demon hunting.

"I wonder if you accidentally did something, or if this is endemic," says Ryan contemplatively. I pour myself a cup of the coffee and he glares at me, and takes it right out of my hand. He drinks it black. He didn't used to drink it black; when he first came to Sally's to guard the Door, he dumped in so much crap that it was almost like coffee-flavored sugar and cream. But I make damn good coffee.

"Is endemic bad?" I ask.

He blinks at me. "Yes," he says, and goes back to drinking my cup of coffee.

I roll my eyes. "If you're going to stand around and accuse me of things, you're going to eat breakfast. *I* am going to eat breakfast," I amend, and cross the room to turn on the grill. I should have heated it before, but I was distracted by Ryan boring a hole in my neck with his smoldering glare.

Okay, so I am prone to melodrama. Sue me.

"There are more Doors in Brooklyn," he says between sips of coffee. "I think the closest one to here is at Maimonides Hospital off Fort Hamilton Parkway."

"Wait, what? There's another Door near here? Do you watch that one too?" I am incredulous—and with good reason. Watching a Door is hard work. Ryan hardly ever leaves here. I can't imagine that he ever has time to watch another Door, much less the energy. Not to mention that . . . well, in the years that the Door has been open, he's never mentioned any of the others.

I guess I knew they existed in an abstract way, but I didn't realize that there was one twenty minutes away.

"No. Owen does."

"Who the hell is Owen?"

"He's a hunter." Clearly not one who's come by

looking for free food. I know all of them by name. "And a paramedic," Ryan continues. "The junkies love him."

I bet this is because all hunters—young hunters, anyway—are sexy. That's my new theory. It would give them a natural defense against really gross stuff—you can't be gross and be sexy at the same time, I'm pretty sure.

Oh, maybe he's better looking than Ryan. Are paramedics likely not to be jerks? Good question. Until I find out, though, I'm officially off my Ryan kick. Cold turkey, baby.

"You should invite him over some time," I say in a way that is not at all suspicious-sounding.

Ryan glares at me. "Not going to happen," he says shortly. A moment passes, and he frowns down at his coffee. "Not that it matters, though. Ask him yourself. Unless he actually answers his phone, you're coming with me."

I am? "I am?" I ask, because I am not one for thinking one thing and saying another. I mean, why bother? If I don't ask, how will people tell me what I want to know? That is logic.

Like now, for instance. Ryan nods, though he doesn't look happy about it. "I don't know what's happening. It's better if you stick with me." I am considering getting my hopes up. "I can always use you as a distraction if a demon shows up," he adds.

I slice the rest of the peppers with a lot more strength than really necessary. Stupid peppers.

I leave the diner in the care of the morning shift—I don't make them come in to prep, because I'm a nice person, but I figure that if I prep, I shouldn't have to work the early shift, with all the surly Williamsburg hipsters coming in for coffee and pancakes before work. Normally I'd be going back to sleep for a couple more hours before I wake up and take the afternoon and evening shifts. Sometimes I wait tables, sometimes I cook, sometimes I run the register—I do whatever needs to be done.

But today I get to run around with Ryan on just a few hours' sleep. Not even run around.

"We have to take the *bus*?" I moan.

"It's that or we go all the way into Manhattan to switch to the D train to get to the hospital."

"I don't want to go to the hospital," I grouch. But really I do, because I want to meet this unknown hunter. I just don't want to take the bus. New York buses are slow, and they smell, and most of the time there are no seats. Plus we're going to have to *transfer*. It means a lot of waiting around, making awkward conversation with Ryan, all because Ryan can't get this guy on the phone.

"I did get him on the phone, but he hung up," says Ryan, shrugging, as we stand in the sun. I'm squinting, because I didn't bring sunglasses. He's got his Stetson on, as usual, and that leather coat. He's leaning against a lamppost. I know he's got weapons, but none of them are showing. Which is good, I guess, because I'm not sure he has a license. Do you need a license for guns in New York? I do not even know. Ryan and I have never actually hung out outside the diner together, so I don't really know if I should be keeping an eye out for the cops or whatever. It is seriously distracting.

"Wait," I say, "why? Were you a jerk? Did you not give the secret hunter codeword or something?"

"Factions," Ryan tells me, like I should have known this already.

"Listen," I say, in what I think is a totally reasonable manner. "You never tell me anything. How am I supposed to know if you never tell me? Bitch."

Ryan snorts. He must be sweltering in his leather gear, but he looks totally cool, like nothing can get to him. He's not even sweating, even though I think I should've reconsidered my clothing choices—jeans? what?—and I can see an easy dozen air conditioners up and down the street practically running water. Ryan just tips his hat back slightly and says, "You never noticed that all the hunters who come into Sally's wear Stetsons?"

"Yes, but—" I never knew it mattered. Instead I noticed that they are all scrupulously polite and treat me like a stupid mundane, and stop whatever they're saying when I come by and start telling elaborate stories about demons they've fought and killed—most of which, Ryan says, are bullshit.

"There are three factions." Ryan stops and nods politely at a passing elderly couple, and I am this close to tapping my foot before he decides they've wandered far enough away to start up again. "Some hunters wear Baseball Caps. Some wear Fedoras. And some wear Stetsons. It has to do with some Scientologists and a loa—" Ryan breaks off—again. This time it's a girl who's wandered up to the bus stop. She's wearing white capri pants, a white halter top, and orange high-heeled shoes with open toes. Her handbag is purple and, seriously, bedazzled. Like, with a BeDazzler, I am pretty sure.

Hipster. She's probably got a trust fund. I used to have a trust fund, before my mother ran away with her tennis instructor. (His name is Rio. They went to Rio. It's a whole thing that I try not to think about—ever since the Great Depressive Episode, I've realized that repression is my friend.)

"And that's why I like the Brooklyn Cyclones instead of the Mets," says Ryan quickly. I have no idea what he's talking about, but hipster girl opens her eyes wide. Uh-oh, time for flirting. It's like his automatic *I am mundane!* defense. He does it in the diner all the damn time. I sigh as she starts talking about baseball.

Ryan smiles more at her in the ten minutes we wait for the bus to come than he's smiled at me in the last few months.

At least there are seats on the bus. Hipster-girl stays on the street, looking miffed. Small mercies. Ryan stands, because that is the Way of the Mighty Badass Hunter, but I slump into one of the seats near him. I don't do very well on no sleep.

As we bump along the streets of Brooklyn, I stare out the window and worry. That is the Way of the Allie.

The girl and his stupid defense flirting. Is that how the other hunters see me? Is that how Owen will see me? What if, actually, I'm just some annoying mundane Ryan's bringing along? What if he's actually breaking all sorts of secret hunter rules? If that's the case, okay, he should be a lot less susceptible to my whining, but what if I lose him his *job*?

Unlikely, but whatever, I am not a new-people person and I don't deal with my issues well.

The bus lights flicker, with those sparks you sometimes get popping up in the window opposite me. They're kind of pretty. I look away from them for a second, and that's how I catch the girl across from me staring at Ryan. Ryan's standing next to me, looking from beneath his hat brim with some middle-distance, thousand-yard-stare type thing that is probably just him reading the Spanish cartoons along the ceiling, but whatever. This girl's checking him out. That's two in one day.

I am not territorial. Not not not.

I squidge down in my seat and stretch my leg out so my calf rubs his. Or hits his—it's tough to get that quite right when the bus is likely to take a sudden turn like, oh, now. But that doesn't matter, because he's looking down at me with a really interesting look on his face, one I can't quite read, and he's shifting on his feet but not, I notice, away from me.

I take a really brief moment to look at the girl— she's pouting. Ha. Take that, sulky-faced blonde girl.

Ryan catches me and my maybe-inappropriate level of smugness. He rolls his eyes and steps away.

Two buses later, and we're at the hospital. I've never been here before, but it looks like the hospitals I *have* been to. Except busy—kind of stuffed, actually. Ryan just walks through the lobby like he belongs there, past the security and the nurses and a lot of sick people who only bother to glare at me in a halfhearted way. Past the lobby there are somehow more people, doctors and nurses, and gurneys lining the halls, and I am starting to wonder if maybe we are getting in the way.

I've never been to Maimonides, because Ryan's got a stoic, anti-doctor thing happening. We've been lucky, so far—mostly the times I've had to patch him up, he's needed weird things done, like his wounds packed with rosemary and sage, or I have to use a soldering iron to melt spelled silver into a cut made by a werewolf claw. Luckily that was only a few times, because I'm not very good with the soldering iron. My hands shake.

Mostly he does his own medical stuff. He's never been hurt so badly that I've had to take him to the hospital. And for that I am grateful to whatever thing is out there that is the opposite of the Hell inside the Door.

It takes me a minute to realize Ryan's keeping an eye out for signs—he pauses at a corner and then takes a left to what must be the cafeteria. There are a ton of people there, too, families eating weird food for the hour, doctors turning book pages with one hand and eating mechanically with the other, and a couple of EMTs with crusty uniforms. One of the EMTs is just reaching a chair at an empty table, and Ryan heads for him.

Owen, if that's who this is, isn't hot like Ryan, and that's a disappointment. What he is is big and rosy cheeked. Before he sees us bearing down on him, he calls out something to the next table over, where some off-duty nurses are sitting, and I hear his accent—he's got a total cheerful British thing going on. He's also taller than Ryan, which is just weird. He's wearing the dark blue uniform, though, which is kind of attractive, if you have a thing for uniforms. I don't, not really, but I can see how he could be getting a lot of play. His name tag says "David" on it, but all hunters have a name thing. He's also wearing a dark blue baseball cap, and I wonder if it's really as meaningful as Ryan tried to make it sound earlier.

He's just pulled out his chair when he sees us coming. His face clouds, and he pushes his chair in again. He doesn't make idle conversation, just like Ryan never does—he doesn't even say hello or introduce himself. He jerks his head back toward the hallway, then leads us into a small room next to a nurse's station. "This is where the interns sleep when they do overnights," he explains briefly. "It'll probably be empty for the next few minutes at least; there was a four-car accident on the Belt Parkway."

Ryan clears his throat. Owen immediately looks pissed. "Listen," he says, and suddenly his cheerful accent is harsh and mean. "I have a *job,* and I don't have to talk to you, Stetson. So either tell me what you want or get the hell out of my bloody hospital."

I snicker. He's got a book of crosswords in one hand and a Styrofoam cup of coffee in the other.

But I do not blame him for being annoyed—Ryan showing up is never really a good sign.

"I need to see your Door," Ryan says, because he is all that is suave and tactful.

"Too bad."

"Hi," I say really cheerfully, because I am crap at keeping out of things and I can tell this situation isn't going to get any better. Anyway, aren't I supposed to be a distraction? Totally fits. "My name's Allie. I run a diner across town. You should come, we have great coffee. Was your Door summoned or was it a spontaneous vivification? I could bring you pie, if you want."

Owen blinks at me, and smiles slowly. "You idiot," he says, which I worry is about me until: "You use the Door to impress girls now?" He winks at me, and then I sort of want to kill him for suddenly turning skeezy. "Never trust a guy with a Stetson," he tells me. "They're not the steady kind."

This annoys me. I don't want to be dragged into the middle of some stupid feud about a Scientologist and a loa. Not only that, but insulting Ryan is not the way to my heart.

"There's a problem. A real one," replies Ryan impatiently. "Is your Door still here?"

Owen's smirk drops off. Now he looks like a guy that you'd expect to see bent over you in an ambulance. Tired, and not as reassuring as he's trying to be. "Yes," he says. "Is there a reason it shouldn't be?"

"Are you sure?"

Owen downs the last of his coffee, tosses the cup into the trash, and leaves the crossword book on the gurney.

Some intern had clearly just been sleeping there not too long ago, because there's still an indentation in the pillow from someone's head.

"Come on," he says. "We need to go to Laundry."

3

There are three ways for demons to come into the world. The way that doesn't involve a Door is when one is simply born among us. (What, you thought *The Omen* was just a movie?) At the right time, and in the right place, cats that jump over cradles can turn babies into vampires. Hungry men can become wendigos, found covered in their family's blood. A walk into a banyan tree can get somebody possessed by a demon with no face. (And, okay, for that last one, the banyan tree has to be in Guam, but you get the idea.)

The second way is when a regular door or opening or whatever goes through spontaneous vivification. That's when it just sparks to life on its own for some stupid occult reason; like the "born into it" way, it's just something in the right place and at the right time—and in this case, the right shape. Those Doors are tough to spot, Ryan says. If a hunter doesn't get to them fast enough, the bodies start piling up, and then it's Hell getting anybody past the police on scene.

Finally, there's my favorite option for bringing demons into the world: Some drunk idiots think they're making up magic spells and, it turns out, they really are.

A lot of vodka, my first tipped dollar from my first diner customer crumpled in the center of a chalk outline, and a shitty attempt to remember lines from *The Craft*. That's what it was. Until the earth shook and a portal opened up in the wall of the fucking diner.

And it spoke.

Ten minutes later, with a lot of crashing noises, there he was, a man in a long black coat, looking like death, breaking through the basement door with a sword in one hand and a gun in the other.

After a bunch of killing and a lot of salt, Ryan, in his delightful way that is somehow terse and sarcastic at the same time, explained the world: Demons are real. Other dimensions are real. He added something nasty about string theory in there, but I was too drunk for that.

The Door I'm looking at now is probably a spontaneous one. I say this because nobody with any hint of gothic drama in their soul would go to the effort of opening a Door in an industrial washing machine.

"I try to keep the nurses from putting anything in there—it just feeds it," Owen's saying. This Door is just swirls of purple and green, like a bruise. The laundry room is deafeningly loud, ten dryers on high, seven giant washing machines chugging along, and the air is muggy and smells like bleach and old people and tears. The lights are bright, and the walls are stacked with pastel sheets, blankets, scrubs, and gowns. Next to Owen is a bright red bucket labeled For Emergency Use Only; I'm pretty sure it's filled with salt.

In the middle of all this stupid weird normality, there's this one machine with an "Out of Service" sign taped on and a small porthole to Hell behind its metal hatch.

A pretty porthole to Hell. "My Door doesn't look like that," I murmur, and reach my hand out. Ryan's quick—he slaps my hand, hard, and it stings, and I snap out of the weird daze I'm in.

"My Door doesn't look like that," I repeat louder, ignoring that I almost *touched* a *Door to Hell*. Am I stupid? Possibly.

Owen either doesn't notice, or is actually polite enough not to call me on it. "What's your Door look like?" asks Owen curiously.

"I thought they all looked the same." I direct this statement to Ryan, who shakes his head a little.

"Most of them do. Some of them don't."

"Very helpful." I turn to Owen. "My Door is a big portal. It's got an arch at the top, maybe a foot wide, made out of stone. The bottom's stone too, a full doorway, and it looks like maybe you could step on it a little without actually going into Hell. Right after is a wrought-iron gate. Or, um, hands. One or the other. They unclasp when the Door opens to spit out demons."

"Wrought-iron hands?" asks Owen skeptically. He crosses his arms and leans beside the washing machine Door. His uniform shirt stretches nicely over his biceps, but I pretend I don't notice. I'm still pissed that he was taking shots at Ryan earlier; only I'm allowed to do that.

"Allie was a goth as a teenager," says Ryan dryly.

Nothing could be further from the truth. I was a pathetic mall rat when I was a teenager, with too much money and too little fashion sense. I had a yellow leather jacket and six pairs of the same high-heeled shoe, each in a different color. And most of the time, my manicure matched my shoes, and my shoes matched my handbag.

Not that Ryan would know that, I guess. When we talk, we talk about the Door, and demons, and what I should ask the day cook to add to the menu for the next week. Not about ourselves. Still. Where'd he get the idea that I was goth?

Maybe it was the summoning Doors to Hell thing. I bet that is it.

"So." Owen lifts a shoulder, then lets it drop. "I don't know what to tell you guys. It's here."

"You can tell us why it's swirling like that. And why it doesn't talk," I say. It's weird, but . . . my ears itch, deep down. Like maybe the Door is trying to talk to me, but can't. I bet I could hear it if I just got closer, though.

"This Door never talks. It doesn't give us anything either, although sometimes people live who really shouldn't." Shouldn't because they're too messed up, or shouldn't because they're bad? Owen sounds like each word is being drawn out of him slowly and painfully. And I'm drifting closer and closer to the Door. It smells—it smells *purple*. What does that *mean*?

And before Ryan can stop me, I reach out a hand again and touch the Door, touch the swirling purple and green, touch its bruise.

There's screaming in my head, shrieks of rage and pain. I feel arms around my waist, pulling me back, but I want to go through the Door. I want to crawl inside and curl up in the purple. It's so *lonely*. But the arms pull me inexorably back until I'm cold and sad and crying.

"Let me go," I say, and I can hear it: I sound hysterical. "Let me *go!*"

I'm thrown to the floor, and I hear noises above me. When I open my eyes, Ryan and Owen are standing over me, and Owen is pouring salt over my head from the bucket by the Door.

"Let me go," I sob. "It's so lonely."

"You idiot," snarls Ryan. "You fucking idiot."

"That was pretty bloody stupid," says Owen, but he

reaches out a hand to help me up. I don't take it, because there's a whisper in my head. *Don't touch him.*

"I won't, I won't, I won't," I say out loud. I'm feeling stupider and stupider the more salt Owen dumps onto me. How much salt can a bucket hold, anyway? Breathing is easier, and my tears are drying up. When I look over at the Door, the door of the washing machine is shut, and I can't see the purples and greens anymore.

I brush salt out of my hair and push myself up. The world spins and I think I'm going to puke. "Maybe I ought to lie back down." And I do, slowly and carefully.

Maybe you shouldn't touch fucking Doors into Hell. I know that whisper. That's Ryan. I look over at him. His mouth is set into a grim line.

"I didn't mean to touch it," I say. "It made me."

"I—" Ryan starts, and then finishes with, *Can you hear this?*

"Yes." I close my eyes to try to stop the spins, and my whole body starts shaking.

Then, out loud, Ryan says, "Did you hear *that*?"

"No . . ." I open my eyes again. The nausea is receding.

"Probably just a side effect of touching the Door," says Owen dismissively. I like him less and less every second.

"It *made me*," I insist.

Ryan looks at me evenly. He doesn't *look* like he's

pissed off, but he's so damn stoic. He could have just eaten six babies and a seventh for dessert for all I know.

"We'll talk about this later," he finally says. I pull my knees up and drop my head between them, taking deep breaths, while he turns to Owen. "Thank you for showing us your Door," he intones. I guess this is a ritual sentence they have to say. I don't know. Hunters are weird.

"You're welcome," Owen says in the same voice, then, "It's never done that before," under his breath, like I wouldn't be able to hear him. "I've never been pulled to it."

"Well, Allie's special," Ryan says. I would punch him, but I'm still having trouble breathing.

"Are we leaving?" I ask. "Because I'd like to get away from here. No offense, Owen."

"None taken!" And the cheerful British accent is back, just like that. "I'll leave you two to it. You know Narnia's back in town, right?"

Ryan blinks. "No. But—"

Owen says, "Her usual place. And you, my lovely," he says to me, "owe me a pie." Then he turns around and just leaves without even saying good-bye. I watch him adjust his baseball cap on his way out. I can see why Ryan doesn't like hunters who wear baseball caps. Also, I will not bring him a nice pie. It will be peach. The peach pies are always mushy.

"Are you okay?" Ryan squats next to me.

"Would it matter if I said no?" I ask, my head still between my knees. I wish I wasn't wearing such tight jeans, but they were all that was clean.

"No," replies Ryan, and hauls me up by the arm.

Even with Ryan's arm holding me up, I'm staggering. I'm *exhausted*. And as we pass the washing machine that has the Door inside it, I can feel the pain again, the crying, the loneliness. I shudder.

I'm two for two now on the young-hunters-are-jerks theory, but Ryan's still the best looking one I've seen. As we make for the hospital exit, him glancing at signs and me stumbling along, I look at him very slyly from the side; his profile is all straight lines and sudden dips, the kind of contours you just want to lick. His face is slightly shadowed beneath his hat brim, and I feel the urge to flick his hat off and touch him.

Apparently I am not that sly. He looks at me from the corner of his eye, and smiles like he wasn't planning to.

God, I love that. He doesn't do it enough. That, and the fact that he's still holding my arm carefully, not letting me fall, his hand curled and warm, is enough for me. I guess I'll keep him. In my kind of wobbly state, this is a pretty big decision. I giggle.

But—

Some part of me, deep on the inside, shivers. Not in a good way. Something is happening.

Do you ever get a chill, just when you shouldn't, and a weird thought just sort of pops into your mind and you don't know why? Here is the thought I have just had, interrupting my stupid daydreams: This is an awfully empty hallway.

"Ry?"

I try to focus. The hallway is silent except for our footsteps, and instead of people I see doors, and doors, and black.

"Hmm?" That's not right. Ryan is . . . distracted? I mean, I'm awesome, but I have vast evidence to support that he is immune. So either I have been taken over by a succubus and am about to have the time of my life before I die by exploding (there was this one time that happened to a hunter trying to sneak a bottle of Snapple while Ryan and I were upstairs, and I got bloody water on my *face* when I was washing him off the basement ceiling), or there is something wrong.

"Are we still in the hospital?" I ask, because based on what I'm seeing this is starting to look like a legitimate question.

He blinks down at me, and turns, and looks—and then he carefully puts down my arm, and says, "Open the door next to you."

I really, really don't want him letting go of me. Almost more than I don't want to open the door. The safety glass window shows it to be a tiny kitchen, cabinets and the top of a coffeemaker in view. I grab hold of the edge of his coat—Ryan frowns but maybe he's glad to stick together too—and push down the handle.

The kitchen door swings out, and—it's a damn kitchen, just a kitchen, and suddenly Ryan's hat slams down over my head. Ryan shoves it down over my eyes, just to ruin his hat completely, I guess, and then he says, "Don't look. Don't even try."

In my head, I hear him whisper. *Please.*

I can't look, I want to say. What with the *gross sweaty hat* over my eyes. But I don't say anything, because suddenly there are voices speaking.

The voices sound tinny and small, far away—the hat partly covers my ears, I notice, because I reach up to rub them, to get the sound out. The voices sound lonely, and sad, and did I mention lonely? The black world inside the hat turns purple. A world of hurt exists out there, and all I want is to reach out my arms and *hold*—

"For Christ's sake, Allie, not *now*," I hear Ryan boom close beside me. I don't have an armful of frightened voices—I have Ryan, and I think I'm holding him back.

What the hell am I doing?

I drop my arms, and he says "thank you" in a really snotty way, and I hear the metallic swoosh of his sword slicing through something gooey. The voices suddenly stop, and I feel something wet and lumpy hit my shoes. I also feel really, really embarrassed, and more sick than ever.

I feel a hand on the back of my neck—Ryan's. His thumb brushes against my throat just once, and then suddenly his hat is yanked off my head and my hair, already kind of gross from being woken up early by a stupid naming-no-names hunter, is now a dandelion gone to seed. I flatten it down and glare at him; I'm going to have to put it in a bandanna if these shenanigans keep up. He glares at me while he tries to reblock his hat into something more Stetson, less poke bonnet.

Behind him is a large purple monster with a lot of tentacles and a sword sticking out of it. One of the tentacles is actually lying across my shoes. The tentacle has a dusting of fur at the very tip, and I am suddenly reminded of the imaginary pet rabbit I had when I was six.

"Um," I say. "Where'd that come from?"

He looks behind him and then turns back to me. He carefully puts his Stetson back on, and adjusts the brim. "Followed you," he says.

He turns back and yanks the sword out of the thing. A small gush of purple liquid, slick as fry oil, comes out along with it. Ryan grimaces and heads into the kitchen I'd opened before. He wipes off the blade with some paper towels.

"How?" I ask.

He shrugged. "You touched the Door. Something on the other side wanted you—or you wanted it. It followed you home."

Ryan hides the sword back in the magnificent folds of his coat. I'm not so blasé. "I didn't want anything like that," I say.

He walks back out into the hall; I follow him. The demon's corpse is collapsing in on itself. We watch it until it disappears completely. Ryan says, "I don't know what that was, but there was something in you to catch its attention, Allie." He looks at me sadly for a moment. "Watch for that."

Then he takes my arm again and drags me toward the next turn of the hallway, and there are all the people, staring at us with their pain, and then the hospital lobby, and the folding doors, and a line of gypsy car service cars waiting to pick up people and take them anywhere they want to go. He hauls me into one of the cars and directs the driver to take us to the Brooklyn Public Library.

Something in me, huh? Great.

I lean my head against the window and close my eyes.

4

The library is huge, and in the middle of Brooklyn. It's right near a park, and the botanical garden. The neighborhood sucks, though; I wouldn't go walking after dark without a hunter to protect me.

The cab ride is nice—even without tentacle monsters, hospitals are pretty unreal. I like the city. I spent most of my life living on Long Island, which is also pretty unreal. It's not even an island—it's a peninsula. Lies, damn lies! I didn't even know that it wasn't an island until I was, like, twenty-five and looked at a map. We weren't taught about that kind of thing in school. Why teach geography when instead we can be taught about . . . uh, other things, I guess. I don't even remember what I was taught in school. I spent most of my time getting manicures and having my hair done and shopping.

I was, basically, your typical vapid New Yorker. I had too much time and too much money. I lived in a house that was really too big for three people—there were six guest bedrooms, a giant swimming pool in my back yard that we kept heated to a ridiculous degree so we could swim all winter, and we even had servants. Not exactly what people think of when they think of New York City—but, as any Long Islander will rush to assure you, Long Island is *not* part of New York City. New York City is the five boroughs, and that's it. Most Long Islanders can't even name all the boroughs, though; everyone always forgets the Bronx.

Stan and Amanda grew up on either side of me. They also had big houses and swimming pools and extreme topiary lining the driveways. We were given matching cars when we turned sixteen, and we drove them too fast while our parents sipped martinis and talked about the stock market and tennis instructors.

The difference now is that Stan and Amanda still live that life. I live in Brooklyn, in a tiny apartment, surrounded by art and literature and philosophy students, minutes away from Manhattan by subway. I had never been on the subway before I moved to Brooklyn.

I wish I could say that I fit right in and there was no culture shock, but I didn't fit in at all. I started working at the diner because it was the closest thing to a job I could actually *do*; it was a favor to Amanda's mother's favorite maid that I was even given a chance in the first place. Amanda's mother's maid, whose name

I don't even know, because that was back when I was still too good to learn anyone's name, despite being completely broke, got a nice bonus for recommending me for the job.

Looking back, I am pretty sure that Sally took pity on the poor little rich girl who showed up for her first day of work as a waitress in head-to-toe white Prada driving a Mercedes. I could barely parallel park, and at the end of the day my feet were so swollen I couldn't drive home. Sally didn't smile too much at my pain, and she let me sleep in her overheated apartment above the diner while she sat up and watched PBS, and eventually went to sleep herself in the old armchair I wish she'd left here when she moved.

That's where the story of the Door starts, actually, because that night Stan and Amanda drove out from Long Island when I didn't come home. Why didn't they just call my cell phone? If they had, everything would be different now. Well, they did call, but from the street outside. I let them in through the back door, and we went into the basement with Amanda's bottle of vodka and Stan's tabs of X.

God, I knew how to repay kindness back then, didn't I?

"We should mem—comm—we should do something, because today is special!" Amanda announced once we'd drank too much for sense. We drank a lot back then. They still do; I don't. I can't—I have too much that always has to be done. Don't think I don't resent the hell out of that, because I do. But what am I supposed to do about it? I have to live with it, just like I have to live with everything else; I've become sage and zen in my old age.

That's a big lie, by the way.

"Yeah," said Stan lazily, stretched out on the floor on top of some broken-down boxes. "You have a job. That's kind of incredible."

"No kidding," I'd agreed immediately. Who ever would have thought that I'd get a job? Not me; my life was so derailed. "We should buy something with my tips!"

"What did you make?" Amanda didn't even bother to try to sound interested, but I pulled the crumpled dollar bills out of my pocket anyway. My gorgeous white Prada pantsuit was stained beyond the talents of even the most skilled dry cleaner, but I felt a weird kind of pride anyway. I'd done a job, and, okay, I hadn't done it very *well*, but I hadn't dropped anything, and only one person complained about getting regular Coke when she'd ordered a Diet.

"Fifteen bucks," I said proudly, and displayed my dollars.

Amanda pulled one from the pile. "We should totally cast a spell over the money so that it multiplies without you having to do a lot of work," she said, spreading the dollar out on the floor.

"You're an idiot," said Stan, but he sat up, clearly interested.

I want to say that I wasn't interested. I want to say that being poor gave me a new sense of purpose. But that would also be a lie. A damn damn damn lie. Because no matter what books and movies and television shows try to get us to believe, there's nothing good about being poor. There's nothing good about living in someone else's house, even when that someone else has been your best friend since childhood. There's nothing to be gained from being in a situation where everyone you've ever known has only pity for you to your face, and nastiness behind your back.

I could have lived my whole life without knowing who my true friends were, and been happier for it.

"Let's do it," I said.

"It has to rhyme," said Amanda seriously, and I agreed. After all, we'd seen *The Craft* about a million times, and all their spells rhymed.

"Um . . ." I stared down at the money. "Shouldn't we make a circle too?" I pulled a tiny piece of chalk out of my pocket; I'd used it earlier to write specials on the board behind the counter. The dinner special was meat-loaf with mashed potatoes, string beans, brown gravy, and a cookie, for five dollars. No wonder the diner was struggling to make ends meet if Sally didn't even charge real prices for the food, seriously.

"Here, give me that." Amanda grabbed the chalk

away from me and drew a clumsy circle on the concrete, put the dollar bill in the center.

"You guys are crazy. Magic isn't real." Stan poked me in the side. "Let's do the X."

"No—not yet," I said, and brushed his hand away from my side, where his finger *kept poking me*. "Quit it."

"Shut up!" said Amanda. "Okay, I think I've made up an excellent rhyme here."

"Go for it," I told her. We dragged Stan into the circle and sat around it, our legs crossed, knees touching, holding hands.

"I think first we need blood," said Stan. "If we're going to do this, I mean, we should do it right, right?"

"Where are we going to get blood?" I looked around, but it wasn't like Sally left knives in the basement or anything.

"I know!" Amanda pulled her purse to her chest. Manicure scissors.

"Very clever," I said approvingly.

"I am the best," she agreed, and scratched the scissors down my finger. A few drops of blood into the cap of her eyeliner. Then Stan's blood, then her own. Our blood looked almost black under the dim lights of the basement, and I felt a little nervous. Who knew what could happen with the blood? Amanda set the eyeliner cap in the center of the circle, on top of the dollar bill.

"Ready?" She looked at Stan, then at me. I nodded

as decisively as I could, which I don't think was very decisive at all, since I was extremely drunk, and if I nodded too hard, I'd've probably fallen over.

"Ready! Steady! Go!" yelled Stan, and started laughing.

"Sun and moon, fork and spoon," intoned Amanda. I giggled, and she squeezed my hand too tightly.

"Ow!"

"Shut up, I'm casting a spell!"

"You guys—" Stan started.

"Shut up," insisted Amanda, and started again. "Sun and moon, fork and spoon, grant our wish for money to cooooooome."

"That does *not* rhyme," I said, and started giggling, then couldn't stop. Too much vodka! I was so stupid, I had no idea what that not-rhyme would do. "Is the chalk glowing? That's awesome, I didn't realize it was phosphorescent."

"That's only in the ocean, dumbass," said Stan. He leaned backwards as far as he could go, pulling Amanda and me off balance.

"Anything can glow," I argued, leaning toward him.

"Wait, there's more to the rhyme: Give us more for less, give us this diner's best, give us the wishes we seek, give us everything we can keep!" Amanda finished triumphantly, and the chalk was seriously glowing.

And then there was a door. A door right up where the wall behind Stan used to be.

"Uh—you guys . . ." I trailed off and pointed behind Stan. "There's like a giant door or something down here. I think—what the fuck?"

Yes, I have a potty mouth.

Still.

"Ha ha, sure," said Stan, and he didn't turn around, and there was something coming out of the door.

Amanda shook her head. "No way! Stan, seriously, no way!"

And Stan turned, and we were all just frozen as something, something with *legs,* came out of the door, and Amanda crowed, "It worked! We cast a spell!"

I don't remember a lot of what happened next—it's all blurry in the way only alcohol can make memories fade. There was a loud bang—it's a wonder the old lady didn't wake up from the noise. There was a bright stripe of light. The next thing I remember clearly is that there was yellow goop all over Stan and Amanda and me. Nothing could save my Prada now. The guy standing over us with a sword in one hand and a shotgun in the other had big eyes, dark eyes, and really sexy stubble.

Ryan has never told me how he got to us so quickly, and I've never asked. I don't want to know how close we all came to being eaten by a yellow slime monster with, I should point out, a *lot* of legs.

"You fucking idiots!" he yelled, and his voice had the tinge of an accent—something Southern and rolling that made me think of ranches and horses and cowboy hats. And, oh yes, he *owned* that cowboy hat on his head.

"You can't call us idiots!" said Amanda, hands on her hips. But oh, man, this guy could call me anything he wanted as long as it was in bed.

Behind him was—well, was what I now know is a Door. Amanda's stupid rhyme opened a Door into Hell. But at the moment, all I could think was that it was pretty.

Helloooo, pretty, I thought, and felt a warm shiver go through me.

"Don't talk to it. Don't—hey! Girl! Listen to me!" Suddenly the guy's hands were on me and he was shaking me. "Do not talk to it, do you understand?"

"I'm not talking to anything—and I'm not an *idiot,*" I said disdainfully. Let me tell you how disdainful I can be: very.

"Yeah? Where I'm standing, you folks sure are, all of you." He stepped back, stood up straight. "You just opened a Door—" I could *hear* the capital letters in his voice "—into the worst place you can imagine."

I looked over at Amanda. She looked half bored and half dismayed at her ruined outfit. Stan was staring at the Door behind the guy.

"Who *are* you?" I asked him. "I mean, you can't just come busting in here and kill some *thing* and get us covered in this garbage, and not tell us who you are."

"You can call me Ryan, and I'm here to save your asses, so if I were you, I wouldn't complain." He looked around the basement, and pulled a towel off the stack. We all watched as he cleaned off the sword. His shotgun had disappeared into his crazy flowing leather duster.

"I cannot imagine," said Amanda in her haughtiest I-am-the-princess voice, "that you could say anything at the moment that I'd be interested in."

"Then don't listen. You can die for all I give a shit after this stunt." He turned his focus on me. "You listen."

"I'll listen." I nodded. "But, uh, I'm drunk. You could be a hallucination. And that . . ." I waved toward the Door behind him. "That could be a hallucination."

"That's not a hallucination—it's a nightmare. It is your worst fucking nightmare ever, I promise. It's a Door into Hell—several different Hells. And you idiots opened it somehow. What did you ask for? Money? Fame?"

"Money," I admitted.

"Don't *talk* to him," Amanda admonished me.

"Something is *happening*," I said to her. "Don't you want to know what the hell is going on? We didn't even take the X!"

"I took the X," said Stan. I ignored him and turned back to Ryan, craning my neck to look up at him.

"I can . . ." I trailed off. "It's, like, is there a whispering? Do you hear it?"

"That's the Door. It wants you to talk to it. It wants to give you everything you've ever wanted. Don't take it. Don't ever take it." He lowered his voice. As he talked, his hand clenched and loosened on the sword. "Hell is real. All the Hells are real. Demons are real. Any kind of demon you can think of—it exists."

"This is the stupidest thing I've ever—"

"Shut up," Ryan and I said at the same time. Amanda looked hurt for a split second, then just annoyed.

"I'm out of here," she said, and stood up. "Come on, Stan."

He stood up too, and looked at me apologetically. "Sorry, Allie," he said, "but Amanda's right. This is totally fucked up."

"You're fucked up," I said, and stayed where I was.

Amanda shook her head. "You can make nice with the unwashed here, Allie, but Stan and I are going home."

And they did.

Sometimes I still can't believe that they left. But sometimes I'm surprised that they stayed as long as they did. Sometimes I'm surprised that I was even surprised that they left. Despite being my best friends, I always thought I didn't have any illusions about them.

"I didn't actually expect them to leave," I told Ryan after the door slammed.

"I did." He sat down in one flowing motion, crossing his legs, mimicking my position on the floor. He laid his sword next to himself; it pointed toward me.

"Tell me what's going on," I requested, because really? "This is the most interesting thing to ever happen in my whole life."

"This is the worst thing to ever happen in your whole life," he told me, and I didn't believe him. I still don't, because—this sounds terrible. This sounds terrible, but as hideous as the Door is, and as horrible as everything that's happened has been, I just can't regret meeting Ryan. I can't regret learning about everything he's taught me.

All the things that being poor are supposed to do, like teach you to be strong and self-reliant and resourceful? I learned all that by fighting demons with Ryan.

From where I'm sitting in the back seat of a cab, Ryan pressed up against me, Brooklyn looks as beautiful and peaceful as it did the first time I drove through it, that first day of work at Sally's. It *is* beautiful and peaceful. It's full of culture and cool shit completely ignored by tourists, like the botanical garden and the tiny Italian restaurants in Bay Ridge and all the old Greek diners and the Verrazano Bridge. But it's also got a couple of Doors to Hell hanging around, and they ruin everything.

The inside of the library is cool and quiet and brightly lit. I can't hear any whispering from Doors, so I am kind of not seeing the point of being here.

Ryan leads me to the right; it's the romance novel section. "Stay a minute," says Ryan firmly, and leaves me.

Yeah, right.

I wait until he's a few steps away, and then I follow him. Up a bunch of stairs, through a bunch of doors, and into a bright, airy room with lots of tables and computers and the slight smell of plasticky ozone. There's no way Ryan doesn't know that I followed him, but he's ignoring me. I press myself against the wall outside the door. No point in pushing things. I peek around the side to watch him lean down and kiss the lone inhabitant of the room on the cheek. She's surrounded by books, but I can still see that she's a tiny brunette, like me if I was made of bones and cocaine. She's got big eyes that speak of a lot of expensive eye makeup, and shoes I know I would've had in my closet back when I had money.

She is not dressed like any librarian I've ever seen. There's no way her tidy dress is off the rack. I'm not a betting girl, and I wouldn't swear to it, but I'm pretty sure she's wearing Anna Sui.

She's also looking at Ryan in a way I think is inappropriate for coworkers.

Unfortunately, I cannot hear them through the damn wall. That's probably why he didn't make a scene when I followed him. Stupid Ryan.

Ryan's back is to me, but the girl is facing me, and when she looks at me, her eyes flash. Not metaphorically. They *flash,* green, sparked through with gold, and when she smiles, she looks *venomous,* like she could kill me with a crook of her finger. Or her *brain*.

I am not one to run away from a fight, but I know when I am outclassed by someone really powerful. If she wants to go one on one, I can pull hair and bite as hard as the next girl, but she seems like she'd fight dirty.

Fine. When I walk away, I am definitely flouncing. Ryan and his stupid cronies sometimes bring out the worst in me.

The stacks of the Brooklyn Public Library look like the stacks of any other library. The books smell delicious, like old paper and ink. I never appreciated stuff like that when I was younger, but I have a new outlook on life since the Door was opened. It turns out that a lot of the stuff in fiction is *real,* and novels can be helpful. Some of them, anyway. Some of them are total bullshit.

I wander through the corridors, down stairs, around corners, until I'm well and truly lost in the stacks. It's kind of nice to be in such complete silence. No one is around, and there's no whispering from a Door, and my nausea is totally gone.

It's not Dewey Decimal, but the book spines near me say that I'm apparently in the BS section. Since all these books are on religious topics, that is pretty funny in a library geek kind of way. (Shut up: Concepts like "vivification" don't just research themselves.)

The yellow overhead lights cast weird angled shadows; I thought I was alone, but there's a dark shape moving along the shelves ahead of me. Student? Homeless guy? Kind of worrying, either way. A shadow is cast along the floor: tall, with what looks like wings, but when I check out the moving thing again, it doesn't have any. That means demon, shit shit shit. What is with today? I've seen more fun this morning than I did all last month.

The only demons I know that cast a winged shadow are the vampires. They're another species that isn't actually sexy. Yet more crap that novel writers get wrong. Vampires are like . . . they're like butterflies. Evil fucking butterflies. They're always gorgeous on the outside, like the goths who hang around the East Village, wearing perfectly applied makeup and knee-high boots with lots of buckles and elaborate corsets even in the summertime. But people forget that butterflies use their proboscis—that's kind of like an antenna that they use to suck up food—to do all sorts of things besides poke at flowers. Some butterflies will drink rotten fruit, or slimy dung, the sweat off your shoulders—they'll drink carrion. Corpse-sucking butterflies, people.

That's what vampires do with their mouth and their wings; they just wrap up their prey and suck all the life out of them. Blood, plasma, souls.

Ryan says the soul is in the throat. I don't know if I believe him or not.

The first thing I learned from Ryan after he stormed the basement is that iron kills, and silver heals. Ryan has all sorts of silver cauter scars on his body—I put some of them there, trying to save him from this demon bite, that demon spit. I even have my own silver scar that Ryan gave me after my first one-on-one run-in with something nasty.

Yeah. After that, and the burning silver, and the smell of my own muscle cooking? I don't walk around weaponless anymore. Even in my last pair of clean jeans that are too tight, instead of a belt, I have a chain made of iron threaded through the loops. I can pull it out and use it to fight almost anything.

"Hey." The vampire moves out of the shadows and toward me, almost purring. She's gorgeous, and, yeah, in a corset. It's red and black, and I'd be jealous, except I know she's a bloodsucking fiend from beyond the grave. From beyond the *world*.

"Hey," I say again, and start backing up, but she's got super-speed and I'm just a human, so the next thing I know, she's nuzzling my neck, which is obvious and stupid, and I make a little sighing sound like I imagine people enthralled do. How would I know? I don't do the thrall thing. Too much silver in me already, I guess. I feel a little nudge on my neck, and that's my cue.

Here is the second thing I learned from Ryan: Salt binds things.

I tuck my fingers into my right back pocket and pull out a dime bag's worth of heavy kosher margarita-quality sea salt, and toss it at my neck, right where I can feel a sharp poke. The vampire rears back, kind of sneezing, and ew, I can *see* this long curled proboscis flapping from beneath the vampire's tongue, and more coming out of the chocolate brown and gold-spotted wings that have spread from her back. The vamp proboscis looks like an old rubber medical tube, the kind nurses use to tie off your arm for blood tests. The very tip is dark red—that's me in there.

I swipe at my neck and get a smear of blood on my fingertips. Not a lot—I didn't really let it go on long enough. I never do, which hasn't ever been a problem, but Ryan bugs me about it every time he catches me at it. I wipe my finger on the nearest squishy thing: call number BS543.A1.

Salt binds; it's called contagion magic. A little salt here, a little salt there, and now whatever happens to my blood in one spot happens to my blood in the other.

This vamp isn't worth my iron belt; instead I pull Betsy, my iron nail, from the same pocket as the salt and shove it through the blood stain and straight into the book beneath. The vampire starts screaming. She claws at her face, ripping at the proboscis.

She collapses, still writhing. Which is when I pull the book off the shelf, take three big steps back, and grasp the nail.

"What are you doing here?" I do my best impression of Ryan's snarl.

"Fuck you, human," it sneers, except the words come out thick and wet because of the flappy feeding tube still sticking out of its mouth.

"That's original." I twist the nail and it squeals. "What are you doing here?"

"The Door—" it gasps, but I'm not buying it. "In the donation room—new—"

"Spontaneous?" I ask. The vampire grimaces. I twist the nail.

"Yes!" Its wings are curling inward. "And more to come, human. Feeding—"

It gasps again, and collapses completely. Its wings crumple, which looks a bit sad, actually—like an expensive dress dumped on the chair after a party. Nothing I was doing should have killed it, though. I look from the nail to the vamp and then there's the brunette from the other room, five feet away and glaring at me. She flicks her fingers, and an iron stake with a wooden handle rises from the vampire. The stake's got dark, coagulated blood on it, and I feel my stomach turn again.

She's killed the vamp before I could get any useful

information from it. "Thanks a lot," I say snidely. The stake twitches in the air, and I start to wonder whether confrontation is really a smart move on my part.

"Don't you know better than to listen to vamps?" the girl demands. Her eyes flash again, *spark!*, and I take a step back unintentionally. Now I'm annoyed at myself. No stupid hunter girl should have me running, even if she can float things. I step forward again; her eyes don't miss anything. She raises an eyebrow before continuing: "They're all liars. They'll just suck you in."

Pun intended? I wonder.

"Just because you have a Door spitting out vampires in, what, the donation room? Doesn't mean you have to be a bitch." I pull the nail out of the book, wipe it off on my salty jeans—now they need to be washed for *sure*—and tuck it back into my pocket.

"Listen, idiot, there's *no* Door here—" She blinks, and then stares at me harder. "Or there *wasn't*. What did you do?"

"Narnia." I didn't even hear Ryan come up behind me. I suck so bad; if I were a real demon hunter, I'd be dead a million times over already. "Leave her alone."

"What the hell are you doing with this mundane?" demands Narnia. What the hell kind of name is that? It's the name of someone who wears hand-tailored Anna Sui dresses. I hate her.

She also stressed the "this" in that sentence. Which makes me wonder what stories have gotten out about me. Aside from being the only mundane who's opened a Door and still has hunters socializing with her, that is.

I have grown up and gotten over my selfish Hell-magic ways, Narnia. God.

"She's killed plenty of demons," Ryan says. "She knows what she's doing." He is totally on my side. I love him. Not *love* love, but, you know, love. Also, it's kind of nice that somebody around here appreciates that I've made up for past stuff.

"Bullshit," she says. Okay, whatever.

"Listen, that vamp might've had something more to say. I salted it. It could've been helpful."

"Vamps *lie*. Demons *lie*." Narnia steps over the vamp and gets right into my face. "I hear you touched a Door. Pretty stupid for someone who knows what she's doing."

"So you know what you're doing?" I ask. "Then tell us why the Door in my diner is gone. Go ahead. Best guess."

Narnia hesitates, then steps back. Score one for me.

"That's what I thought." I turn to Ryan. "Can we leave now? Something smells bad here."

I rocked the junior high social drama scene, let me tell you.

Ryan rolls his eyes. "We're leaving. I've got what I need."

I try desperately to think of something that would be semi-insulting to Narnia while still sounding innocent, and fail miserably. I raise an eyebrow and hope for the best.

"Narnia says that she doesn't know how the Door closed. That means it's something new. That's information we didn't have before." Ryan turns on his heel, duster flapping. "Come on," he calls over his shoulder. He doesn't say good-bye to Narnia. I smirk at her before I follow Ryan out of the stacks.

I'm pretty pleased that I don't have to get rid of the vampire corpse. Poor Narnia, all alone in her Anna Sui and Clinique face powder.

I rush to catch up to Ryan.

"I don't think the Door closed," he tells me. "It'd be one thing if Owen's was gone too—that would mean the world was ending in water and fire, and we don't have the manpower for that." I cannot even tell if he's joking. "But it's just your Door—and if Narnia doesn't know how it could have got gone, then it's not gone."

"Because Narnia knows everything," I say sarcastically.

"About this? Yeah. She's psychic. A witch."

Psychics? I didn't know *they* were real. "Are all psychics witches?" I ask, and that gets me an exasperated glare. "Okay, I guess not."

"She feels the Doors. Kind of the way that you do, but professionally." What I do? Huh. Allie, Amateur Psychic. I could make millions. But now I'm wondering how that kind of skill could be helpful to hunters.

Maybe she "feels" the Doors and knows when new ones show up? Maybe she assigns hunters to Doors. That would make sense.

Except the idea that Ryan watches my Door just because he was assigned there and not because he wants to protect my poor mundane self is . . . really kind of gross.

Okay. Deal with the issue at hand, then wallow in self-pity.

Ryan's still talking. "It could have moved. That's what she suggested. That it moved."

"Okay. So say it moved. How do we find out where my Door moved to?" Look at me, dealing with the issues. I'm still rushing to keep up with him as we burst out of the library. Even though it was well lit, the sunlight is even brighter. I squint, my vision blurring. Everyone's out and about today. Why aren't all these people at work? They've probably all called in sick to take advantage of the first nice day of spring. No rain, it's over seventy degrees out, and the air smells fresh and clean. Especially after all the death of the Doors.

"*We* don't. You're going back to the diner. Now that I know you had nothing to do with this, you stay out of it. No more touching Doors for you. No more going near them until I figure out what's going on." Ryan pushes the Stetson back on his forehead. He has a little hat line, and a little tan line, both in the same place.

"I'd rather stay with you," I tell him, not even thinking, but the moment I say it I know it's true. He stops to wait for the light to change; he's heading for the subway. I can tell he's mulling this over.

In the last few years, I've gotten to know Ryan really well. Or as well as anyone knows him, I guess. We've spent a lot of time together. When he's not sleeping in front of the Door or watching the Door, he's in the kitchen with me. He tells me stories of demons he's fought sometimes, when he's in a good mood. When he's in a bad mood, he sits and chops potatoes, or scrubs the heck out of pots. Once I woke up late and came down to the kitchen in a rush only to discover that Ryan had done almost all the prep work for the day and when I looked at him with my eyes wide, he just shrugged and said, "Couldn't sleep."

I've slept in the same bed with him more times than I can count—just slept—and when he can't sleep, I know it's because of nightmares. I have them too, but I bet his are worse. Mine are almost always about him dying—sometimes about me dying. Almost never about me dying, though, because in my nightmares? He always saves me. He *always* saves me. I have never had a nightmare about dying in which he did not at least try to save me. When I die in my dreams, he's always dead first.

The first time I almost died in real life was about a year after we opened the Door. I always want to say "after the Door was opened"—I never want to take responsibility for it. But I make myself, because I'm an adult now, and that's what adults do. Adults take responsibility for the dumb shit that they do.

That first time I almost died, Ryan jabbed me with a syringe full of something that made me feel like I was floating, but I could still feel the pain. The demon—a *semyazza,* he later told me, which I had to look up on the Internet because I didn't know what it was—had ripped open my stomach.

The *semyazza,* if you don't know, is a demon that eats humans. It starts with the intestines. I was in the basement getting rice, and Ryan, it turned out, was in the kitchen. The Door just opened, just spit a demon out, and wham, I was down, screaming, and Ryan, just like in all my dreams, saved me.

This was before I knew how to fight, before Ryan decided I had to train, had to quit smoking two packs a week. It's been years, and I'm down to a little more than a pack a month—I always smoke when I count out the register. One cigarette every day.

It's all fuzzy and hazy, but I know what he did. I know he pulled out the soldering iron that he kept in the basement, and a piece of silver that he muttered some Sumerian over, and dripped the silver into my stomach. I have a huge scar, bumpy, still red after all these years. It's kind of ugly, but I also like it. I know it's fucked up, but I like all the scars that I have. They mean that I've survived.

I've got scars on my arms and scars on my hands

and a really bad scar down my spine. But I've never been to a hospital, because Ryan's always gotten to me with the silver cauter in time. And sometimes I've had to do him. I know exactly how to do it now; he made me practice on oranges.

But it's like I said: My hands always shake.

The scars look just like the scars I've gotten from cooking—from cutting myself with knives and burning my hands on the grill. That's the way it goes in a kitchen. That's the way it goes with demon hunting. I can give a shot of morphine with the best of them now, and sew up cuts with a needle and thread. My first aid kit doesn't look like anyone else's, I guarantee you that.

I think that if it had been anyone else, anyone besides Ryan, I probably wouldn't have learned as well how to do all the things that need doing when you fight demons. But—and I know this is stupid, I know it's wrong, but . . . but I learned how because I wanted to be able to save Ryan. I couldn't stand it if something really horrible happened to him, if he was out of commission, if there had to be another hunter in my basement.

Maybe, like baby kittens or something, I imprinted on him that first night he showed up. Maybe it really is love—I don't know. I've never been in love before, so I couldn't say. But I busted my ass learning how to fight, how to stake a vampire, how to cut the head off a jinn, how to sprinkle blood in the right pattern to trap a shedu. I did it all so that I could save Ryan, I think. I don't even know. I'm not even sure. But maybe, maybe that's why I did it.

I look over at him. His nose has been broken a bunch of times, and he has scars on his face, on his neck. Some of them look like they were maybe done on purpose, but he's never said and I've never asked. I did ask once if I could tattoo talismans all over me to prevent demons from getting me, and he just laughed and said that stuff like that only works in movies and on television. He gave me a talisman to wear after that, though; a Seal of Solomon. It's inscribed on a huge silver disk, and I never wear it because it is so heavy that it hurts my neck, but sometimes I sleep with it under my pillow.

The Seal was the first sigil I ever learned to draw. It's a six-pointed star in a circle, with a dot between every two points. Very easy, very protective. The trick to make the magic strong is to interlace the lines, rather than intersect them; the more intricate the design, the more protection, the more magic. He told me the triangles represented elements, and he said it reminded him of me. I'm still not sure what that means, and Ryan hasn't said, but I hope it's more than just a nice thought.

"You have to promise not to touch any more Doors," Ryan says at last.

"I swear." That could possibly be a lie. It wasn't like

I *chose* to touch the Door at the hospital.

The sun is high in the sky and beating down on my head. Sometimes I wish I were blonde; I bet blondes don't get hot as quickly as brunettes do.

"Sure," he says, and clearly doesn't believe me. "I'm—"

I've never seen him at a loss for words before, but he stops right in the middle of a sentence. The traffic light's changed and everything, but he's not moving.

"You," I prompt.

"I have no idea," he confesses. I've never seen him look so unsure. "There's a place the Door could be, but it's just—I've never actually seen a Door move before. Ever. I've never even heard about it. But most of the Doors are—this sounds so stupid, even to me. But most Doors are in malls."

"In . . . malls."

"A lot of people, a lot of noise, a lot of confusion. A lot of basement rooms no one goes into." Ryan ticks these points off on long, well-shaped fingers that I've had more than one fantasy about. His nails are always clean, and that's pretty impressive considering what he does for a living. "Malls are great places for demons," he finishes. "They blend in with the disaffected youth. So if your Door moved spontaneously, maybe it went there."

"Well," I say brightly, "I am great at malls. Let's go."

"Is there even a mall in Brooklyn, or do we have to

go into Manhattan?" He resettles the Stetson on his head.

"Oh, there is definitely a mall in Brooklyn, and it's full of disaffected youth," I assure him. "But . . ." I stop and sigh.

Ryan eyes me warily. "But what?"

I scowl. "It means getting back on the damn bus."

5

We actually have to take both a train and a bus. Luckily, the train is mostly above ground at this point. It's not the 1970s; the New York subway system isn't very scary anymore. But it *is* a haven for demons. All those catacombs, tunnels that aren't used anymore . . . It's like demons have a homing device. The ones that get past Ryan out of our Door always seem to end up in the subways.

I don't want to get on the train, though. I really don't want to. It's not like I can hear a Door whispering or anything, I just . . . don't want to get on the train. I feel like I did in the hospital hallway. *This is a bad idea.*

Ryan takes my arm and gently tugs until I step through the open doors, and I hang onto him, put my face in his chest. He doesn't smell like blood anymore; he must have showered in my apartment above the diner when I was dreaming about werewolves. He smells like sandalwood.

Out of the corner of my eye, I can see shadows with wings, and I swallow back the bile that rises in my throat.

"Ryan," I whisper urgently.

"I see them," he says calmly. Too calmly. "They won't come near us. You still smell like the dead one."

He murmurs quietly to me about demons and animals and the importance of smell identification to largely noctural creatures. It sounds like garbage, but it's comforting. When the subway stops, we get out, even though we're not at our stop yet. We get into a different car. This one feels wrong too, but there are no winged shadows, so I just stand with my face in Ryan's chest, and breathe in the smell of sandalwood.

As soon as we step off the bus and onto the mall grounds, I can hear the Door whispering. We find it easily; it's in the basement, right underneath the first-floor Bath & Body Works.

This Door is ugly, and it's not the one from the diner. I don't recognize it—but it has the wrought-iron fence inside it. I mean, it can't actually be iron, because then nothing would ever be able to come out of it. Or maybe it *is* iron, and that's why stuff doesn't come out 24/7 and require legions of hunters to contain. Maybe the demons have to figure out ways to slip through the iron bars without killing themselves.

I don't know.

All I know is that all around us are the bodies of dead teenagers and mothers and babies. I can't look. Some of them have had all their blood sucked out. Some of them are only bones. Some of them are just dead, maybe hunters who didn't make it past their last fight.

Dead people, in case you're wondering, don't look like they do in the movies, or on *Law & Order,* or even at the open-casket funerals. The dead we see at funerals aren't what death really looks like—they're all made up and pretty, ready for a show.

Death looks like wax, and weight, and grease. Death looks like what I'm seeing here.

The smell isn't, though—it's the fruity floral chemicals from upstairs, filling the air.

On top of all this, the whispering of the Door is really getting to me. While Ryan is poking around like there isn't a giant pile of rotting people in the middle of the room, I sit down on the dirty concrete floor, nice and far away from bodies and Doors and grossness. The nail in my pocket digs into my butt, but I can be uncomfortable for a little while. I'm hungry and thirsty and tired, and I'm still angry that Narnia killed that stupid vampire while I was talking to it, and that I freaked out on the trains where Ryan could see me, and—

Allie, whispers the Door. A different, smaller voice says, *Allie.*

I ignore them both.

Allie.

Allie.

Allie.

What? I snap.

We can give you what you want . . .

What I want, I grumble in my mind, *is some french fries.*

The Door . . . it snickers. That's the only word I have for it. The Door laughs at me. A tiny titter comes from the second voice, and I am thinking about doing something unwise.

We know what you want, the Door says. *Your mother. Your family. Your money. We—*

"Allie," snaps Ryan. From his tone of voice, I'm guessing he's said my name more than once.

"What?" I draw the word out. Doors make everything move in slow motion. My stomach roils as I remember what it was like to touch the Door in the hospital.

"What's it saying?" he asks. He kneels down in front of me. "Don't listen to it."

"I think I know better than to listen to a couple of damn Doors to Hell," I say before I think better of it.

"But you don't know better than to touch one?" Ryan puts a hand on my knee. "Allie, don't listen to it."

"I'm not."

"What's it saying?" That question seems counterintuitive to his order not to listen to the Door, but whatever.

"Nothing," I lie. "Just my name."

Ryan looks at me for a long moment, then he stands and goes back to the pile of bodies around the Door. With his boot he starts nudging them, separating them, turning them over just enough to see their faces.

"What are you doing?" I ask.

He looks up. "Checking their wounds. I need to make sure we won't have to deal with a werewolf in the next ten minutes. And . . . I want to know what kinds of demons come out of this Door." He rolls over a body, a woman, and I can see tiny punctures all over her. "Looks like this one's mostly vampires, with some *mandurugos* mixed in." Before I can ask, he says, "Filipino. Like our vampires, except their victims only have the one mark on their throats—*mandurugo* wings don't have separate suckers."

How does he even know this stuff? Where do you go to learn it? I've asked before, and he never tells me. I think he is secretly going to Kinko's and printing out Wikipedia pages to crib off of. That is my theory and I'm sticking to it.

"It's strange, though," Ryan continues, almost to himself. "Usually you get *mandurugos* with other *Aswang*—the Filipino demons."

"Maybe they came out of the other Door."

He looks at me sharply. "Other Door?"

The tiny voice says, *Allie!* "Never mind," I say quickly. "Is it bad that it's not what you were expecting?"

Ryan looks hard at me, and then back at the bodies on the floor. He shakes his head. "I don't know. It's . . . different. I don't like different." He pulls off his hat and runs his hand through his hair.

The Door, very quietly, laughs at me.

We head back upstairs to the food court. I wasn't kidding about the fries. I get a giant order of them after Ryan steals my cell phone. Grease and salt and the smell of ketchup clean out the smell of rotting bodies and the horrid Bath & Body Works perfumes. When I get back to the table, Ryan is now on my phone. I put a Coke in front of him—always regular, never Diet. Me, I like the diet stuff. I like the aftertaste, and the way there can never be any other taste in my throat.

I ignore his conversation and eavesdrop on the teenage girls sitting next to us. They're all wearing their jeans a size too tight, with pink belts and tiny T-shirts that wouldn't even fit on one of my arms.

"I don't even *know* what he thought he was doing," says the one with blonde hair. "He was, like, all totally over me, and I was like, hello, get your hands *out* of my pants."

"Oh my *god*," says the brunette. "Like, what? In your pants? That is so gross!"

Oh, they will learn.

I turn my attention back to Ryan when he snaps his

phone closed. "That was Narnia. Another Door just opened, somewhere in Bay Ridge. A hunter reported it. She thinks it's in an Italian restaurant."

"That's two that have surprised her. Is that weird? Isn't she, like, supposed to *know*? Isn't that her job as the psychic witch or whatever?" I munch on a french fry and offer the container to him. He waves me off. I don't know how he's not starving to death already; it's way past lunchtime.

"It is weird, but she'll figure it out in a little while. She has to do spells."

"And then she has to hop on her broom and cackle," I say sagely. Ryan looks annoyed. I point my half-eaten fry at him. "Hey, this whole time you never said anything about psychic witches. Bad witches, yes. Kids pretending to be witches? Yes. Kids who watch movies about witches and try to make up spells? Yes. But real witches who do real witchy things? No."

He sighs and rolls his eyes. I eat more fries, and say, "Okay, what do we do now?"

"About the Door? We can't do anything. Narnia will find a hunter and—"

"Why does Narnia get to decide?"

Ryan shrugs. "We track the demons; she keeps track of us. And replaces us when we die, of course." He says this like I'm supposed to know it.

"I don't like to think about that," I reply, mouth full of salty greasy goodness.

"Well, I don't like to think about it either, but it happens all the time. And someone's got to know where we are, how we got there, and whether to be worried if no one's seen us for a month."

"So, in conclusion, Narnia *does* assign hunters to Doors." I hum a little. "That's what I thought."

"Are you satisfied with yourself that you guessed right?" He grins at me a little, the best kind of grin where he just lifts one corner of his mouth. That's the grin he uses when he's laughing with me instead of at me.

"Look, you've been doing this a lot longer than me. I say that I get points for anything I get right these days." I grin back. Then I have the best idea ever. "So if there are hunters all over New York City, let's get them all together. Maybe one of them has an idea about what's going on."

"Get them together how?" Ryan stares at my fries and then takes one and chews it thoughtfully. "It's not like we have a bat signal or anything, Allie."

"There's not one single way to get hunters all in the same place at the same time?"

"I've never seen it happen—not even once. Hunters don't trust each other, you know that. The only way I know how to contact the local crew is through the paper. An ad in *The Village Voice*."

"Is *that* why you read it every week?" I knew it couldn't be for the Savage Love sex column.

"Yeah, but I've never seen the ad. I've been doing this a long time, and I've never seen the ad even once. I don't think—not since that thing with the Scientologist and the loa. Active hunters just don't get together." He takes another fry and swoops it through the ketchup.

"Maybe it's time for that to change." I swoop my own fry through the ketchup, use it to draw a little heart. "Maybe there's a spell to make a bat signal."

"I don't want you doing any spells," he says severely.

"Maybe *you* could do the spell. Or Narnia. Maybe we can make the letters of whatever the hunters are looking at spell out the address of the diner," I suggest.

"That's the stupidest—well, it's not the stupidest thing I've ever heard, but it's close. But maybe Narnia knows a way. Or knows someone who knows a way." Ryan takes a long sip of his Coke. "Smoke signals or something."

I snort. "Smoke signals? Seriously? And you think *my* idea was stupid? Jerk."

He lifts one side of his mouth and grins at me again.

6

We split up: Ryan says he's going to hunt, but I don't know *what* he's going to hunt. Maybe he's going to track down Narnia again and divest her of more information. She was so very helpful the first time. I have made him promise that this is not ditching, and he has assured me that it is instead a two-pronged attack. I couldn't tell if he was laughing at me.

I head back to the diner. Time to get on the bus again. When I first started working at the diner, I drove one of Amanda's cars out from her place on Long Island. Then I saved up, found myself a cheap little apartment in a crappy neighborhood off the train. I never took the bus until I met Ryan. For some reason he really likes it. Maybe because he can watch the world go by without ever having to get involved. I imagine demon hunting is enough involvement in the world for him.

I don't live in the crappy neighborhood anymore.

I live above the diner now. When Sally left, she said I could stay in her place, and I took her up on it. I can keep an eye on things up here, and make sure Ryan actually gets to shower with hot water, and that there's a decent mattress he can use at least sometimes if the Door is quiet and his cot gets too lumpy. I can do my bit.

I let myself in through the back and go up to my little apartment. It's stiflingly hot, even though the day is nice and breezy. I pour a line of salt in front of the window and strap the salt in place with a length of mailing tape—which means the salt'll only work for about twenty-four hours, but it's worth it for the breeze—and I open the window wide. The salt won't keep out everything, particularly in the neutered form, but it keeps out the weak, generic demons—any kind of demon–human hybrid.

I strip off my shirt—there's a little blood on it from the vamp earlier, plus it's sweaty, *plus* it smells like *bus*. I trade it for a black tank top, and pull my hair back into a pink bandanna, then head downstairs.

The place is empty of customers. It feels like I've been gone forever.

I want to get down on my hands and knees and kiss the ugly black-and-white tile floor. I think the waitstaff would think that's weird, though. They're sitting in Ryan's booth, playing with mozzarella sticks and looking bored. The place *is* weirdly empty; not even my Homeless Guy hunter is at the counter. I ask how things are going, and when all I get is a shrug I steal one of their mozzarella sticks, tell them to all go home, and head into the kitchen. I use the stick to poke the blonde beside the chopping block. She shrieks.

When she finishes punching me in the arm and eating the stolen cheese, she says, "Weird shit's been happening today, Allie." Her name is Dawn; she's my day cook. She's got wild streaks of color through her hair, and an incredible attitude.

She started out in the front, dealing with the customers, because I thought her attitude was entertaining. The customers did not. She's better in the back, anyway. She can cook anything; sometimes I think it's too bad that the Sally's menu doesn't extend to the experimental. Sometimes when it's slow Dawn will make crazy things—once she made cappuccino with mushrooms instead of coffee. Okay, it was disgusting, and sometimes I still have nightmares about it. But one day I am sure that I'm going to lose her to some gourmet restaurant and she'll be the next Bobby Flay.

She was reading what looks like one of Ryan's books about evil. It could be a novel, it could be a history book; I have a hard time telling them apart when it comes to Ryan's reading habits.

"Have you read this?" she asks, holding it up. There's silver on the cover, so I'm guessing it's a novel. Not too many history books are decorated.

I shake my head. "Has it been dead out there all day?"

"This is *wild*," she tells me. "There's a fairy who looks like David Bowie."

"Is that social commentary?" I reply. I would wink, but when I wink I look like I have an eye twitch, so instead I just smirk. Which makes me look like a bitchy homophobe, I am sure.

But Dawn takes me seriously. "I don't know," she says contemplatively.

"No, really," I say, and lean a hip against the counter. "The grill looks practically clean."

"That's because there haven't been any orders. Nothing all day." She puts the book down on the chopping block, and I wince for its binding. And for my diner.

"Nothing all day? What the hell? Well, in that case . . ." I sigh. "Just go home, Dawn. I'll close up myself."

"It's not even closing time yet," she protests. "What if someone comes in?"

"I'll handle it myself. Really, just go." I wave a tired hand. "I'll pay you for the full day."

"If you're sure . . ." She sounds dubious but she hops off the stool and grabs the book. "I'm going to borrow this."

"I'll let Ryan know." I rub my eyes with my hands.

"Is that—is that a *hickey*?" Dawn comes closer and pokes at the vampire bite on my neck. "Oh my *god*, Allie. You and Ryan? Finally?"

"I *wish*," I reply fervently. "It's just a bug bite."

"It's a bug bite that looks like a hickey." She sticks her face closer to my neck and I pull away.

"Seriously, Dawn. It's not a hickey. Ryan would never."

"I wish he would already. It's been years, you guys dancing around each other. Like you're in orbit or something. It is way past time for your orbits to start decaying." Dawn tucks the book under her arm and pulls off her apron.

"When that happens, don't things explode or something?" I was never very good at science.

"That's the point, baby. *Explode.*" She laughs lasciviously, and winks as she picks up her bike helmet from the worker shelf by the sinks. She does *not* look like she's twitching. Her wink is totally smooth. She waves as she heads out of the kitchen.

Exploding. I'd like to explode with Ryan. Dawn is right—we've been dancing around each other for years. Six years. But he turned me down *both* times. The first time I was drunk, and, okay, I can understand that. We were both covered in goo and had only just met. The circumstances weren't good.

I pick up a knife and start chopping carrots and onions for beef stew for the hunters. As I dump them in the pot, I think about the *other* time. I don't think about it very often; who likes to torture themselves with memories of horrible rejection?

We were both down in the basement; he was guarding

the Door, and I was doing inventory for Sally. We were so silent; I was just listening to him breathe. Every breath he took turned me on more and more, so I kept my eyes on the stupid cans of black beans and tomatoes.

Then he said my name: "Allie—" and I turned around, and he was standing up, and seemed so . . . so . . . so into me. So ready for me. And I took the few steps over to him, and slid my arms around his stomach.

"God, Ryan," I said, and lifted my head.

And he kissed me. Oh, did he kiss me. It was a moment like no other I'd ever had. Like a movie, like a novel. My whole body felt like it was burning. His hands were hot on my skin. He slid them under my tank top, had one hand pressed to my lower back and the other hand on my spine. His fingers dipped under my jeans, and he pressed my back so I was arched against him.

Then I moaned, and he jumped away like I was the flame and he was the moth, instead of the other way around. We looked at each other for a moment—a long moment, a never-ending moment.

"No," he said, and he looked like I'd cut him. *"No."* And then he turned away and strode across the room, kicking over his chair as he went. He pounded up the stairs, and I heard him jump over the salt. I thought I could hear him slam the back door as he left.

I just stood there, fingers pressed to my lips.

That was year one, and that was the night I almost died for the first time. A *semyazza* came out of the Door not five minutes later, and thank god Ryan had only gone upstairs, hadn't left at all. He was in the kitchen. He came running when I screamed. He saved me. He scarred me.

And he never kissed me again.

"Allie." I turn around. I was expecting Ryan—not Dawn again. "Allie," she says, "I'm really sorry, but—could you look outside? Seriously."

"Seriously, Dawn, go home." I am busy in here, doing prep work with my good knife. The knife because I'm feeling the need right now for some comfort weaponry (and can you tell I spend all my time with a hunter? Did I really just think "comfort weaponry"? I cannot even believe it)—and I'm doing prep just in case someone shows up. Which I am pretty sure that no one is going to, but just in case Ryan and Narnia figure out how to get the hunters here, I am going to be ready with food. Ryan packs it away, and so do the older hunters who come visiting. I mean, I guess I could just put up a big sign saying "Meeting moved, go to IHOP" on the front door, but that seems uncharitable. You save humanity, you get a decent meal. This seems fair to me.

If Doors show up in populated locations with a lot of bustle and confusion, I wonder if there is a Door in the IHOP that Stan and Amanda and I used to go to out on Long Island. Sometimes we liked to go slumming at three in the morning. Before the smoking ban in New York, we could stay awake all night chain smoking and drinking vodka out of water bottles. We never ate anything, of course. Sometimes we'd split a plate of french fries. Mostly it was vodka, sometimes we'd mix it with our Diet Cokes.

We were so hideous. I was hideous.

What's strange is that I hardly remember who I was back then. I remember the highlights—fighting at parties, doing drugs, drinking too much. I have no idea how I'm not dead from drunk driving, really. I'm like the poster child for the spoiled rich kid—or I used to be. Stan and Amanda are still the same people they were when we were in high school, but I'm completely different.

Or I like to think that I am.

But it's like . . . it's like I really became alive when the Door opened and I met Ryan. It's like that's when my life really started. All my memories from the last few years are sharp and true—the happiness is brighter, the pain hurts more, and I am pretty sure I remember every single time Ryan smiled.

I can't remember what my mother looks like, but I can remember every single time Ryan has smiled at me.

"Allie." Dawn sounds worried. "You're going to think I'm a huge baby, but I kind of don't like the look of the street outside. So it would be really good if you could look, and tell me I'm nuts, okay?"

I bite my lip. Dawn's never been nervous about biking through the city. She's a New Yorker to the bone. So hearing this? I am concerned. I've seen a lot of demon activity today, and now I'm wondering if maybe I brought it home with me.

I put down my knife but, on second thought, pick it back up again. It's high-carbon steel—that's an iron alloy, and good enough to kill or seriously maim all kinds of things. I wave Dawn behind me and then slink out toward the window booths. I flick open the blinds, and take a look.

At first, I don't see anything. I mean, there's traffic, but no creatures of the night hanging around, you know? It looks normal.

Except. There's a bright green leaf on the sidewalk. I think it's oak.

If you've never been to the Williamsburg area of Brooklyn, maybe you don't understand why I'm staring at that leaf. It's because leaves imply the presence of trees. There are no trees in Williamsburg.

Why are you here? Like it can hear me, the leaf floats up in the air on a bit of breeze, and turns in place.

The world shivers. Really. Like a picture in an Etch A Sketch, except instead of going blank, it's a brand new picture. There's a woman standing right in front of me, dressed in green, and the leaf's attached to a long stalk coming out of her hand. She twitches her hand and the "leaf" starts to float around, drawing the attention of a teenager with big sunglasses walking past. He smiles, and reaches for the leaf.

He doesn't see the woman. Or can't see her. And she's smiling in a really creepy way.

I jerk open the blinds and knock the butt of the knife against the window. "Hey!" I yell. "Do not eat the mundanes!" The woman-thing shoots an irritated look at me. She starts walking backward toward the alley next to the diner, drawing the guy along with her.

Not for the first time, I wish that Ryan didn't live off the grid. If he didn't live off the grid, he'd have a damn cell phone, and I could call him to come kill the demon. But he's not, and he can't, and it's just me.

Shit.

Okay. I look around. Ketchup. I flip the top, squirt out a ton onto the table, and toss the bottle. Fingerpainting time! Two intersecting triangles on the window, and dots all the way around, and I stare through the ketchupped Seal of Solomon to the woman outside and think, as hard as I can, *Please go away!*

Look, Ryan never said how to actually *use* the Seal.

But it must be good enough, because the woman suddenly hisses and the leaf zips up into her hand. She turns and runs—that's how I see that she doesn't have a back. I mean, there's nothing there, except ragged edges. She's made of hollowed-out wood, all splinters and rot.

I turn to look at the teenager, just to make sure he's okay. He's staring at me. I smile apologetically. He reaches up and takes off his sunglasses, revealing big, black eyes with a thousand facets. He's a werewolf. He bares his teeth at me, and then lopes off after the woman.

So. Um.

I cannot figure out whose meal I ruined in that encounter.

I look behind me. Dawn's still in the kitchen, thank god. I close the blinds again without wiping off the Seal, and then go back to the kitchen.

"I don't know what to tell you, kid," I lie. "You can stay here if you want, or we can call you a cab to take you home."

"I have my bike." She stares at me, eyes rimmed in too much black eyeliner. It's smearing; she needs to learn to put on foundation and powder before she applies it.

"Leave it here, in my apartment." I point to the door that goes upstairs. "I'll call you a cab to take you home. My treat. Seriously. If it's getting scary out there, I don't want you biking home. You never know who's gonna knock you over, you know?"

Dawn swallows hard and nods. "I'll get my bike," she says.

"Take this," I say, and hand over a knife. She takes it, but not without giving me a look. I shrug. "Call it psychology. You'll feel more confident. And you're going to give it right back in two seconds, so why not?"

"I guess," she says, leery, and heads back out front and, hopefully, not to her death.

Because now that I know there's something wrong outside, I can tell there are other demons hiding around; I can *smell* it. And I'm feeling really bad about sending my waitstaff home through this without anything to protect them. I hope one of them made it, at least. I hope I didn't get someone killed just because I was dumb again.

I call a car—we keep the numbers for different cab services handy, just in case a customer needs them, but this time I call the service Ryan recommended years ago—and Dawn comes back wheeling her bike in, the knife clutched awkwardly in one hand. I take it back, and because she looks like she's going to jump out of her own skin any second now, I decide to go for a distraction.

"Seen Stan or Amanda today?"

She leans her bike against the door to my apartment and then jumps up onto the counter and looks at me worriedly. "Nope, neither one's been in today. Amanda called, though. I wasn't kidding when I said it's been dead." She has a really heavy Brooklyn accent, and it's coming out even more now. She sounds like a character on a television show, her accent drawn out—a caricature of herself. She says, "Why do you ask?"

A car horn honks and I look behind her. "That was fast. Your car is here." I open the cash drawer and hand her a twenty. "Bring the change back tomorrow."

She hesitates before taking it, and the silver rings on her fingers glint in the fluorescent light. "You sure?"

"Sure." I push the twenty at her again, and this time she takes it, jumps off the counter. Considering just who recommended this service, I add, "Listen to the driver if he's telling you something life-or-death, okay?"

Dawn may be too clever for her own good. She nods thoughtfully. "Be careful, Allie," she says, and then she's gone, and I can breathe again.

Let's fix that: I pull my pack of cigarettes from the shelf under the register and light one. Screw the health department and the smoking ban. It's my fucking diner and I'll have a Camel Light if I want one.

Then I pick up the phone to call Amanda. That used to be the very first thing I did whenever something weird happened. Now my first instinct is to call down the stairs for Ryan. Since I can't have Ryan right now, I'll take what I can get. If all I can get is my drunk best friend, I'll take her. She won't be able to do anything, but maybe she'll come to the diner and keep me company while the vampires mill around outside looking intimidating.

She doesn't answer the phone. I let it ring until it goes to voice mail and then I call her again, and again, and again. She never picks up. That is so weird, because Amanda is, like, chained to her phone.

I leave her a voice mail asking her to call me, and then I call Stan.

"Hey, baby," he greets me.

"Hey, Stan. You still coming to the diner for closing?" I ask.

"Yeah, of course."

"And have you heard from Amanda?" I continue.

"Amanda? No, not at all today. But I've been . . . busy." I can hear his leer.

"Ugh, don't tell me, I don't want to know. Just— it's almost sunset. Why don't you come a little early, okay?"

Now he sounds suspicious: "Is this a trick to make me do work?"

I sigh. "No, I just don't want you wandering around outside after dark. Seriously, there's shit happening that you need to know about."

"Don't worry about me, Allie, I've got an iron nail." He cackles. He still thinks this whole thing is a big fucking joke. And one of these days that's going to get him killed. The very idea of it twists something in my stomach. Stan isn't a good guy—I'm not going to lie, okay? I love him, but he's not a good person.

That doesn't mean that he deserves to die at the hands of vindictive bitchy demons.

Starting at sunset, hunters start trickling in. I have no idea how Narnia is doing it. Does she even know where the diner is? Okay, evidence is suggesting "yes," but I am still suspicious. And how is she getting everybody together without the benefit of this week's newspaper? Maybe she really is using smoke signals. I mean, if she's the one who assigns hunters, she's got to have a list of them and some way to contact them.

Maybe, and this is just a wild and crazy guess here—maybe she's using a cell phone.

Most of them look like normal people who have a few extra scars. A lot of them are wearing retail uniforms, like for Target and IKEA. I guess it's hard to hold down a desk job when you're constantly being called to fight demons—or maybe the Doors open in retail outlets like they do in malls, and this is just the most convenient solution.

I want to ask Ryan, but he's milling around, going to each group of hunters and speaking to them in a low voice. I can't even eavesdrop.

The girl hunters are my favorites, I have to be honest. They take Girl Power to a whole new level. They all look kickass, and have muscles. And I, okay, am selfishly comparing myself to them—none of them are as skinny as I'd expected. Too much science fiction television, I guess, and I'm as vulnerable to social programming as anyone else. *I* am not skinny by any stretch of the imagination. Never have been.

I tried for a few years, when I was a teenager, but no matter how many meals I skipped, I never lost an ounce. I'm just naturally curvy, I guess.

By the time we lock the door for closing, every single seat is full. All the demon hunters from the area and beyond are here.

Stan's shown up, too—he and Amanda usually always show up for closing, whether any hunters are around or not. They grew up the same as me, selfish and spoiled, but coming to the diner at closing time is something I can always rely on them for. Mostly I think they do it to make sure that I'm alive, that a demon hasn't killed me yet. Sometimes I think they do it because they feel badly that I'm poor now, still poor even though the diner does well.

Instead of buying Brazilian leather shoes, now I buy new aprons and T-shirts that say SALLY'S DINER on them for the odd tourist who stops by. Sometimes, if I have some money left over, I get a manicure, but there's not really a point to it when my fingers are always crushing tomatoes or cleaning up demon guts.

Except instead of being here when I need her,

Amanda is probably out at her house on Long Island, sitting by her pool, drinking something alcohol-heavy, and . . . and not being here when I need her, basically. I can't figure out if I'm bitter because she's not here when I need her (not that she'd be very helpful, but a girl needs her best friends at times like these), or if I'm bitter because she gets the option of sitting around and doing whatever she wants whenever she wants. The diner's mine, sort of, and she's my best friend, but that doesn't mean that she has to be committed to it the way I am. I know that. And I resent the hell out of it.

"I wish you had come before dark," I say to Stan while we're waiting for the coffee to brew. When he asks why, this time I fill him in a little, and tell him about all the vampires—who disappeared from the block at sundown, way before all the hunters showed up.

"I know you're, like, worried about all this stuff," says Stan, "but maybe you're overreacting."

"I don't think I'm overreacting." I reach around him for a loaf of Italian bread and start slicing, just for something to do with my hands.

"Chillax," he tells me, and sweeps away with the coffee cups. I want to punch him in his stupid face.

He does the coffee, I do trays of stew, and we're ready to go. Everyone is well into their food and coffee when Ryan stands up and leans against the counter.

"Narnia probably told you all why we were gathering here tonight," Ryan announces. "That while I was being distracted by a shedu, the Door in this diner disappeared. We can't figure out if it's just gone, or if it's moved. I've consulted with Narnia, and she's damn near positive that it's just been moved—but we don't know where, or even why."

Stan turns to me, his eyes wide. *"What?"* he mouths.

"Later," I reply, and tilt my head toward Ryan, hopefully conveying that later means "away from where Ryan can call us mundanes and be mean to us in front of the other hunters." Not that I necessarily think that Ryan would do that, but it's always a possibility. I spent a really long time living the life that Amanda lives now—the one with the pool, the alcohol, the drugs, and along with that went being really nasty to other people for no reason at all except their differences.

It sounds like I'm different now. I'm not. Just quieter.

Ryan kept talking while I had my introspective moment slurring his character, and then one of the hunters in the back, the only tall, black, gorgeous woman in the crowd, yells out, "Magic?"

"I think so," says Ryan. "I'm pretty sure that someone's moved it, but I don't know how, and whatever magic they're using is preventing me from finding it. That's some serious stuff, and I don't like not knowing who has it, and why they wanted a Door. But while this is a problem, it's not our biggest."

"That's a relief," says one of the hunters sitting up front. He sounds sarcastic, but how to be sure?

"What about these idiots, the ones who opened the Door in the first place? I bet they did it!" called out a guy wearing a Fedora and a cape. A cape. Seriously. A cape.

"We learned our lesson!" I reply angrily. "We had nothing to do with this."

No one believes me, that much is clear. Sometimes I wonder how much the demon hunters hate us. Us being the mundanes that they protect. I think they only protect us incidentally—maybe they just all have tiffs with the demons. If they hate mundanes, people who aren't hunters, people who don't know about demons, then why fight the demons in the first place? Why not just let everyone die?

On the other hand, really obnoxious twelve-year-olds could have opened the damn Door. They're lucky it was me. The ones that show up here to shoot the shit with Ryan? I give them a discount on food, let them sleep on my floors *and* use my shower.

"Don't even bother trying that shit," yells one of the hunters from the back. Yeah, they hate us.

I scowl at them all. "As sick and freaking tired as I am of having a Door in my basement, I would never even consider moving the Door without talking to someone first. Or, hell, moving it at all! Demon guts suck, it's fucking true, but what about all the unsuspecting people who'd get hurt if the Door moved unexpectedly?"

"Yeah," says Stan. He sounds a little stoned, and his bleached hair is standing straight up off his head like he's just rolled out of bed. Probably he has. "Anyway, we wouldn't even know *how*. Ryan never tells us anything."

"Well that's something he does right," a Baseball Cap in the back snickers. I look closer; it's Owen. And seriously? Shit. List.

"Hey, assholes," says Ryan, as rudely as I've ever heard him talk. "*Forget* the moving Door. We have a bigger problem, bigger than Narnia or I realized. *Many* bigger problems." His eyes sweep over the group. "Haven't you noticed? There are more Doors, spontaneous ones. Ten years ago there was, what, three in the entire state of New York? I've seen that many new ones *today*."

The hunters *do,* to give them credit, start looking around and muttering to each other. I even see a Baseball Cap say something to a Fedora. Oooh, evil brings people together.

"Who works the Door at the Kings Plaza mall?" asks Ryan. "Allie and I were there today, looking for *our* Door, and—"

"That one's mine." A Baseball Cap in a security guard uniform stands up. "Christian, at your service."

"It's been more active lately," says Ryan. It's not exactly a question.

"Yup," drawls Christian. He's gotta be from the Midwest somewhere; his accent is sharp and twangy. And he's gorgeous, but he looks like he could be really mean. I know how to spot people like that. Hunter or no hunter, I've got a nose for the snotty bitches.

"When Allie and I were there, the bodies showed signs of multiple mythologies at work; I went back later, and as of two hours ago there is a second Door beside the original one, and it's brought friends. Definitely spontaneous, though—Allie talked to the fledgling one when we went looking for her Door, before I realized the bigger issue. But there are definitely two Doors at Kings Plaza now."

"Shit." Christian says it with feeling. Then he pauses. "She can talk to them?" he asks, and suddenly there's a lot more interest in the room directed toward me.

"They don't really say anything," I say, but my voice is a squeak. "They just like to . . . I don't know, *chat*."

"The Doors like to chat with you?" A Fedora looks skeptical. "Jackson." He's the same Fedora who talked to the Baseball Cap guy earlier. "Doors don't just talk to anyone."

"They talk to me. I try not to talk back." I paste a

smile on my face, my ditziest one. "I don't want what they're offering."

"And what do they offer you, *chère*?" This is from the woman from before. She adds, belatedly, "Call me Roxie. I guard the Door in the movie theater in Sheepshead Bay."

I've been to Sheepshead Bay. Once. Accidentally. I was looking for Manhattan Beach, which butts right up next to it. It's sort of a little fishing village, built around a bay that drains into the ocean, and it's full of Russians. Roxie, who is six feet tall at least, wearing a leather vest and leather pants, and has a thick scar bisecting her face diagonally, must stand out.

"They just want me to ask for things. All the Doors are the same."

"Because," says Jackson, "the more you ask for, the more demons they can send into the world."

I know that. "I know that. I've had a Door under my diner for six years. And I know better than to ask it for things."

"It's just," Ryan tells me, "that most people can't actually hear the Door talk to them. It's just an urge, an urge to ask for something."

"Okay, I didn't know that," I admit.

"Listen, 'educate the mundane' is all fun and games," says a Baseball Cap rudely. They are rapidly becoming my least favorite faction. There's something to be said for civility in times of crisis. "I'm thinking we need to find out what's going on, though. If Door activity is on the rise, there's got to be a reason."

Ryan nods. "And if it's because the Doors are preparing to multiply, then we might be looking at something a lot worse."

"I talked to a vampire——" I was cut off from finishing my sentence by angry mutterings. I exchange a glance with Ryan. He's just as annoyed with the hunters as I am. Good, someone will have my back when I go rage blackout on these assholes. Jeez. I raise my voice.

"As I was saying! I talked to a vampire who said that there *are* going to be a lot more Doors to come. It also started saying something about feeding—"

"That's it? Rumors from a vampire is all you know?" Christian snorts. I knew it: snotty bitch.

"Unfortunately, Narnia killed it before I could keep talking to it," I say repressively.

"Hey," says Stan, and the room quiets. "But if there are Doors in the mall and in the movie theaters . . . why don't you just leave them alone? Like, who cares? It's just the *mall*." He says *mall* the way other people say *cockroach* or *dial-up Internet*.

He's got a cigarette hanging out of the corner of his mouth, and looks like he's about to go over to New Jersey to hit one of the dance clubs. Then he has to open his mouth and say dumb shit? And not stop:

"People who shop in Bath & Body Works deserve

whatever comes through the Door," Stan announces, and steps up to stand next to me. "It's Darwinism in action."

I really resent being put in the position where I have to be the logical, responsible one. It's been more than a few years already, and I'm getting tired of it. When do I get to sit around and smoke as many cigarettes as I want and arbitrarily decide what matters and what doesn't?

"Shut up," I tell him. He's making me look like a moron.

"So there are really two problems," Ryan says to the hunters, ignoring us. "Problem one is that the Door here is missing, and we don't know where it went. Problem two is that there are more and more Doors popping up. Best case scenario with that one: Eventually we run out of hunters, and the world is overrun with demons." This is the best case scenario? Ryan resettles the Stetson on his head. "Worst case scenario: The world ends in earth and air." The hunters nod soberly like that makes *any sense whatsoever*. Except the world-ending part. That sounds bad.

"I'm already guarding two Doors," volunteers a youngish looking hunter. Seriously, is he, like, sixteen? Or am I just getting so old that everyone looks young to me?

While the hunters talk about whether or not these problems are related—the consensus seems to be that they are, because otherwise two mysterious and shitty things are happening at once for no good reason, and that's just too depressing to think about—I lean against Ryan. Just a little. Just enough to feel that he's there. He smells like blood, like he's been hunting, but he also smells like my sandalwood soap, and a little like sweat. It is the sexiest shit I have ever smelled in my life.

My pheromones want his pheromones.

I stand on my toes and say, very quietly, in his ear, "What's 'earth and air'?"

His head whips to the side, and he's looking at me like he's never seen me before. Surprise surprise, I was listening. But I am also distracted, because there's this fantastic cheekbone of his, right there, inches from my mouth.

Which is right when Stan decides that he is not done making me look like a selfish idiot. "Does it really have to come back *here*?" he asks, and I settle back on my feet and Ryan turns back to the crowd. And, look, I guess I *am* a selfish idiot, but I don't need any help displaying that to the public, and Stan is *still talking*. "Allie doesn't need any more of this hunter shit," he says. "And it's *boring*."

I close my eyes, take a deep breath. I open them again and say, "Stan, why don't you go home?" *And,* I add in my head, *just forget all about this.* It's not like he's helpful anyway. It would make my life a lot easier if he didn't remember anything about the Door or the hunters, really. I'm not sure *how* it would make my life easier, but I am pretty sure that it *would*. Like, maybe he'd stop saying dumb shit that just makes me look like another idiot mundane who played with things she didn't understand.

Because you know what? That was six years ago. And since then, I've killed at least as many demons as a green hunter. I don't just sit around and let Ryan do the fighting. I'm not very good at it, but I do it. I helped open the Door. I'll help close it if they ever figure out how. Ryan has slept on a cot in my basement for six years—sometimes, mostly when I am not in it, he sleeps in my bed. Hell, he helps out in the diner when it's really busy and the Door is dormant. It's not like I don't understand the situation we're in, how dire it can be. It's not like I don't understand that at any time, if Ryan or I are just a moment off in our reactions, just a split second, we could be dead.

Stan glares at me. *Go,* I think at him. "Just go," I say wearily. "The hunters and I will handle this."

"Fine," he says, and storms through the hunters. They open up to make a path for him. I hope and pray that's not what I look like when I flounce off, because he looks like a spoiled brat.

Once the door closes behind him, Ryan's hand comes down on my shoulder and squeezes gently. I'm hoping that the squeeze translates into something like, *You just did the right thing,* and not something like, *You are monumentally stupid.*

The hunters are all arguing among themselves, and their faces are grouchy. I tune them out. I'm interested, but hunter politics are bullshit. I've only been exposed to them for the last day, and I'm already tired of all the drama. It's just like government—they're going to talk and talk and fight and bicker and be annoying and loud, and in the end, the decisions are all going to be made by the one or three people who yell the loudest, are the meanest, and aren't afraid.

Ryan pulls out tobacco and rolling papers, and starts rolling a cigarette. I know I'm not supposed to find it hot, but he looks really good smoking. And it's not like hunters really have to worry about dying of lung cancer; something else inevitably gets them first. I don't know how Ryan has made such peace with inexorable death. Sure, anyone can get hit by a bus in the middle of the street at any time, but that's the kind of death we can ignore. Ryan's death is in the cards; it's going to happen. It's just dumb luck that it hasn't happened before now.

He looks up and catches me staring at him. He stares back. It's like the world goes away when he looks at me. The world just goes away. He licks the rolling paper, seals the cigarette, and offers it to me. I hate unfiltered cigarettes because the tobacco is always getting into my teeth, but I take it anyway. He lights it with a Zippo. The smoke hurts my lungs and stings my eyes, but I blow smoke rings and wait for the hunters to stop arguing amongst themselves.

Here is the thing: Like I could smell the badness on the trains, and hear the Doors whispering in the mall—I know that I'm going to have to do something dangerous. I can tell.

I have a really bad feeling about it, too.

7

When we opened the Door, six years back, for a while I lived in a tiny apartment near the diner because old Sally hadn't gone to Florida or whatever and left me in charge yet. I'd just broken up with Jimmy— I'd caught him and Amanda more than halfway to doing it next to the grill. It would have served them right if they'd accidentally burnt themselves, but I had to stop them. We'd just gotten in seven orders for pancakes from some high school kids, and with them in the way, I couldn't fill the order.

I don't blame Amanda. She can't help it. It doesn't occur to her, ever, that she can't have something she wants. I used to be like that, so I can appreciate the difficulty. And Jimmy should have known better, but no man can resist Amanda's stupid mouth and pointy elbows. Honestly, I was more angry that they were messing up my kitchen.

So Jimmy was history, and Amanda had the sense to

stay out of my sight for a while. But little by little, I let her back, and she came.

That's why I really keep up with Amanda and Stan. Because even though they have no idea who I am now, and have just the slightest clue what I have to deal with on a daily basis, they stick by me. They could've laughed off the whole Mom-and-Rio thing—and they wouldn't have been the only ones by a long shot—but they didn't. They stuck it out, and they're still sticking it out, and for that kind of loyalty, the least they deserve is a little something back.

I'm sitting on the floor behind the counter, back against the shelving and feet up on a pile of collapsed cardboard boxes I haven't tossed out yet, and I'm flipping my phone open and closed. I have a cell phone, but Ryan doesn't. I bet Narnia does. I bet everybody does except Ryan, because having a convenient way to contact him would be too easy.

No, I'm not being fair. I understand that he needs to stay off the grid. It would be a pain in the ass for him to have a cell phone, to have bills to pay every month, to have a driver's license. He can't vote, because he can't be registered to vote, because what a pain in the ass it would be for him to have to do jury duty or something. It would suck and be annoying, just like it is for everyone else—but twice as bad for Ryan, because he'd spend the whole time worrying about the demons coming through the Door while he's gone.

I'm worried about Amanda. I guess I'm worried about Stan too, but he's been a bitch more recently, and so he gets to have some downtime before I go bugging him. Amanda, on the other hand . . . when did I last see her? Dawn said she called, but it was the diner number instead of mine. I am seriously confused. Maybe I did something?

Maybe I'm not doing enough.

But, jeez, it's hard to have a lot of patience for drama when you run a diner. Diners are hard work. It's a lot harder than I ever thought it would be, frankly, because I guess I believed a little too much in how diners ran on TV, like on *90210,* how they just magically made the Peach Pit a success.

Little did I know. I had a lot of ideas when Sally left town, and implementing those ideas led to a lot of interesting misunderstandings. For example, if you write the menu in poetry, you get a lot of truckers and demon hunters ordering what they think is steak and potatoes, but turns out to be steak tartar with asparagus.

Let me tell you something. If you ever serve a truck driver steak tartar with asparagus and herbed new potatoes with ghee, they will send it right back and ask if you have meatloaf.

That was the last time I let Dawn write the menu. From then on, we went right back to using the original Sally's cookbook. No one can go wrong with Sally's steak and potatoes—or her meatloaf.

I am behind the counter right now because, seriously, listening to the hunters is really boring. From what I understood, the Baseball Caps didn't trust the Fedoras or the Stetsons, while . . . well, you can guess the rest. It's one big show of mistrust. Who screws up the most, who gets killed the most, their philosophies of hunting. I think it's not a surprise anymore that Ryan doesn't want to have sex with me—I am pretty sure that I'm a Fedora. They're the ones who keep demons alive and torture them while asking questions about the underworlds, and that's the suggestion of every Fedora in the room—find a demon, capture it, torture it with holy water, and make it answer some damn questions about what's going on. That's a plan I can get behind.

The Baseball Caps think nothing is wrong. They're all easygoing like Owen, with an undercurrent of meanness. They kind of make me think of the little kids who pull wings off butterflies. Not to get anything, not for information, not because it has to be done—but because they *like it*.

Eventually, things get quiet. I pop my head over the counter. The diner is empty except for Christian, Jackson, that tall black female hunter—Roxie—and Ryan. They're talking quietly in Ryan's corner booth. They all have coffee, clearly gotten from the bodega down the street. Ryan *hates* having to make his own coffee, and clearly no one thought to ask me. I make great coffee. A little smoky, a little bitter, a little dark, a little mellow.

I stretch, and stand. No one looks at me. Fine. I flip open my phone and call Amanda. No answer. Her voice mail is full. I call Stan. He, at least, answers.

"Heeeeyyyyy." It's all long vowels. "Whas-saaaaaaap?"

I cringe. "Stan, the hunters are gone, you can come back now."

"What hunters, Al? What are you even talking about? Crazy girl. Nobody hunts in Brooklyn. The B-K-L-Y-N!" he crows. So high. So so high. Or drunk. Or both.

"The hunters, Stan. You know. Like Ryan."

"Oooh, is that your *boyfriend*?" says Stan.

"What? You know Ryan." I pull the phone away from my ear and check the caller ID to make sure that I actually called Stan and not some random accidental person. But it's Stan.

"Sure I know Ryan. Surrrrre."

"Don't forget to drink some water, Stanley," I say, in my bossiest voice. I hear people in the background calling to him. "I'm going to hang up now."

"Bee-*oy* friend!" he chants, and I click my phone shut.

Boyfriend indeed.

Why does Stan not remember anything about the hunters? Maybe he's just high. Or maybe—

Oh shit. I drop down behind the counter again.

Okay, this is stupid, but I am trying to work through this. The Door in the hospital told me to touch it, and I did, right? It used its voice, the one that sounds directly in my head. I told the leaf thing to tell me why it was here, and it did, in a weird way. I even told the hollow woman to go away, and she did.

I said it in my head, with my thoughts.

Maybe I *told Stan* to forget. That cannot possibly be what happened, though. Right?

Okay, so maybe now I'm psychic. That would be good, right? Then I can help assign hunters, maybe beat up Narnia without getting my own ass kicked—except how the hell did I just become pyschic, like, *now*?

. . . You know, I've been around a lot of Doors today. A lot of wish-granting Doors.

I do not like my random logic chains. Hunters in my diner, saying you can ask a Door for things without really asking . . . and the diner became *really* successful once the Door opened in the basement. Once Stan and Amanda and I opened it. I thought—okay, what I thought my Door gave me, when we first opened it, was Ryan—and I hate thinking that, hate thinking that I owe a Door to Hell for the best thing that's ever happened to me—but what if I was secretly asking it for my diner the whole time? That would explain why the diner was empty today. No Door, no successful diner.

And what if I haven't stopped asking it for things, and the Door's just been giving, and giving, and— What if I asked for something to make me important to the hunters? What if I asked to be important to *Ryan*?

On top of that, Ryan's always told me that wishing for things from the Door dries up your soul and turns you into a demon. But sometimes he says a wish lets the Door open to release another demon. I've never bothered to find out if either one of them's the truth.

All I know is, if I become some kind of psychic demon, I am going to be *pissed*.

When I pop back up and look over at Ryan and the others, they are still talking in low voices, not looking at me. So I open the dessert case and pile black and white cookies onto a paper plate and bring them out. I need to ask them about this. I need to know if I am accidentally turning into a demon and if that is making me kind of weirdly psychic, or if I'm weirdly psychic and only coincidentally turning into a demon.

Ryan is the one talking, but he falls silent when I come up.

"Well, what's the verdict?" I say. I will enter into the subject of my possible demon-ness with subtlety.

"The Baseball Caps are idiots," snorts Jackson.

"Shut up," says Christian, but he says it like he knows that his crew sucks.

"We're . . ." Ryan stops, sips his coffee, grimaces. Yup, he wishes he had my coffee. "We've decided to go with the worst case scenario. Which means that some of us have to go into a Door and ask for help."

"Uh. What?" I cross my arms over my chest. "What?"

"You heard me." Ryan takes a bite of a cookie. He only likes the chocolate halves. I only like the vanilla halves. We're meant to be, in some other world, some world where there are no demons.

"It's the only way," says Roxie around a mouthful of cookie.

"I think I need to go back behind the counter until you are no longer crazy," I say, even though I know it won't do any good, because this is the kind of hare-brained scheme that has Ryan written all over it. Not that he's ever had a really stupid plan before, actually, but he's like me in that way: one minute he seems perfectly logical, and the next minute his logic has gone to a completely bizarre place that nevertheless still makes perfect sense. "Did you say that instead of doing magic, torturing a demon for information, or waiting to see what happens, you all want to actually go in through a Door into an actual Hell dimension to see if you can find *help*? In *Hell*? For a world-ending 'scenario' that no one has yet explained, by the way."

"In Hell dimensions, there are avatars that come down to protect you," says Christian, ignoring my obvious play for the whole earth-and-air info. "I'm not sure exactly how it works, but that's what I've heard.

We'd ask them for help, and they'd—do something. Maybe talk to the gods for us or something."

"This sounds like one of Ryan's cheap novels." My arms are still across my chest, and I still can't believe what I'm hearing.

"Sometimes the novels get it right," Ryan tells me. "You know that, Allie."

"If we can get to one of the nice Hells—"

I cut Jackson off with a shriek. "One of the *nice* Hells?"

"They're not all Hells," says Roxie. She has some kind of drawl. It's different from Christian's midwestern twang; more of a Deep South thing. What's she doing in Brooklyn, of all places?

"What do you mean that they are not all Hells?" I am totally suspicious of this new information.

"They're not—" Christian stops and frowns. "They're not *Hells*. They're underworlds."

"And the difference is . . . what exactly?"

"The difference is that not all underworlds are scary and evil. The underworld of the ancient Egyptians is fields and rivers." Ryan leans back and offers me the vanilla half of the cookie.

"I shun your cookie," I tell him. "How the hell do you know what an underworld is like?"

"The Egyptian Book of the Dead," chorus all three of them.

"But you don't know if that's *real*!" I protest. They

exchange *oh, what a stupid mundane* looks, and I scowl. "Listen. I think it's really cool that you guys are so into protecting humanity—which you clearly all hate and disrespect all the time—but I think this is going a step too far. What's in a Hell that can tell you anything about what's going on? Not to mention that if you go into a Hell dimension, you're going to die. You'll be attacked by demons, and they will kill you. This is totally straightforward. It's not like it's a surprise or something."

"There are avatars, and we think there are gods there. And it can't be any worse than trying to live through the end of the world." Ryan pushes the cookie toward me anyway, even though I shunned his cookie! I shunned it. But it's the vanilla half of a black and white cookie. It is inevitable that I am drawn to it. I reluctantly take a bite.

"You're idiots," I say around my mouthful, then swallow. "You don't even know if the worst case scenario is going to happen. You don't even know what your avatars *are*. What kind of word is that anyway? And don't get me started on this whole gods idea—"

"So you're coming with us, then?" Ryan smirks up at me. Roxie rolls her eyes. When I look at Jackson and Christian, they are both studiously looking elsewhere, not at me.

"God, of course I'm coming," I say with a lot more confidence than I'm feeling, and I take another bite of cookie. I know I should say something, should tell everybody what's going on with me and my worries, but . . . Ryan asked me to come with them. Like I'm a real hunter. It's sad, and it's pathetic, and he probably didn't even mean it like that, but maybe, *maybe* he did. And I'm surprised to find that that's really good enough for me.

In my head, I say, *And by the way, I think that maybe I am turning into a psychic demon a little bit.*

Out loud, I say: "Who wants root beer?"

"Look, I've got to know." I plant a giant root beer in front of Roxie, and she sniffs. Whatever, it's barely four in the morning. Now is not the time to over-caffeinate. The boys are at the next table over, poring over Ryan's notebooks, making lists, and swilling down coffee because they do not accept my wisdom. "Did her parents actually name her Narnia, or is it just some kind of stupid thing she does to impress fanboys?"

Roxie grins up at me. Her scars move in really cool ways when she does that. "Her? She never calls herself that. *We* call her that."

I lift an eyebrow. Roxie takes a big swallow and makes a face.

"Rich bitch like her, you have to give her a big house, a big wardrobe, and a dozen fur coats before you get in her—and then she's *still* cold."

I blink a few times. "I have no idea what to say to that," I tell Roxie, and take a sip of my own root beer. "But I totally did not get that vibe from her."

"That's because you were with Ryan, weren't you?" Roxie sniffs again, this time a lot more disdainfully. "She's got a thing for Ryan."

"Everyone's got a thing for Ryan," I grumble.

"Uh-huh." Roxie's eyes are wise, and I avoid them.

"So tell me about the thing with the hunters. I just don't understand. I'd think that demon hunters would all get along, have a union or something, but Ryan says that's not true." I sip at my root beer. It's got too much fizz and not enough flavoring, but I'm going to drink it anyway.

"It's got to do with a Scientologist and a loa," says Roxie like she knows more than that, but when I press her, she stays silent. "Instead of talking about shit that don't matter—"

"So you're a Stetson?" I guess. Otherwise she'd have a problem working with Ryan, right?

"Well, I'm not a *Baseball Cap*." Roxie glares at me. "You got a problem with the Stetsons? Gods, Ryan didn't tell me that you're a Fedora."

"I'm not a Fedora!" I protest. Only *maybe* I am a Fedora. "I'm not anything. I think I own a pair of sunglasses. That and this bandanna is as close as I get to covering my hair."

"Uh-huh."

"Seriously," I say, but I can tell she doesn't believe me. "Look, we don't have to get along, but you don't have to insult me."

Roxie takes a sip of root beer and makes another face. Oh, whatever. "There's fucked-up stuff happening all over the city, not just here," she says thoughtfully. "But Doors appearing, earth and air—why would your Door disappear? It should be really happy here. It has someone to talk to, plenty of people to wheedle into asking for things . . ."

"That does make sense," I admit. "But what's all this earth and air—" I feel fingers on the back of my neck. I shiver. His fingers have calluses, gorgeous calluses, from swinging a sword and using daggers and shooting guns. He squeezes my neck for a moment, then trails his fingers down the exposed knobs of my spine.

I *melt*. But I want to remain firm. "Thank you for asking me to go through whichever Door you eventually decide on," I say resolutely. Best offense and all the rest of that stupid phrase.

Ryan slides in next to me, and keeps sliding until I move over, but I can't move far enough away. He's pressed up and down my side. "You're not," he says. Guess I'm not hunter enough for you after all, huh. My tiny little fantasy begins to wither. Well, screw *that*.

"I am. You said I was and I said I was and I'm going to," I insist.

"I wasn't serious when I asked. And no, you're not.

You have nothing to do with this. Your Door probably only moved—"

"So I should just care about my Door? Forget it. Stan and Amanda and I opened the stupid thing in the first place, and thanks to us there's who knows how many demons and deaths and hunters out of comm-mission, and I can't just—I can't just go to sleep and forget what I owe." Damn, I hate being an adult.

"Who do you think it's going to help if you get hurt yourself?" demands Ryan. "It's not going to help any-one. You'll just be dead."

"So I'll be dead," I reply with a calm I don't feel. I do not want to die. *Not.* "At least I'll know that I helped fix the mistakes I made. That's one of the things—you *know* that's one of the things I've learned these last few years. And you trained me yourself. I can kill a vam-pire, destroy a werewolf—"

Roxie is watching this with growing interest, but when I mention that I fought demons, she jerks her chin at me. "You fight?" she asks me. I nod. "You fought an elemental yet?"

"Uh . . ." I look over at Ryan.

He shakes his head. "You've done kid fighting. It's chump stuff. Hell plays with your mind, Allie. There's big monsters there. There's things so small you'll never see them get you. It's not smoke and mirrors. It's *real.*"

"I think I know that already. I did touch the damn Door, you know. I felt it."

"And you *fainted*." Ryan is heating up, where he's pressed against me. He puts a hand over mine on the table. Roxie's eyebrows almost hit her hairline. Mine too. "I can't let you do it, Allie. You're not ready."

"And you are?" I snatch my hand away. I hope he doesn't think I'm rejecting him. I'm not. I'm just mad. I'm just—um, I guess I'm rejecting him. But just for the moment! "I don't think *anyone* is ready to travel through a Door into Hell. So I might as well."

"We need you here."

"Why?" I am full of challenge. And I think I'm winning, too, because Ryan is not making a lot of sense. I take another sip of gross watery root beer. Ew. When next I am not fighting for the survival of humanity, I will adjust the ratio of soda water to syrup in the root beer.

Ryan says, "Allie—"

Roxie thunks her root beer down. "Listen, you two. As fun as this is for me, we really need a plan. And we need it soon. Argue this later." Roxie pushes her glass aside and leans across the table. "If we're going to go through a Door, Ryan, we've got to have supplies. We don't know what kinds of Hells we're going to end up in."

I frown. "I thought there were only nine?"

"Each Door," Roxie says, "leads you to one Hell. But you have to go through nine Hells before you can come back to our dimension—if you can get out at all. We think there's hundreds of Doors in every Hell, and they lead to *hundreds* of different Hells. It's a spider web of choices, and we need to be prepared for any of them."

I frown. "So how are we going to find what we need? I mean, won't we just get lost?"

Roxie frowns back. "It's a quest. They're all structured differently, organized differently, and they all do different things to the people who take part in them. So maybe being lost is part of that. Or maybe 'lost' doesn't mean the same thing there."

I throw my hands in the air. "But you just said we might not get out of Hell anyway! So we go in, have no idea where we're going, and have no way of getting out? That is *insane*."

"Glad you think so, because you're not coming," says Ryan. He slides out of the booth and stands up. "Roxie. You coming with me?"

"No," she says. *That* is what resolute sounds like. But she's looking at me oddly, and I feel—worried. "I do think we need to talk," she says to him, "about some of what Allie's just said—because she's right—but if she wants to fight and die, she needs to be allowed to." Roxie's voice softens. "No one gave us training or engraved invitations when *we* started, Ry."

"I can't let her, Roxie. I can't." Ryan's voice is low, and he's got an actual expression on his face instead of the grim visage he normally sports. He looks . . . pained.

"Yes, you can," I say, and jump out of the booth. "Although now that you've made it sound so attractive . . ."

"Shut up," Roxie and Ryan both snap.

Ryan resettles his hat on his head and has what looks like a totally silent conversation with Roxie via their eyebrows.

"Okay," he finally says. "Okay. You can come with us. But—Allie. I'm in charge."

"I'm in charge," Roxie corrects.

"One of the two of you is in charge. Got it." I nod.

Except now I don't want to go. I'm not even half interested. Because now it sounds like I will probably really actually die a real and actual death once we step through a Door. And I don't think I'm ready for that. I haven't even talked Ryan into bed with me yet.

Roxie looks at us, then says she's going to check out the basement. Ryan stops me with a hand on my shoulder when I try to follow.

"What's going to happen if you get killed?" he says quietly.

"You know what's going to happen. The diner's going to close, Stan's going to get HIV, and Amanda's going to die of an overdose."

"Those last two things might happen anyway."

I can't look at him; the sympathy in his eyes makes me want to puke. Puke or cry.

"Ryan . . ." I sway toward him, and he steps away.

"We have to get ready," he says, back to all grim business.

8

So Roxie said she was going to tell me what was going on. This, it turned out, was a fib.

Roxie and Ryan talk and talk, to each other, sometimes in English, mostly not. Stupid Sumerian.

Okay, actually I think they're speaking French. Which might as well be Sumerian. I took Spanish in school, and I remember this: *Hola. Yo me llamo Allie.*

If they really wanted to teach us something helpful in school, they would have taught us Old English. There are tons of magic books written in English that I can't understand because it doesn't make a lick of sense to me at all. It's all spelled wrong—S is F and F is Y, except when it's TH. Seriously.

Christian and Jackson show up periodically with new piles of stuff, get told things I can't understand, and then go out again.

Ryan and Roxie don't chat, they don't grin, they just exchange theories on what we need to bring. There's nothing for me to do except listen—listen and then wander downstairs to sit on the floor of the basement. I guess that I could have gone upstairs to my room and gone to sleep—it's almost dawn now—but somehow that would mean that I was leaving the field, going off to do a normal thing. I don't know. Maybe if I stare at where my Door used to be, it will magically appear and then nobody has to go to Hell at all.

I am so pathetic.

There is a rubber mat down on the part of the floor where we keep the extra canisters of soda water. I sit there because I'm worried I'll fall asleep if I sit on Ryan's cot, but apparently it is still way too soft for my sleepy self. I wake up, a little, when I feel someone cup the curve of my hip.

"It's just me," murmurs Ryan into my hair. "Meeting's over for a while. Relax."

I cannot relax. "How can I?" I roll over. Ryan's lying beside me; I must've been dead to the world for him to manage that without waking me. His coat is off, and his black T-shirt is showing off those fantastic arms. So now it's him and me, face to face, on the edge of a rubber mat on the basement floor. He's got a lot of stubble, and I want to run my hands over it. I want to kiss him. I want—

"Allie," he says softly. "Allie, when I go through that Door—"

"When *we* go through the Door."

His eyes are sad. He raises a hand and touches my cheek. "It's not a good idea," he says.

"Which one?" I ask. "You going through the Door without me, or you coming all the way down here to convince me otherwise?"

He smiles like he doesn't mean to, and all I can think is, *Score.* His hand is resting on my cheek now, and his thumb is teasing my mouth. "At least the coming down here one," he says. "I think I'm bruising."

"You are such a baby."

"You sleep on basement floors."

"And you joined me, cowboy."

His smile drops away, but not in a bad way. "You made it look good," he says.

My brain kind of shuts down.

Ryan gets an intent look, not quite like any I've seen before. His draws his hand away from my cheek and instead tucks it under my hair, and I'm pulled to him like I was pulled to the Door yesterday. I'm drawn to him like I couldn't stop even if I wanted to, and I move until I'm almost lying on top of him, and we're breathing the same air.

We're breathing the same air and then our mouths are touching. His mouth is hot, and his jaw is just as scratchy as I thought it would be. Where he rubs up against me, I know I'm going to be red.

His lips are soft. I usually think they're hard, maybe because he's always pressing them together. Maybe because the first time we kissed they were. I moan a little—I don't mean to, but my body is on fire—and I press against him harder, moving so I'm straddling him and he's on his back. I move my hands to his shoulders, like to hold him down, but he's got both hands in my hair—he's not going anywhere.

He licks at my lips, and I open my mouth. He tastes like dark, strong, black coffee. No sugar. He tastes like heat and passion, he tastes like everything I've ever wanted and nothing I've ever had.

"Please," I say into his mouth. "Please." I don't know what I'm asking for, but he must, because he sits us both up with me straddling his lap. He strips off his t-shirt, then he strips off *my* T-shirt. He brushes his thumbs across the silver scar on my stomach, and it's numb and tingly and embarrassing and amazing, all at once. His hands drift around and he runs his fingers up my spine—I shiver.

He takes a moment to very carefully remove my bra, and he lets out a breath when he sees my bare breasts. I think hysterically that I hope Roxie isn't around, because I'm not into giving a show.

When Ryan pulls me back down, my nipples press against his chest, his scars, and I moan again. His mouth captures mine, and he rolls us over until he's settled between my legs.

"Yes," he says tightly, and his hips buck into mine. He's hard, I can feel it through his leather pants, against my jeans, hitting me right where I want him—where I *need* him to be.

"Yes," I repeat, and get my hand between us. His pants are all buttons, and I fumble and swear. He laughs breathlessly. The leather is tight, and uncomfortable to *me*; I can only imagine how uncomfortable they are to him. He raises himself up on one hand above me and unbuttons his pants. He's not wearing anything underneath. Jesus. I never was good at keeping my hands to myself—he's hot and hard, and I just want to taste him, but he doesn't let me. When I struggle to move, he gets *his* hand between us, and unzips my jeans. I push him off, and wriggle out of them, pulling my plain white underpants—work underpants, not what I would have worn if I'd thought this might happen—down too.

When I look up, he's standing, totally naked. How he got out of his pants and boots so quickly, I have no idea, but he has, and he's standing there and staring at me like I'm everything he's ever wanted and couldn't have. His fingers are digging into his palms, and he's breathing like he's running a marathon.

"God," I say. "I can't even."

"Me either," he replies roughly, and kneels beside me. His movements are smooth, unhindered by any old injuries. I can't imagine . . . he's fought demons for so long, and despite his scars—mental, physical, whatever—he's relatively unscathed. And he's hard. And I really *really* just want to lick him all over.

"I just want to lick you all over," I say, and he shudders, and that's hot too, because, god, what is sexier than being wanted? I never knew.

"Jesus, Allie, you . . ." He's too far away for me to touch. I kind of want to cover up, because the scars that are so sexy on him just make me feel exposed. All my flaws for him to see under the stark light.

But his eyes are hot, pupils dilated, and suddenly he looks young, and wolfish, and—

He leans over me, his arms to either side, and his breath touches the skin of my belly as he gets close, so close. "I'm going to touch you," he says, and his voice is low and deep and I can feel it all up and down my skin, up to my breasts and down to my clit and I can't help but move my hips to the sound of him. "I'm going to know every part of you," he says, and it sounds like a threat; it sounds like a promise. My breath catches in my throat.

"Now," I say. "Now—please—" I rise up to meet him, pull him down to me, get him in me, *in me*—

He puts one hand behind my back and brings me up, moving me easily until I'm sitting upright, my legs spread around him. He's kissing me again. I can feel him between us, and I don't know if he's holding back or if he's holding on, but I don't want to wait any longer. Now it's me rising on my knees, pushing *him* back off our rubber bed and onto—yeah, it's his leather coat, where he must've dropped it before joining me on the floor, and he's watching me with wonder, his hands rubbing my sides and curling in my hair and he's whispering my name over and over.

I brace myself with one hand and hold him with the other as I lower myself on him, and then—then he's inside me. I fall against him, nothing left to hold myself up, and the only thing keeping me alive is his arm strong and hot across my back, his hand on my head. My breasts are crushed to his chest, and the hot sparks of pleasure from that offsets the small hurt I'm feeling where we're joined—not that he's so big, but that it's been so fucking long. It's been so long, but he fits in me like a second half, and it's all I can feel, him inside me, his breath hot against my face. I dig my fingers into his shoulders and slide down as far as I can, until he's so deep inside me I can't tell where he ends and I start, my legs straddling his hips, my thighs stretched.

"Oh, god," he says. "Oh, god." I can feel myself start to sweat. If he doesn't start to move, if he doesn't let *me* move—I just want to *move*.

"Please," I moan, "oh, god, Ryan, please—I want, I want—"

"Yes," he mutters, and puts both hands around my hips, and then he *presses*—

It's awkward at first; we can't find the rhythm. My knees are getting rubbed raw, even through the coat, and he's shaking from keeping it slow, keeping it good for me. I don't have the muscles for this. But here is the thing: It doesn't matter. He's whispering to me, but I can't hear him, I can't hear anything except the thrumming of my body, the slick sounds of skin on skin. I plant my hands on his shoulders, and I press down, and he pushes up, and it's uncomfortable, but we're so close, so close to being amazing.

"I want you," I groan, "I want you, please—" and at last we're moving together. I can thrust my hips down, and he's coming up at the right angle, and it's all I want, us, moving together, fast and hard, my fingernails in his skin.

Breath and beat and our mouths together; I don't see stars when I come, but it's a damn near thing. He cries out into our kiss and I bite my own tongue, and I think I'm crying.

It's minutes and minutes before I come back to myself, sprawled over Ryan, my hands in his hair, his hands like wings on my back. Then his muscles tense like he wants to get up, but I keep my head on his chest, listening to his heart beat. Thump. Thump. Thump. We're sweaty and gross, but I don't care. I don't want to move. Ryan and me together was just as good as I always thought it would be. Six years, we'd been building up to this.

"Allie," he whispers. "Allie, come on."

I let myself go loose and pliant, melting into him. "Come on, Ryan," I whisper back. "Just a few more minutes."

"We can't."

"Your duster is probably toast." I stick out my tongue and lick his nipple, and feel his interest pique. You *know* what I mean. I'm not a prude or anything, but it's kind of weird to think about; I haven't been with too many men, not enough to be used to this whole *I am interested in having sex with you again, like, right now* thing. I decide I am in favor of it.

"The coat's lamia skin," Ryan says, which would be more reassuring if I knew what a lamia was. Ryan twists his hips a little. "It can stand up to more than a little bit of you."

I decide I do not care what a lamia is. "I love the way you said that." I twist my hips back.

"Allie . . ." He runs his hands up to my hair, digs in lightly, lifts my head until I'm looking at him. "We *can't.*"

"I want to," I mutter, and he drags my head down for another kiss. His tongue in my mouth is never going to get old.

"I want to too," he says when we finally break off the kiss to breathe. There's something in his voice that's not quite right, but Ryan doesn't lie to me, so it must be true. "But we can't," he says, "so it's better if we just . . . *don't.*"

It wouldn't be an interaction with Ryan if there wasn't some level of annoyance, and I see that we have reached that portion of the evening. I roll off him and push myself up. "Is that how you live your life?" I say. The concrete of the basement floor hurts my feet, but I'm too indignant to care right now. "Because you can't have everything you just take nothing?"

"It's easier." He leans up on an elbow. God, he's gorgeous, all tan skin and scars and worried eyes. And I'm sad for him, because that's a terrible way to live. I want to make him change; I want to be the change in his world.

Boy, am I in *trouble*.

"That's a sad way to live." I run a hand through my sweaty hair. But he's already getting up and getting dressed again, which just shows that I have made a tactical error by getting up first. Dammit.

He's pulling on his clothes and watching me pull my jeans back on when I realize: "We didn't use a condom. Fuck—we didn't use a condom."

Ryan stops buttoning his pants. Holy shit, the man can rock a pair of unbuttoned leather pants, hair trailing down into them. The part of me that never remembers words like "responsibility" just wants to follow that trail of hair with my mouth and make him writhe under me. Again.

"I didn't even—it's been—it's—I—" he stammers, and I am pretty sure he's *blushing*. What? The great and composed Ryan is *blushing*.

"I'm on birth control." I suck a breath in through my teeth and pull my jeans the rest of the way up. I am *gross,* and I need a shower, and okay, I am on birth control, but we *did not use a condom*. Of all the stupid shit. "We should fucking know better, we're fucking *adults*."

"We do know better, we just . . ."

"Got caught up in the moment?" I ask sarcastically. "Yeah, that's great, we're like every sixteen year old in the tri-state area. Shit." I pull my shirt over my head, forgoing the bra that I can't see anywhere on the floor. Someone is going to find it at exactly the wrong time, I just know it.

"I'm sorry." He looks at me from under his eye-lashes, head bowed.

"Yeah." I sound a lot angrier than I am. "I've never . . . shit." I sigh. "I've never forgotten before. I'm clean, for whatever it's worth."

"I'm clean too. It's been . . . a long time." He sounds almost shy, and it is so. Hot. So. Hot. I almost can't stand how badly I want him again.

"I feel like an idiot," I say, and walk toward him, slide my hands under his pants, around, until I'm almost hugging him. And, honestly, it feels more intimate than the time we just spent rolling around on the floor like animals. I don't know why. We've got our clothes on and everything, but this just feels . . . like more.

"I want you again," he whispers into my hair. "This is such a bad idea."

"I want you again, too," I reply in a low voice. I lean my head into his neck, lick his skin, taste the salt of his sweat. "What if—"

"Don't borrow trouble." He pushes me away, steps back, finishes buttoning his pants. "Seriously. Don't borrow trouble. We have enough already."

"I'm *not*, I just—" I put my hands on my hips and watch him pull his shirt on. He walks toward me and I back away. There's nothing like forgetting a condom to make a girl feel vulnerable and hideous. Not that I've ever forgotten a condom before in my *life*. Ryan makes my brains leak out of my damn ears.

He grabs his coat from the floor and swirls it over his shoulders, sliding his arms into the sleeves. I swear to god, everything this man does looks like magic all the fucking time.

"I'm not a slut," I say, "but I sure feel like shit."

"Don't feel like shit." He's coming toward me again, and I want to back away again, but I will *not*.

"Don't feel like shit," he orders. "I—" He stops, and I wait. We're standing close enough again that I can feel the heat of his body through his clothes. He runs his hands through his hair. "Where's my goddamn hat?"

"I don't fucking know."

He stares at me, and I want to cry. Stupid emotions.

"Allie . . ." I look down at the floor, at my bare feet.

I need a pedicure; the last remnants of neon orange toenail polish glow up at me. "Allie." His fingers slide over my chin, cup my cheek, lift my head. I close my eyes so I don't have to see his stupid face. "Allie, this was a mistake. We shouldn't have."

"You're right, it was stupid," I agree in a monotone. Way to make a girl feel special.

"I can't regret it, though."

When I open my eyes, he's smiling. I don't think I've ever seen him smile at anything before, not like this. Not like there's something wonderful in the world.

"Me either," I whisper, and stand on my tiptoes to kiss him.

He doesn't pull me close; the kiss is almost chaste. Our mouths are closed, our eyes open, yet when we pull away, we both take deep breaths.

"We have to get ready," he says. "We should have been before—it's why I came down here, to tell you. I'm sorry. I didn't mean—"

"Enough," I tell him. "We made a mistake, and we won't do it again."

"But being inside you . . ." His voice is scratchy and rough, and it scrapes over every nerve ending I have. "Being inside you wasn't enough. I meant what I said. If we . . ." He swallows, and closes his eyes, and when he opens them again there's a light shining in them. "We're gonna take our time next time, Allie, and I'm going to taste every part of you."

When he walks away from me, his coat flaps, and I'd rather think about how sexy that is than whatever that "if" might have meant.

Roxie lifts just one eyebrow when Ryan and I come back upstairs. I shrug. She smirks. It's like we're having a conversation, except I have no idea what we're saying. I totally smell like sex, though, and I know it. "I'm going to shower," I tell her.

"You need it," she says, and I scowl at her, but I'm not really angry. As I head upstairs, I hear her tell Ryan that maybe he should shave next time and leave me some skin. I wish I could go back and see his blush.

I shower as quickly as I can; I don't linger, I don't shave my legs. I just wash up, wash my hair, get the basement dust off me, all the sweat. When I'm done, I don't smell like Ryan and sex any more. Well—I don't smell like sex. I smell like my sandalwood soap that Ryan is always stealing. When I first started using it, it was the cheapest soap in the little Indian market around the corner, and I associated it with poverty. Now it's the sexiest thing in the world because it's the way Ryan always smells.

I am *so* gone. So gone. I have fantasies of, like . . . I don't even know, actually. I'm not fantasizing about babies or white picket fences. I'm fantasizing about us *not dying*. That seems so grim. But as long as we don't die, we can be together. Our orbits can decay around each other until we explode.

Unless Ryan gets really angry that I might be a little psychic. Whatever I did to Stan . . . that has got to be fixed, I think. That shouldn't have happened, he shouldn't have forgotten everything about the Door and the hunters.

When I get out of the shower I step into jeans, pull on a T-shirt, and towel dry my hair. I'm still damp, but I want to get downstairs, out of my stiflingly hot apartment. What I really want is to curl up on my bed in front of a fan and sleep for about a week, but in lieu of that I'll take helping Roxie get what we need to get through the Door . . . and I want to talk to someone about Stan.

Roxie seems like the obvious choice, but Ryan is the one lingering in my doorway when I step out to go back down into the diner. The wood is a little swollen from the dampness and heat in the air, but I force it closed.

"What?" I say, and it comes out sounding really bitchy. Dammit. I lean my face against the door. Ryan puts a hand on my back, and when I breathe in, it stays firm against me. For no reason at all, I want to cry. Or maybe for every reason—we're probably going to die, if not in some random Hell somewhere, then here, fighting demons. Because even if we close a million

Doors, there will still be a million Doors open, and Ryan will never stop fighting.

I'll never stop fighting either. How can I, now that I know what's out there?

"Stay here. Don't come with us," he murmurs into my neck, into my damp hair.

"How can you ask me to stay here? Really, how can I possibly—" I cut myself off before I say something stupid and sentimental, but I lean back against him so that he's pressed all against my back, and his face is hidden in my neck. His breath is hot on my skin, and I'm sweating and uncomfortable, but I love that I am allowed to touch him now.

"I know. And that's something I—" He stops. What was he going to say? Is it something he *likes* about me? Something positive? I am practically slavering for a nonsexual comment from him. "You're really strong, Allie. And that—scares me. Because the women around me . . ." He stops again.

"We—" I clear my throat. "We don't have to have a Hallmark moment, Ry," I say, and it kills me to say it, but we don't. I know how hard it is for him to talk about his feelings. I'm dying to know more about him—six years and I still don't even know his last name—but I'm not going to push it. I'm not going to push him. At the rate we're going, if we're still alive in ten or twelve years, maybe I'll know things like if he has a family somewhere, how he became a hunter, what he wanted to be before he discovered demons. Maybe I'll make him laugh without that undertone of bitterness and sarcasm.

Maybe the hunters will declare me Queen of the Hats. Fuck the loa *and* the Scientologist.

"No," he tells me, and turns me so that my back is pressed against the door, and he's holding me. I'm between his legs, and his arms are against the door, his forehead pressed against mine. "Listen, I want you to know. I want to tell you. I don't want to make all the same mistakes. I—"

"Okay, lovebirds."

I look up, and there's Roxie, her face twisted in irritation.

"That's e-fucking-nough," she continues. "Let's get this show on the road so we can get some sleep before we have to throw ourselves into the birthplace of evil, okay?"

I close my eyes, and when I open them again, Ryan is staring at me and grinning. A real grin, not a nasty one, or one of those ones where he only lifts half his mouth. Then, in a blink, it's gone again, and he's Ryan the Badass Demon Hunter who turns to face Roxie.

"Whaddya got, Rox?" he says, and it's back to business. I slump against the door and take deep breaths. Of course she had to interrupt just as he was about to open up and tell me . . . something. Something important. Shit. Thanks a lot, Roxie.

I take a deep breath, square my shoulders, and follow Roxie and Ryan down the stairs into the diner. It's time to get started saving the world.

9

Roxie is methodical. There are stacks everywhere: leather bottles, wooden stakes, nails, giant pendants covered in script I can't read, piles of rocks, bunches of herbs. There's even a stack of clothes.

"What's this?" I touch the dark fabric; it feels like what Ryan wears, the leather.

"It's lamia skin," says Roxie. She's got a cigarette in her mouth, but she's not smoking it. It's not even lit. It's just hanging there.

"What *is* a lamia, anyway?"

"*Chère,* pray you never find out." Roxie picks up the topmost garment and holds it up against me. It's a coat, a bit too long in the arms. "You wear it for protection in this dimension, but for where we're going," she says, "it also gets around the rules."

"There are rules?"

"Sure. No unnatural fibers, no holy water, no metal alloys, no farmed wood, no—"

"Where are you even *getting* these? They seem pretty arbitrary."

She shrugs. "Can't change the Door-hounds, *chère*. They catch on to man-made things." Door-hounds? What? She hands me the coat and starts pawing through the pile for the rest of my leatherwear. I run my hand over the skins, gearing up to have to put that shit on. I wonder about my underpants; do I have any that are pure silk? Or maybe cotton—cotton's natural, right? Except I don't think thread's made out of cotton anymore, so that cuts my clothing choices down to nil. But I really don't feel like going commando in some dead hunter's suit, because I bet that is the only way they got some lamia skin clothes for me so quickly; there must be a stack somewhere of stuff that's been stripped off dead hunters.

I'm sure it's going to better use than if it had been, like, thrown out or given to a consignment shop or something, but it's still creepy.

"Earth and air," I say to Roxie. "Gimme the straight dope."

She gives me a look, which I guess I deserve. Then she shrugs. "Lots of ways for the world to end, *chère*. One is when all the Doors begin to close and disappear. That ends the world in fire and water. We can work with that, if you get enough hunters together. Just need to open more Doors."

"But why? I mean, no more Doors, no more demons or supernatural hijinks or—"

She shakes her head. "Rookie mistake. The Doors lead to Hell, and they release the supernatural—but that is the way our dimension is supposed to be. We have Doors. We have a balance. No Doors, and the world starts to destroy itself with fire and water. Very messy, from what I've heard."

"So when Ryan was looking for Owen's Door this morning . . ."

Roxie nods. "Seeing if it was fire and water."

"Okay," I say. "But the Door wasn't gone. And now we know there are *more* Doors than there should be. So . . ."

"So too many Doors is the same problem. No balance. The world will end in earth and air, our entire dimension eaten by Hell. And there aren't enough hunters in the world to stop that."

I look out over the pretty impressive array of goods Roxie's got laid out over the tables, and think about it being crushed into worthlessness under a horde of demons. "I think I see now why we're skipping straight to going through a Door to find out how to fix this," I say.

"Exactly. Ryan tell you about the blood?" Roxie asks.

"Blood?" Ryan was supposed to tell me about blood?

Roxie looks at me for a long moment, and she puts down the lamia vest she's holding up. "We talked it out while you were downstairs, went over the angles, Christian even called up Narnia when Ryan was off waking you up." She goes back to picking out clothing, and now she's not looking at me at all. "The only way to get to Hell is through a Door. The only way to travel through the Hell dimensions is through Doors. None of us has ever opened a Door before—none of us but you. You're already tainted with that knowledge, and your blood is already on their tongues. The Doors, they're like animals, yeah? They've smelled you. They know your taste. They'll open for you."

She hands over a vest and a pair of pants, and then starts setting out the things that need to go in all the pockets of my coat: a leather flask filled with salt, sharp knives knapped out of obsidian and carefully wrapped in lamia skin.

"If *we* open Doors, we'll unleash untold demons and probably die in the attempt. You've already done that—the damage is done. No new Hells are going to grow from your sacrifice. So we need your blood, one way or the other, if we want to get in and get out alive."

I don't know what to say to this. "Just me? I mean, I made the Door with Stan and—"

"And Amanda. I know. We could get by with one, we think." Roxie stares at me frankly. "More of you we have, though, the better. If one of you dies, then there'd be a backup."

Then there'd be a backup.

So . . . so. Now I know. I'm not a hunter. No one thought I might be a hunter. I—I am right up there with a flask of salt and a chipped knife. A tool. And if I break, they want to make sure they have replacements. To save their own skins.

"Where's Ryan?" I ask.

"Out," says Roxie, and takes back the coat. She starts packing it with all the gear she's laid out. Gear to keep me alive. Because I am so very valuable.

I turn away and start wiping down tables.

"I think I did something bad," I say. My back is still to Roxie. "I think I did something to Stan's mind earlier. I *pushed* him, I told him to go and to forget, and the next time I talked to him, he didn't remember the hunters or the Door, or anything—"

"Shit," says Roxie.

"Yeah, that about sums it up." I turn around and look her square in the eye. "So maybe Ryan won't have that easy a time finding Stan. Whoops."

"Found Stan," Ryan calls out, coming through the front door of the diner. He's practically frogmarching Stan, whose head is lolling. To complete the picture of Stan as a totally debauched young idiot, he's even drooling. "He was outside, wandering around like he wasn't sure where to go. I thought he wasn't doing anything that hard, anymore."

"It's not drugs. Not all of it, anyway," I say. It's hard to look at Ryan, but I can't keep my eyes off Stan. "I told him to forget." Aw, Stan, I am so sorry. I did not mean for this to happen. "I said it the way Doors do. I *told* him to *forget*."

"Great." Ryan sounds really angry. Too bad. "Take him and hold him, because I still have to get out there and find us—"

"Amanda?"

He shoves Stan at me and I catch him, staggering a little under the weight; Ryan leaves. "Heeeey," Stan says. His pupils are completely blown. "Aren't you friends with Amanda?"

"Shit," breathes Roxie. At first I think it's about me, and Ryan, and all of this. And then I see what she sees. On Stan's arm, by his elbow, there looks like a mosquito bite that's been infected, all red and white and puffy, with a little greenish pus oozing out of it.

It's a werewolf bite. There's a demon in Stan. And very soon, it will take him over, and he'll die, if he doesn't take out some of us first.

This is my fault, because I told him to forget, and he did—he forgot everything, including how to be safe. He's not even wearing any silver or iron; I can't feel it on him. And he's stoned. Really incredibly stoned.

"I don't know what's worse—the drugs or what I

did," I say out loud, and I hate that my voice is shaking, but I did this—or part of it—to one of my best friends. Sure, he's not the greatest friend in the world, but he tried really hard, and this is no way to repay that.

All this, and these fucking hunters wanted to use him as an escape hatch.

Roxie helps me set him down gently in one of the booths. I wish she wouldn't touch him. He drops right off to sleep, or falls into unconsciousness, and I'm jealous of that.

"How long," I ask.

Roxie shrugs. "Long enough."

I suddenly hate her. As if she can hear me, Roxie rubs her face and pulls the cigarette out of her mouth. "Fuck," she says. "How'd you do this to him, Allie?"

"I don't know," I say quietly. I sit down at the booth where Roxie's stacked the talismans. They're all made of silver, I can tell by the weight of each one. Oh, the things I never knew that I needed to know to survive in the world. How to calculate sales tax and what pure silver feels like in my palm. "I can feel it, though." I look up at Roxie. "There's more of it in me. I could do it again. I don't know if the Door gave it to me or what."

"Door's gone, and you still have it," says Roxie. She pulls a Zippo from a hidden pocket in her lamia-skin pants—ugh, that will never stop being gross—and lights the cigarette, puffs contemplatively. "Maybe the Door just brings out what you got naturally."

"After six years?" I glance over at Stan. "After six years, I just suddenly become psychic?"

"After six years you just suddenly *use it,*" Roxie corrects. "You need another psychic to help you learn how to use it completely. But . . ." Roxie taps a long finger on the table. Her nails are short and unpainted, but in perfect condition. I notice these things, I can't help it. "But maybe we can use you. Your blood will get us through the Door, but once we're there, maybe we can make things go a bit faster using your new skills."

Great. So glad to help.

Roxie goes back to putting together supplies. I sit next to Stan, pull out my phone, and dial Amanda. To tell her about Stan? To warn her about Ryan coming? To sit and whine about how she was right all along about these fucking hunters?

None of it, it turns out. Just as I suspected, she does not answer.

I shake my head. While I've still got the phone open, I check the time on the display. "We've got to get this junk out of here." I wave my arm at Roxie's stockpile of stuff. "Jake and Tiara are gonna be show-ing up to open the diner soon, and, you know, they take a lot of stuff in stride, but I don't think they've ever actually seen stakes before, you know?"

"Yeah." Roxie takes another long pull on the cigarette, and drops it to the floor, crushes it out with her boot. Tiara is going to be pissed that she's going to have to sweep before opening, but I am not telling this Amazon warrior of a demon hunter where to put out her cigarettes. Even if I really, really want to.

Roxie has a big white Econoline van, the kind that people are always getting kidnapped into on cop shows. And it's full of *stuff*. I really hope that we don't get pulled over, because I am not sure how we're supposed to explain the crossbows to cops. And Stan. Really not sure how to explain Stan.

I sit down clumsily next to one of the crossbows. A moment later Ryan heaves Stan's unconscious body next to mine—at least Stan's head lands on my calf, and not on the floor. I hitch Stan up and put his head in my lap. He looks asleep. Sort of. The werewolf bite on his arm is shrinking. I really hope he doesn't wake up while we're still driving.

Ryan came back from wherever just as we were finished loading the van. He looks unhappy. Good. I don't think he could've actually gone all the way out to Long Island to look for Amanda, but he could've checked out her usual clubs. He's done it before, when we were worried about her. Or when I was worried about her, and he was just a gigantic faker.

Bitter? You bet.

But he's back now, and I guess he's noticed that I'm pissed, or he's pissed because he doesn't have a triple backed-up escape route out of Hell, or . . . I don't even know.

As soon as Ryan gets out of sight, I wiggle around uncomfortably. I'm still not used to the duster, or to the leather pants, which are too tight around my thighs and too loose around my waist. The pants look kind of stupid with my ugly white cooking shoes. They are the kind that nurses wear, and they are super-comfortable. And there is no way that I'm going to wear brand new leather boots that aren't broken in to wander around Hell; I mean, come on, who wants to be dealing with blisters while fighting demons? Not me.

There are no seatbelts. Now I *really* hope that we don't get pulled over, because no seatbelts in New York City equals trouble-with-a-capital-T, and that rhymes with P and that stands for points on your license. Is that more points or less than for monsters-in-the-making in the back? I wonder if demon hunters care about that kind of thing—losing your license, I mean—or if one of their psychic witches can magic the problem away.

I bet there's a Door in each DMV location. I bet the Doors in the DMV slow down time and that's why it always takes so damn long, and why there are always such long lines. I bet demons love shit like that. If I were a demon that's the kind of mischief I'd make, for sure.

Something's poking my leg. It's one of the crossbow bolts, short and blunt and hopefully it can't actually rip these pants. The bolt has a tiny Star of David carved into the end of it. That's awesome. Mostly Ryan fights with Christian and pagan stuff; I think maybe once or twice I've seen him fight with things like the Star of David and the Seal of Solomon, but those demons don't come through the Door very much. Not through my Door anyway—my Door gets a lot of vampires and werewolves. The boring stuff, except for the last couple of days (because seriously, a shedu? Come on).

I kind of like that I've been doing this for so long that I am totally blasé about certain kinds of demons. Oh, a vampire, yawwwwn. I push the bolt away and try to settle in with a bunch of weaponry and a werewolf wannabe draped on me.

Christian and Jackson climb in and sit across from me. Ryan and Roxie get in up front, because clearly, since Ryan and Roxie are vying to be in charge, they should get to sit in the seats with seatbelts.

"You excited?" Christian asks me, pushing aside a bag full of wooden stakes. I've never used a wooden stake before; I wonder if they give you splinters.

"I'm totally excited," I reply. I am. I am still really angry, but I'm getting over it. Except for Ryan. Ryan is still on my shit list. "But I feel like I'm not supposed to be excited. You know?"

"You shouldn't be," says Jackson. Thanks, Jackson.

He's sitting next to Christian, with a box of salt between them. Both he and Christian are rocking their leather look—*their* pants look like they fit properly. I wonder if there is a tailor I could bribe with pie. Jackson suddenly cracks a smile. "But I'm excited too."

"Yep." Christian slides his baseball cap so that the brim is in the back. If he wasn't wearing leather, if he was wearing, like, a tracksuit or something, he'd look just like all the guys I went to high school with on Long Island. Every time he opens his mouth and that drawl comes out, it's a surprise.

Jackson doesn't really have an accent, which is also a surprise. With his high cheekbones and soft mouth, I want him to be French, and kind of slick, and maybe a little smarmy or flirtatious. But he's not—he's just a regular guy. Maybe he's from California or something; he's got that no-accent like people on television. And he has really dark skin, like a permanent tan.

Christian pokes me with his boot. "You're not bad for a mundane," he says as Roxie starts the car. Christian has a nice smile for a jerk. I think he is the flirt.

"You're just saying that because I fed you," I say.

"Everyone ready?" Roxie calls, but doesn't wait for an answer before she peels out. She's got a lead foot, and we're definitely going too fast.

The car swings wildly around a corner. "Hey, do we need a cover story?" I ask quickly. "Because I'm wondering how we're going to explain the crossbows to the cops when they pull us over to ticket Roxie." I am only half joking, and Christian and Jackson both laugh.

"We work for Medieval Times," Ryan calls from up front. I wonder if he really does? Maybe that's where he goes when he disappears. Sir Ryan of Pennythwaite. I would make fun of him until the *end of time*. "And if it comes up at all, Stan's drunk."

"But don't worry about it." Jackson shakes his head. "Cops don't ask. And when they do, they're not mundane cops anyway, just other hunters giving us a hard time."

"There are hunters who are cops? Seriously?" I don't know why I'm surprised; hunters seem to like jobs that come with uniforms.

"Of course. Hunters do everything. We're everywhere— or we try to be. It makes things a lot easier. A hunter who's a cop can pull strings to hide evidence better than a hunter who works at Target." Jackson grins, but Christian scowls. That must be a dig at the Baseball Cap hunters.

"So most of the hunters who are cops wear Fedoras?" I guess.

Christian scowls again. "Yeah, but they don't guard Doors."

I am slowly learning about hunter hierarchy.

"So . . . hunters who guard Doors are better than hunters who don't?" I guess out loud.

"Hunters who guard Doors just have standing positions. Hunters who don't guard Doors do other things, like make sure that the demons who do escape get caught," explains Jackson. Christian snorts.

"The good hunters who guard the Doors don't *let* anything escape," says Christian. His accent is getting thicker so he must be pissed off.

"I am not trying to start shit here," I say too loudly. Ryan turns around from where he's talking to Roxie, and glares at me.

"Allie, just shut up," he snaps.

"You shut up," I reply. Jackson and Christian look from Ryan to me and laugh; Christian laughs the loudest, and shakes his head.

Jackson punches Christian in the arm. "So that's how it is," says Jackson. "She's off-limits."

"I'm not anything." *I* am in a crabby mood, and do not want to talk about this. "I just want to know—"

"Can we have some quiet please?" asks Roxie. She sounds snippy too. Great, we're all in terrible moods. It's sure going to be fun to fight back to back with everyone. You know, if they let the blood bank fight. "Allie, put on your damn hat."

"I refuse to take part in the ridiculous partisan hat wearing," I snipe. "You all can keep your hats to yourselves."

"You need *something* for when we go through the Door," says Christian. He pats my leg. Apparently I am not so off-limits. "We won't take it as you siding with one faction or another."

I pull my sunglasses out of one of the inside pockets of my duster. "I have sunglasses. I'm starting a new faction," I declare.

"I can get behind that," nods Jackson. "We need some fresh blood."

"Allie will train up a bunch of badass sunglasses hunters." Ryan sounds like he's trying not to snicker. He also sounds his age, which is just weird. "They'll fight the forces of bad fashion everywhere."

That's harsh, even for Ryan. "Well, you never know." I smile sweetly as I slide my sunglasses on. They're from the drugstore, and have rhinestones on the sides. "My fashion sense could save your life."

"*Sure*," replies Ryan. "And then—"

"Y'all just *shut up*," snaps Roxie, and we do. I guess she's in charge after all.

Roxie likes her Door, inasmuch as any hunter likes a Door. She justifies this by saying that it's very defensible. We're going to her Door because it's big enough for us all to walk through, and there's a parking lot that doesn't charge for parking. Hunters are cheapskates.

When we get to the Sheepshead Bay theater, Ryan goes back to being Dark Knight Hunter Guy and looks over the situation. The Door—wrought iron like mine and the mall's, and it doesn't talk to me, but I hear it hum something almost friendly to Roxie—is pressed into the far corner of the main screen's balcony. To the left is carpeted wall, and to the right is a big pile of storage boxes labeled BUTTER FLAVORING, blocking that side's stairs to the balcony seats. The pile's a mess—I bet Roxie put it together, and has to keep making it every time the theater workers pull it down again.

Ryan nods. "Good setup. Very Thermopylae."

I have no idea what that is, and I don't think Roxie does either, because she scowls at him. She points at the Door with her knife, maybe only coincidentally cutting off a tendril of blackness I've just noticed inching out of it. Not so friendly, then. "Things come out," she says. "They've got nowhere to go but toward me. I kill them."

Ryan blinks at her. "That's what I said."

Christian and Jackson snicker. For crazy faction foes, they're having a great time watching the Stetsons implode. Roxie scowls at them too, and then at me because I guess I am being left out. I smile brightly. She slices off another tendril, this time without looking. I think to myself, *Someday I want to be that badass. Also, that scary.*

"Come on," says Ryan. "We've got places to be. Any last information?"

Christian raises his chin. "Me. I called Narnia again while you were . . ." He slides a look at me, then goes back to Ryan. "Out. She said she's been looking at entrails. They said to bring something we need to find our way through the Doors, and to leave something of ourselves behind to find our way home."

Jackson nods gravely. "And not to call her anymore."

Christian steals Jackson's Fedora and pops it out of shape. They grin at one another. Total bromance.

"Something we need? We don't *know* what we need. That's why we're *going*." Roxie kicks the butter flavoring boxes, and then mutters darkly as she carefully restacks them.

"Witches," I say sagely. They all look at me. Shit, that means I have to say something smart. Um. "It's an allegory?"

Ryan rolls his eyes, but he looks at the Door and then back at me. "What do we need to find?"

I know I'm angry, but . . . this is what we do. I raise my eyebrows. "An answer?"

"To what question?"

"Where my Door went."

He waves that aside. "We don't even know if that's related. We need to fix the symptoms before we can even start thinking about the problem."

"Okay," I say. "Symptoms. Why there are more Doors?"

He shakes his head. "I think we need to save the metaphysical for Narnia. Forget the 'why.' "

Roxie's watching the both of us now, and she looks

less frustrated. "We need action. How to stop them multiplying," she suggests.

I chew my lip. "Too simple. That's just one thing. We want the whole shebang. Slow down the increase, slow down the activity—"

"Control," Ryan says.

Christian gets into the swing of it too. It's like they've never heard of group brainstorming. Where were they during the three AM leadership seminars on PBS? "Can't," he says. "The Doors are Chaos—they're *Hell*. That's god territory, the gods that know the true names, and I don't think we'll find a helpful one of those through the Door."

"True names?" I ask, because I am easily distracted.

"You think Roxie's my true name?" Roxie says with a quick smile.

Ryan is now studying the Door with a lot of attention. A lot a lot.

"I know you all have a name thing," I say slowly. Oh, if Ryan is not his real name, I am going to kill him. Or call him Nigel.

I will call him Nigel *forever*.

Christian shrugs. "And your true name isn't Allie, right?"

"My name—"

Ryan whips around and in seconds is by my side. His hand covers my mouth. He looks into my eyes.

"Don't tell anyone your true name. It's *you*," he says. "It's stronger than salt."

His eyes are . . . I just. I just can't. His eyes are searching mine, worried, young, old, scared. I nod, and because I can't help but remember six years of wanting him, I touch my tongue to the palm of his hand.

He closes his eyes and takes a ragged breath. So I know this: Whatever his name is, he likes that.

"Come on, lovebirds," Roxie says. "You'd think we weren't standing at a dark abyss."

Ryan steps back. "Stronger than salt," he says again, and then looks at Roxie. "That's the leaving behind part. To find our way home again. Bind our blood to this dimension with salt, and we'll find our way home."

Roxie thinks about it, and nods. "That's good. I like that. But what do we bring with us?"

If salt's the answer to the second riddle, then . . . I bet I know the first. "Salt binds, silver heals. We want to heal the Doors—right now they're out of whack. Everything's out of balance. We want to heal *everything*." And that's when I think: including Stan. I don't say it, though. He's a lump on the floor from where Jackson dropped him, curled up and small. He looks like he did when I first met him, twelve years old, all tousled hair and freckles.

And now he's unconscious. And he's forgotten. And he's bitten.

We'll heal everything.

"Silver," I say now. "We bring silver with us."

Jackson looks uncertain. "Silver brings the Door-hounds. We'll die."

Ryan says, "Only unpure silver, and we were screwed with that to begin with, unless you thought ahead to get all your silver cauters done with the pure stuff?" Everyone looks embarrassed. I just press my hand against my silver-scarred stomach. Ryan continues, "But maybe not all of us will die. And anyway, I think Allie's right."

While I am gratified that as a poor silly mundane I still get to be right once in a while, I still want to know: "Door-hounds?"

"Stop asking questions," Roxie says. She narrows her eyes and looks at all of us. "We're five. I'm thinking only one of us will die, not more."

"We're six," I say. "Stan's coming too."

She makes a face. Even though it was her idea, to her, he's already evil. "Six, then. Maybe we'll be able to keep one of you two." She's talking about the blood. Thank you for the reminder.

Ryan's looking at me. And then he's looking away. I guess he's remembering too. Fine.

I slide my sunglasses down over my eyes. I can't see for shit, but who cares? I'm just here to party.

"Let's get this done," I say.

* * *

Jackson has a smaller knife than Roxie's pigsticker, and he says it's clean, so I don't flinch too much when he cuts my finger. Blood wells up—I sprinkle some of my margarita salt on it (larger salt doesn't sting as much—these are the things you learn), then swipe the theater wall. Uck. *That* stings.

When he's cut everybody else, and while they're marking this dimension as home, I take Jackson's knife and cut Stan. Someone has to. He needs to find his way home too.

His blood is dark, and oily.

I remember Stan's fourteenth birthday party. We snuck away from the kids his parents made him invite, and the "friends of the family" his parents wanted to schmooze, and drank raspberry-flavored wine coolers in his room. He cried, and told me he thought he might like boys. Later, I stood support on the three-way call when he told Amanda. Amanda didn't say anything for a second, and then she talked and laughed and started gossiping about all the boys in class she thought he should make out with.

I don't want Stan to die.

"Do we have silver?" Ryan asks.

Roxie nods, and pulls forward one of the duffle bags I helped her pack. She'd explained to me that she wanted to leave a store of silver outside the Door for when we came back out, to heal any of the wounds we might have gotten inside the Hells. I think it's very forward-thinking of her to believe so firmly that we're going to make it out of the Hells without dying. She doesn't even call them Hells—she calls them "the underworld."

While she's bent over the duffle bag, a larger tendril of blackness comes winding out from the base of the Door, and wraps itself gently around Roxie's ankle. She reaches down to the tendril and I could swear that she pats it before she rips it off her leg.

The Door whimpers. Their relationship is very, very odd.

"Here," Roxie says. "Silver for everyone."

The talisman on string—it feels like silk, to my practiced hand—that Roxie hands me is an ankh. I finger it for a moment. It's portentous. The ankh stands for life everlasting, and I am a sucker for symbolism. So instead of putting it over my neck, I put it over Stan's. I'm wearing silk underwear, anyway, I don't need a silk necklace. And Stan needs life everlasting more than I do. He's got maybe an hour in this dimension before he changes into a werewolf for good, maybe two, tops. The greenish pus that had been oozing from the bite is gone, and it is about as big as a pinprick, but glowing green. Not a good sign, not at all.

Roxie shakes her head at me, but hands me another talisman. Ah, a Seal of Solomon. I wish I'd thought to bring the one Ryan gave me. This Seal is the most intricate one I've ever seen, and it has a bunch of lettering on it that I don't recognize. Maybe Hebrew. The one still under my pillow is a simple set of lines and dots. Still powerful, less pretty, a lot heavier. This Seal's necklace is leather. I slip it over my head.

The silver is cool against my chest. I look totally badass in the lamia leather—no bra, but the vest is tight enough that my cleavage is to die for. If this were an action movie, I'd totally be the heroine. Or at least the heroine's best friend.

Except Amanda is my best friend, and she's not coming to Hell. Thank god. I called her a bunch of times on the way over to the movie theater. No answer at all, just right to voice mail. And I'm glad. At least she has a chance of not dying, you know, right now.

Ryan looks at me. "Are you ready?" Ryan pulls out *his* knife—I am the only person in the world without a knife at this point, I swear—and hands it over. "There's strength in pain freely given," he tells me. I grimace and prick the tip of my finger. I have to press really hard to get a drop, because, once again, I didn't let it go deep enough, but I am not going to wuss out. I let my blood drip down, and then I sling it at the Door. Am I supposed to be doing anything else here?

The Door laughs at me.

It laughs, and it does nothing, and everyone's staring at me, and this—this is not cool, Door. This is not right. If this is all I can do for these people, if this is all I'm worth, you will *take* this fucking blood and you will *open* for this goddamn crew of people, and—

"Take it!" I finally scream. In my mind, I speak like Doors, and say, *You know me. Open. Now.*

The Door growls, a long, low growl like thunder, and then it's *open*. There are no gates. There's no purple bruising around its outside. It looks just like a Door that I'd walk through, if I were to walk into a cold basement, or a silent attic, or all the other human places that we just don't feel right about.

Roxie steps in front of me, takes a deep breath, and steps through the Door.

She's gone.

There's icy air blowing out of the open Door. Jackson and Christian are next, carrying Stan between them. It's just me and Ryan now. He takes my hand.

"When you get through, wait until I come out, and then spill another drop of blood and say whatever you said to the Door just now. That should do . . . something. Probably useful. You ready?" he says, looking down at me, his hand in mine, his eyes . . . I surge up and take his mouth with mine. If I'm gonna go out, I'm gonna do it with style. At the press of my lips, he pulls me in toward his body, his fingers threaded through the belt loops on my leather pants.

I pull away first. I pull away, and twist to look

through the Door. I'm so angry—it's taken so much from me. It's even made this kiss something different than it should have been.

You bitch, I think at it. *There's no way you're ever going to win.*

There's something like laughter back at me, but fuck it. Fuck this.

I take a deep breath of brimstone, lean back against Ryan, and then shove myself through the Door after Roxie, and Ryan is right behind me. He's so warm, he's radiating heat, and I'm burning up too, I'm burning from the inside out with all the fire, all the blue fire that never stops burning, all the blue fire that kills the demons, the blue fire that's killing me.

It's suddenly very quiet.

10

I open my eyes when I feel Roxie's hand on me. I know it's her. I can smell her the way I can smell demons and Ryan. The way I can smell Amanda (vodka and a slowly rotting liver and the Dr. Pepper–flavored lip gloss she used for years because I gave it to her); the way I can smell Stan (stale makeup and stale sex that never quite washes off and the burned plastic smell of a perfectly executed wallride on a really top of the line skateboard); the way I can smell the diner (bleach, pancakes, pot roast, blood); the way I smelled the dead underneath Bath & Body Works (blood, blood, copper, iron, blood, and horrible horrible flowers).

I never realized I could smell this before, but standing in this freezing cold valley of red sand, with ash, like snow, floating in the air, I can smell everything, and I can remember smells I never knew I had stored in me.

Roxie smells warm like a snake, hot like scales in the sun, slithery. With all this cold, I kind of want to wrap her around me like an electric blanket. Except suddenly I can see her, really see her, when I open my eyes to her hot hand; snakes on her palm, snakes on her arm. Snakes all around her.

Maybe I won't wrap myself with her just yet.

But those snakes . . . are they the avatars? The hunters said there would be avatars, but I was kind of expecting shimmering figures to come out of the sky or in our dreams or something, leading the way and talking mysteriously. Maybe they still will. Maybe Roxie is really just a snake deep down.

I look down at myself. No snakes. Thank god. Just skin and blue fire . . . and maybe something moving quickly out of view. I will have to ask somebody what it is I can't see. I don't want to be something I'm not, particularly if it's something gross. Who wants to be gross? Been there, lost the money, gone through the redemptive poverty stage.

I look down at Stan. His breathing is getting easier, which is good? Bad? He doesn't have anything different about him. Nothing new, extra. Except this: He smells like he belongs.

I don't like that he belongs in Hell, now.

A popping sound comes from behind me; I turn and it's Ryan stepping through the Door. When I look at him there is a woman, like a transparency, overlaid on him, moving as he moves. She looks like—okay, she looks like an ancient Egyptian, like all that Egyptian stuff we've all seen our whole lives. She's beautiful, but she's kind of scary at the same time. She carries a staff, and she's wearing something red and tight and much too light for the current temperatures.

Ryan steps closer to me, away from the Door, and the transparency moves with him, except a beat behind the Egyptian woman is another woman, with wings, and she's surrounded by stars. When she moves, behind her, finally, the last ghost in the train, is an honest-to-God lioness, tawny fur and big gold eyes. Ryan is apparently complicated. Color me surprised.

He's the last one, so I nick a finger on my hand and let a drop fall on the ground. "You know me," I say out loud, and feel really stupid doing it. But it worked before, and in the distance (a really long distance), I think I hear a Door say, *Hello, Allie*.

It's the only thing that happens after I drop the blood, so I shrug, and I point. We're in a valley now—there are mountains, with fire, where the next Door is, through a blizzard of ash and below a reddish-black sky. That's where we need to go. Allie, Amateur Psychic, now with extra Compass Feature. It looks a long way off, and there's nothing to block that biting wind from hitting us the entire journey.

"I think this is Kur," says Ryan. He's got at least two voices speaking through him, maybe three. "Which means we're in the Sumerian Hell sequence. Get your kerchiefs on."

Sumerian? What? Apparently I say this out loud, because Roxie says quietly, "He doesn't know, *chère*. Not really. Just go with it. I'll let you know if we need to change plans." She sounds like hisses. I am not sure I am comforted.

I pull my bandanna off my head, and the wind whips my hair and stings my cheek, but I don't want to breathe whatever is in the ash. My bandanna is pink; everyone else's is black. I'm totally an individual. I bend over and pull up Stan's kerchief too, not that anyone cares. I care. That's what's important. Only then do I take a band out of my pocket and pull my hair into a ponytail.

Christian clicks a little underneath his voice. He's like a giant spider, or he *is* a giant spider, or there are thousands of tiny spiders crawling all over him. I'm not sure; it shifts when I blink, and I can't get a good look. "Jackson, where's—"

He's not here. I finally notice. Did he chicken out? Did I do the recognition spell too soon? Didn't he come through with Christian? He—

Ryan looks at me, and lets out his breath, and turns away. Oh.

Jackson must be dead. The first of us to die. I knew someone would, Roxie said one in six, if we were lucky, and I hoped it wouldn't be me, and Jackson said the silver would kill us, and—*This is my fault,* I try to say, words pushing, everything is my fault lately, but all I say is, "Jackson—"

"Let's go," orders Christian. He pulls down his baseball cap over his eyes and hoists Stan in a fireman's carry. He heads in the direction I pointed at earlier, and he doesn't look back.

We walk through sand, the cold leaching up through my shoes and numbing my feet, and the sky is dark. I run my fingers over my chain-iron belt. I feel better with the iron. Iron kills, iron kills, ironkillsironkills.

In front of me, Christian clicks and clicks. We're on an incline now, heading closer to those mountains. Doors make everything slow, but in Hell itself, things move fast. Is that irony? Or just an '80s power ballad?

We've hit a path, now. Hell must have mountain goats. Around a corner—and there's Jackson's body. It's been impaled on five spikes—head, heart, genitals, both palms. He's surrounded by fluttering wings; tiny, tiny vampires. Or just butterflies. I don't know. He's dead. That's all.

Hell is cold, and it is mountainous, and I want to stop but I don't think we can. We leave Jackson behind.

Roxie reaches out and squeezes my hand. I feel the snakes slither over me, hot and dry. Every time I close my eyes, I see Jackson's hand with a spike through it, his iron knife on the side, his lamia leather completely untouched except for the spike through his back.

We can't take him with us. Part of it is that we're already dragging Stan's dead weight, but part of it is that we always leave men behind. Hunters can't come back.

I'm scared and I'm shaking.

The valley where we entered is a long way back now, and I can barely hear its Door. (Though what I do hear, softly, is a hum like lullabyes. Shudder.) The next Door, though, doesn't sound any closer. I don't know. We've been walking a long time, and Christian's already handed Stan off to Ryan to carry. I offered to do it instead, but Ryan shook his head and Roxie said, "We can't group you two together."

I guess that means if something jumps out and attacks, she'd rather one of us survives instead of both getting eaten at once. Glad to see that pragmatic approach still going strong.

Though for a Hell, it is awfully empty. What kind of demons does Roxie get, anyway? I wonder about her scars.

Ryan pauses; beside the path is an outcropping, a bare expanse of stone that the wind has scoured of sand and ash. There's a cliff face along one side of it—Ryan heads toward that, and sets Stan down. Ryan wraps his coat more tightly around himself, then beckons to me.

"Here," he says, except with the Egyptian woman's

voice. He pulls an old, worn-down crayon out of his pocket and hands it over to me. I did not know that there was a crayon color called *flesh*. Dammit, Ryan, stop being weird.

I want to say that out loud. Want want want. I can't seem to talk. Egyptian Woman says, "Draw a circle. Drop your blood. Protect this space."

The crayon—it's more peach than flesh, and not everyone has flesh this color *anyway,* oh my god, thank you very much—is almost too light to see on the red rock. Whatever. I draw a kind of lumpy oval along the entire bluff, because who wants to be cramped? I have to pull Stan away from the cliff face first, and he thuds over sideways in a way that is almost totally funny. When it's done Ryan waves Roxie and Christian into the center with him, and I drag Stan over to their feet. I look for a knife to stab my finger with. I am going to be so sore after this—

I am looking for Jackson's knife, because his was the cleanest. Dammit.

Roxie holds out her big knife, which I have seen her slice nasty things with and not clean. I shake my head and pull Ryan's knife out of my belt loop.

I nick my thumb and let my blood drop onto the ground. Who cares if I get staph? I'm already in Hell.

The second my blood hits the ground, my voice comes back with a vengeance. I almost choke on the words I want to be saying—how dare Hell or Kur or

whatever take the ability to talk from me? *Fuck* them—
but I know that what I say first is probably important.
"You know me," I say again, and the flesh crayon sparks,
and I hear whispers, whispers.

Allie.

Hello, Allie.

We know you.

We're waiting.

Allie.

Allie.

There are so many Doors. So many. They're everywhere. The loudest one is still against the fiery mountain, which suddenly looks a lot closer, so I think that's
still where we have to go. But—how many Doors, to
how many Hells, are there?

Here is the bigger thing I am worried about now:
I've only dropped a little of my blood here, and I'm
being serenaded by Doors. I've got a lot more still to
do. When does it become too much? And what happens if it does?

Whatever freed my voice frees up everyone else
too. Ryan says, with his own voice, "Ereshkigal might
visit. We'll need to keep a lookout." Roxie snorts, and
then sits cross-legged away from the rest of us to look
at the mountain we're heading toward. She rubs her
knee with one hand, and I wonder how old she is.

Christian goes and sits nearest the path, and faces
where we came from. The spider clicks and clicks and

clicks. The spider has been clicking for hours, and it's getting on my nerves, but it must be upset because Jackson is dead.

Ryan stays and sits with me, and Stan, in the middle.

"If Jackson were alive," I ask out loud, "what would I see?"

Ryan glares at me, and Christian's spider clicks some more, but Roxie shrugs without turning around. "I've never been in a Door with him. Hell, *chère,* I've never been in a Door with *me.* I didn't know I was a serpent."

I address Ryan. "Ry, you knew about the women, right?"

"No," he says. The women have spread out to either side of him, and the lioness is standing erect behind him, staring at me over his shoulder.

"Who are they?" I ask.

He frowns, but before he can talk, Roxie laughs low. "I know Isis," she says. She looks over her shoulder at us. Her snakes hiss. "Underworld, saves her husband. Goddess of magic. Everyone knows Isis."

Egyptian Woman—Isis—smiles. It's creepy.

I totally ignore her. "Who's the other one? What's with the wings?"

She smiles at me too, and it's even creepier than Isis.

Roxie stares at Ryan, squinting. "Ishtar?" she offers. When *Ryan* smiles at us, it's with the two women smiling beside him, and the lioness opening her mouth.

Okay, yes, creepy.

"You're creepy and it's scaring me."

"Ištar." It sounds different when Ryan says it, there's a slither, there's death. "And not Isis. Ūsat." It sounds almost exactly the same. Plus one point for having his avatar be three women goddesses, minus a million points for being *a jerk*.

"Okay, whatever," I say. "And the lioness?"

Roxie shrugs. "Got me."

Ryan turns and looks at the lioness for a minute. When he turns back to me, he changes the subject. "I think Stan won't wake up," he says.

Stan mumbles, "Don't wanna."

He's alive! But he's got a demon in him. I am very torn. Ryan bends over and tugs Stan's kerchief into a roll, up and over Stan's eyes. Ryan looks at me. "Don't let him see any of this, Allie."

"Why?"

"Because I said so, dammit." He looks tired, and not like he's my age at all. He rubs his face and tries again. "Sorry," he says. "He can't see where he is, because he won't be the only one looking. The werewolf is inside him now—it'll see Kur, and worse, the things in Kur will see it. They'll track him here."

Ryan stands. He pulls at his Stetson's brim, half-hiding his face, and he walks over to Christian.

I look down. Stan's trying to sit up. In a slurred

voice, he says, "Allie, what the fuck . . . ?" He reaches up to the kerchief, and I yank his hand away.

"Hi, Stan. Don't touch that."

"But I can't see," he whines.

"I know," I say. "But it sucks to be seeing things right now, anyway. Just listen to me, okay? Okay?" He nods finally, and I lean him up against me. I put my nose in his hair. He smells like cigarettes and glitter. "What do you last remember?"

I can feel him make a face against my shoulder. "I was coming home. No—I was coming to the diner. I just had an *amazing* time with Matt—did I tell you about Matt?"

"No," I say.

He sounds almost shy. "I met him a couple weeks ago. He's so great, Allie, he's like—remember when we were kids and we used to describe who we wanted to marry? He's like the guy I always wanted to marry."

I always wanted to marry someone handsome and rich. Amanda wanted to marry someone exciting and famous. Stan, of course, wanted true love. I don't remember much more than that, because I'm a terrible friend.

I stroke Stan's hair.

"Tell me about him," I suggest, and try not to make it an actual *suggestion,* but just the kind of thing one friend might say to another.

"He's got these eyes, Allie, and he can *dance*. He

likes the same music I do, the club stuff, but he also likes classical. He plays the piano. His *hands* . . ." Stan trails off and makes a snuffling noise into my neck. I start to cry. Because here is my friend, one of my best friends, and he's dying. He's dying and there's nothing I can do. He doesn't have an avatar. He smells like he belongs here. And his arm has stopped glowing. There's not even a pinprick where the werewolf bit him. It's all in him now.

So as he tells me about Matt, I cry, because there's no way. There's no way anything is going to be able to fix this.

"And then there was a weird buzzing, Allie, like you know how my ears got when we tried that amyl nitrate?"

"Nitrite," I correct automatically. I sniff and try to dry my eyes with the sleeve of the leather duster. Not exactly what it was made for. "Yeah, I remember."

That's what they sound like—buzzing, like flies or bees or anything with really fast-moving wings. Demons seem to love taking on the forms of insects, the kinds of insects that have been pestering humans for thousands of years. It's the perfect disguise, isn't it?

"The buzzing . . ." Stan trails off and curls into me tighter. "Matt was buzzing, Allie. And then he scratched me with his fingernail, and then *I* was buzzing, and I don't remember—there was this guy in a leather coat, and he brought me to you."

"That's Ryan," I tell Stan. God, he doesn't even remember Ryan. I can't even.

"Is Ryan your boyfriend?" Stan's going for light-hearted, but he sounds like he knows something's wrong. I doubt he knows he's going to have to die or turn into a demon, a buzzing insect parasite of a demon who'd kill me as soon as he'd look at me.

I doubt Stan knows that, but he's got to know that something is really really wrong.

"Yeah, Ryan's my boyfriend," I say into Stan's hair.

"Hey, go you," Stan says, and I think he's actually happy for me. Even with all of this, he's happy for me. God, I am such a bitch.

I hear a chuckle, and when I look, there's Ryan, squatting next to me. "I prefer 'significant other'," he says seriously. " 'Boyfriend' is so trite."

I laugh and laugh until I cry again, and then I'm leaning against Ryan and sobbing into his fucking coat, because my best friend is going to die and it's my goddamn fault. Jackson died and it's my fault. Everything sucks, we're in Hell, and the world feels like it's ending, and it's all my fault.

Stan goes to sleep. I do too. Maybe it is not wise to sleep in Hell. With a transitioning werewolf. In the freezing cold.

Maybe I don't care.

The light never changes. The ash-snow hits the edges

of my circle and swirls in little dances. I close my eyes. The last thing I see is Roxie, rubbing her knee. The last thing I feel is a light touch against my hair.

When I wake, it is because there is someone talking really, really loudly.

When I open my eyes, there is a fucking snake-faced *dragon* slithering its way through the black sky above us.

Stan says, "What the hell is that?" and he tries to pull the kerchief down *again*. I put my hand over the kerchief, and press the cloth against his eyes.

"I will tell you really soon," I say, and I hope it is not a lie.

Rites! the dragon is screaming. *There are rites to be performed in the netherworld!*

"Stand back!" Roxie says. She is standing at the edge of our bluff, her knives out, her scars like snakes burning bright and silver. She flexes, her weight balanced, and her grin is wide and fierce.

Christian moves slowly, but he ignores Roxie and gets into a support position behind her, his spider crouching, spread-legged, poised for the catch.

Ryan doesn't move to support. Instead, he comes to me, and I don't know why—and then I remember what Roxie said before, about grouping the blood kids together.

"I know," I say angrily. "Take him." I help Stan up

and thrust him at Ryan. Ryan grabs Stan clumsily. Stan clutches Ryan's lamia coat and murmurs something I bet Matt would really love, and Ryan's expression is nothing, nothing.

Fuck him.

Shit, I did that already.

Rites! The dragon is slithering its way through the sky, a beacon of angry muscle and scales that swims through eddies like an eel through water. It's coming closer.

Ryan turns away from me and drags Stan along with him. "Are you Ereshkigal?" he shouts to the snake. Great. Roxie doesn't turn away from the dragon coming toward us, but her snakes all turn and shriek at him in a way I never, ever want to hear again. At any rate, the dragon doesn't answer. "Are you Neti?" he tries again, because he is made of stupid.

The dragon's mouth is the size of five of me, stacked head to foot. I know this because it has just opened that mouth and I can see exactly where I'd fit in it.

Ryan is shouting more things, this time in a language that must be Sumerian. The dragon is shaking its head, and coming closer. Roxie's knives are glinting. She's going to step over the circle. Christian just looks up, his hands bare, waiting.

And then there's me.

I am a girl who runs a diner. It's not even my diner.

I slept with a guy I've wanted for years, and right now all he wants me for is blood magic. One of my best friends is going to die unless we can fix him in Hell. I don't know where my other best friend is, and whether to be grateful that her hiding out from me means that maybe she won't die today.

There is a dragon above me, and I can smell its anger. But I am angry too, damn it.

Allie.

It's just a whisper. But it's a whisper I know.

It's the Door across the mountain.

Allie. Is there something you need, Allie?

The dragon reaches us. It balances in the air in front of Roxie. As it opens its mouth, Roxie screams and jumps at it, cutting at the dragon's eyes and snout. She gets one slice, along the edge of its mouth; boiling blood spills over the rocks and runs perilously close to our feet.

The dragon screeches, losing speech, and Roxie tumbles back onto the bluff, breathing hard. The cut on the dragon closes as if it had never been.

Is there something you would like, Allie?

There is only one thought now: Out out outoutout—*Done,* the Door whispers, and the mountains fold around us, and the whispering Door opens beside me, and I grab Stan from Ryan's arms and push him through. Ryan is staring at me, and he looks—whatever, he can

be disappointed in me later, after we are alive and somewhere else. Ištar, the woman with wings and stars, puts
her hand on his shoulder and he nods abruptly and turns
to get Christian.

I turn and jump through.

11

The fiery mountains weren't where the Door was, it turns out. It's the Door that has them.

I pop out on the edge of a crater. Sand and smoke and heat, a lot of heat, and I am already sweating. A belch of steam comes out of the crater, and it is *loud*. Stan calls out, "If nobody tells me what is going on, I'm gonna take off this stupid blindfold."

"It is a bandanna," I say loudly. "And don't do that. I'm here." I turn in circles—I see two, four, six immense cones of black stone rising from dark waters in the distance, and I'm standing on the summit of the seventh—and Stan has crawled away from the Door and is, I kid you not, like five steps away from tumbling into the gigantic crater and into a pit of lava many, many feet down.

I skip around the Door and pull him away from the edge. "There is a giant pit of lava to your right, FYI," I say to him. "Do not fall into it."

"Sure," he huffs. "Where's Ryan?"

That is a good question. Pop. I look. There's Christian, and his creepy spider. Pop. And there's Ryan and his women. Ūsat looks around, dizzying, and stops when she sees me. Ryan doesn't look at me, but keeps his eyes on the Door.

One minute. Two. And then Roxie pops out, and she's got a brand new cut on her. Ryan finally looks at me, and nods like I'm a soldier. Whatever. I know my place. I poke Christian until he gives me a knife, and I cut the pad of my other thumb. "You know me," I say, and the Doors light up—they literally light up. When I close my eyes, I can see a map of Doors, each Door a different color light. I didn't know there were that many colors in the world.

Maybe there aren't. Maybe there are just that many colors in Hell.

I can hear some of them laughing.

The loudest one is a Door on the closest cone-island. Only about a day's walk, maybe, except for the part where there's all that water between us and it. I point. The others sigh.

Steam bursts from below again, and the sound blocks out everything else for a moment. It is not the best place for talking, but Ryan turns to me. "What did you do?"

He asked me that—what, yesterday morning? He sounded so different then. More worried, less . . . whatever this is. "We were going to be dragon meat," I say. "The Door offered something different."

"Idiot," Roxie snarls. Her hand is pressed up against her side, where blood is leaking out of a long, wide, shallow cut—a tooth that missed its mark. Her snakes are coursing over it, their silver tongues licking out, and I can see the cut growing slowly smaller. "I had it," Roxie says.

"Bull," I say. "It was a million times our size and a *dragon*."

"What do you *think* I fight?" she says angrily, and stalks away, heading down the black island.

"She fights elementals," Christian says to me—no, his spider says it, clicks and hisses. "She fights the giant things with no names, that come from the snow and wind."

Excuse me, but I am under the impression that I just named it by calling it a dragon.

I do not say that out loud.

I turn to Ryan, and he nods. "She would've stopped it."

"I—" I just can't.

Christian turns without a word and heads after Roxie. Hell has not improved him.

Ryan says, "Stan, can you walk?"

"Yeah," says Stan, and he stands carefully and holds out his hand. Ryan takes it, and he looks at me.

"You won't need your bandanna here," he says quietly. "We're not following the Sumerian Hells. This is something different. Keep your eyes open."

And he carefully leads Stan away.

I am concerned about how we're going to get to that other island.

The others don't seem to be, though. It was an easy climb down—just walk, and avoid the gushes of lava that come from random breaks in the cone, and hate everyone around me. Very easy. I wish I had a Snickers. I'm not the biggest fan of candy, but I feel weird, dizzy.

At the bottom now, on a shore with no sand, just ugly lumps of what must be cooled lava reaching into the water, they turn and look at my expectantly. Even Stan, and he can't even *see*.

I pull the flesh crayon from my pocket. There isn't actually much of it left. I hope Ryan has another crayon with another gross name, because otherwise we are going to be out of luck. I refuse to draw smaller circles.

This is because I am stubborn, and possibly stupid. As has been demonstrated. I am living up to my peers' suspicions and expectations.

I draw the circle. I drop the blood. I say the words. And nobody says anything. Roxie sits facing the new island; Christian sits facing the old Door. Ryan drifts between the two, and I am a hub in the center with Stan.

I am getting really hungry.

When Ryan passes me next, I grab at his pant leg. Lamia leather, let it be known, is super-slippery. I end up catching at the lioness instead. Her fur is rough on top, but my fingers dig in and I find a kind of softness under it. Is that normal for lions? I have no idea. She looks at me, and does this giant rumbling thing which I think is actually a purr.

Ryan shivers.

"What is it," he asks. He's looking at Roxie.

"I'm hungry," I say.

He sighs, and drops down beside me. The lioness curls around him, but close enough that I can keep scritching the top of her head. "No," he says, "you're not."

"I am," I say. "I totally am."

"Me too," Stan says. "But it's weird."

Neither of us knows what to say to that, except maybe *Do you feel like rending us limb from limb and drinking of our soiled flesh?* That is awkward to say, and might make Stan feel bad.

"You might be hungry," Ryan says at last to Stan, "but you're not, Allie. You can't get hungry here. It's all in your head."

I narrow my eyes at him. "I *am* hungry," I say, "and

I am tired of not knowing what is happening. There are rules that I am breaking, and not on purpose either, and that is making me very cranky. I want to help, dammit, but I can't if you won't tell me anything!"

"I—" Ryan looks over at Christian, whose spider is skittering its legs up and down the rock, up and down the rock. Ryan shoots a frustrated look at me. "Roxie will tell you. I have to go for a moment."

Sure she will. But Roxie is apparently listening, and maybe she doesn't hold a grudge, because she stands up from her view of the lapping waters and comes over to our side.

I slide my sunglasses up on top of my head. Roxie watches me. I hate to admit it, and I won't ever say it out loud, and I will deny it if asked even under blood oath, but she was right. I need a hat.

"So tell me what I don't know," I start with, which proves I win at conversational gambits.

Roxie shrugs. "There's not much. When it comes to fighting, odds are we know more than you do, so let us handle it. Don't let yourself and Stan get bunched together, and not just because we need you—he's a werewolf now. And if you see a god, ask it for help. Nicely."

"But *why* am I asking for help?" I reply with exasperation. "No one has told me the worst case scenario yet!"

Roxie frowns thoughtfully, pulls out her knife, and

starts drawing spirals into the dirt in front of her. "There are a lot of ways for the world to end, *chère*. Some maybe we can do something about, some we really can't. Some ways were meant to be, and we can't change them. The world ending in fire and water—that happened once in California about a hundred years ago. The Doors started closing, then disappearing. Ruined the balance of things but good. Hunters from all across the country came to that, and fought the Doors open again. And this was back before any fucking loa got in the way of a hunt."

I am imagining rows upon rows of leather-clad hotties marching in tandem. With shotguns. And salt.

"Now," Roxie continues, "the other end of that, is the world ending in earth and air. And there's no hunter trick that can fix that. When Doors open, and open, world without end . . . like Christian said before, that's god territory. Nothing human can fix that, and maybe nothing human should." She sighs. "But we're hunters, and that's what we do. Which is why we're in Hell, looking around for any gods who might be able to change fate. If fate needs changing, anyway."

I am trying to pretend that we just did not have the scariest conversation of my life. "So we're just going to wander through Hell dimensions forever?"

"Yes," says Roxie. "That's the idea. But we're hoping to talk to a god or something just as useful before then."

"Okay, you guys, seriously, are we really in a Hell dimension? Because this is a little elaborate for a practical joke." Stan is smiling, but it's pretty weak.

"Shut up," says Roxie.

I am trying really hard not to agree with her silently, because what if I tell him to shut up with my mind and he does, forever? I just can't be responsible for anything else in this lifetime, okay? I can't take on anything else. Not ever.

"Look," I say, and take a deep breath. Calm. Calm. Calm. "Look," I repeat. "I'm not trying to piss you off. I've done that enough times today. But wouldn't this be easier if we had more of a plan than 'wander through Hell dimensions waiting for a god to contact us and tell us what to do'?"

"Absolutely," Roxie tells me. She draws little spirals on the ground between us with her knife. "But what kind of plan could we have? We've never done this before."

"Most of us, anyway." Ryan is back, and settles closer to me. "Allie, you've come the closest to going through a Door before this of anyone I know. Who lived to tell about it, anyway. Most people who touch a Door have their soul sucked into it and turn into a demon."

His lioness is back. Ūsat waves. "Great," I say. "Could I still turn into a demon?"

Ryan nods. "With what you've been doing lately,

definitely. But at any time any of us can turn into a demon." He glances over at Christian, who is still clicking quietly by himself. "Looks like Christian's already started."

I look over at Roxie, shocked, but she's looking down. "Seriously?"

"Yeah." He pulls out his own knife and starts crosshatching Roxie's spirals. Maybe this is what hunters do for fun.

"I thought . . . I don't know what I thought," I say. "I don't think I believed you when you said that souls can be sucked out and people can turn into demons."

"You should've believed me. I don't lie," says Ryan, and Roxie snorts.

"Sure, *cher*." She looks over at me. "You know enough not to summon Doors. That's all I'm going to say about that. I don't know what all we're supposed to be doing here. But if Narnia says it will help—"

"Narnia talks in riddles." Ryan rolls his eyes. "If she were less of a pain in the ass, that might be less annoying, but—"

"I doubt it," says Roxie, and rolls her own eyes. "Stupid bitch."

Ryan's lioness moves, shifts her weight so that she's leaning against me. I lean to the side, against her. She's totally solid, and huge, and comforting. She yawns. I yawn, and I don't mean to.

Roxie yawns too. I read somewhere that serial killers

don't yawn after other people do, because group yawning is an empathic response. Points for not going to Hell with a serial killer?

"You sleep with me," Ryan says, and I think he's talking to Roxie because he's looking at her.

There's sleeping now? I don't care if she's not a serial killer: "No—I don't want to sleep by myself." I know I sound childish and whiny, but *I do not want to sleep by myself in a Hell dimension, oh my god*.

Roxie looks at me like I'm a baby, which I know I am to her. "You're sleeping with Ryan," she says. "I'm sleeping with Stan."

"Ew," says Stan, and Roxie pinches him.

"Shut up," she says. "You're not my type either."

I take a deep breath and let it out slow. I feel a lot better knowing that I'm going to sleep with someone. "You'd better not dream crazy," is all I say, "because if I wake up screaming, I'm going to have to punch you."

"That's okay." Ryan yawns big, like how the lioness did. "You punch like a mundane."

"I hate you," I grouse, but when he opens his coat, I hesitate for a minute. I smell bad, like blood and sand and sulphur. There's ash in my hair from Kur. I'm sweaty from the lava.

"Come on, Allie," he says in a low voice. "It's okay." Like he knows what I am thinking or something.

I crawl into his arms. My coat is still on me, and it's sticky from sweat, but this is nice.

I know I keep saying "nice" when I talk about the little things Ryan does, but it *is* nice. It's nice to be protected. It's nice to know you can protect someone else. I've got my arms around Ryan, and even though we sort of hate each other right now—the kind of hate you feel for someone you *know* can make you feel something that's not hate, do you know what I mean?—we're going to stand by each other. I can feel his weapons down his back, the guns replaced with iron and obsidian.

"I'm sorry," I say to Ryan, my face in his neck, and his face in mine. I wrap my legs around his hips and settle into his lap, and we lean against his lion. It's not comfortable at all, and I'm not tired, but I'm slipping into sleep, softening into him.

"Don't do it again," he says to me. His voice is raspy. "I like you human." That is possibly the most romantic thing he's ever said to me.

His heart thuds against mine, and I'm asleep.

I wander through a field of grass, freshly cut. It smells wonderful, like spring, and there are stars overhead.

"Ryan worries, you know," says a deep voice. I turn around, in a complete circle, but there's no one there.

"Who's there?" I call.

"You know me. I am the goddess of Babylon, the goddess of courtesans, the goddess of—"

"Um. Ūsat?" I guess.

I hear a snort that sounds just like Ryan's, and suddenly the voice is a lot less O-So-Powerful. "Ištar. And rest your head, child, you have nothing to fear from me. I prefer lovers, and my lovers a bit more . . . a bit *more*."

"Thanks. I think." I sit down on the grass. It's damp. I lie back to look at the stars. There's no moon, and I don't recognize any of the constellations. Not that I would anyway, but maybe I could pick out the Big Dipper.

I can feel a hand on my forehead, stroking the top of my head, but when I twist around to look, I can't see anyone.

"Do you know my story?" Ištar asks me.

"No, I don't know anything about you," I say apologetically.

"I went through a Door, a gate with a lion on it to bar the entrance of anyone who would dare confront Ereshkigal, the goddess of the underworld. But I was prideful and thought I could have anything I wanted."

Sounds like my friend Amanda, I wanted to say, but I kept my mouth shut.

"Yes, very much like Amanda . . ." The hand on my forehead pauses, then continues stroking. "Ereshkigal let me through the six gates of Hell, but at each gate I had to take off a piece of clothing; that's why I'm naked now, always. Once I was through, she—that stupid cow—imprisoned me and killed me with sixty diseases, and no one on Earth could have sex anymore."

"That sucks for them." I turn over and rest my head on my hands. Ištar's not-really-existing hands are cool against the skin of my neck.

"Finally the other gods were annoyed enough that they demanded Ereshkigal sprinkle me with the waters of life, and I came back to Earth, at each gate receiving my clothing back. But still I always feel naked now." She heaves a deep sigh.

"Ereshkigal sounds like a bitch."

"Well, I breached her domain. Surely if she were to breach mine, I'd act much the same. And yet . . ."

"And yet," I prompt, when Ištar doesn't seem to want to keep going.

"And yet I never did get what I came for in the underworld." Her hand tightens on my neck. The waters of life came from the hand of the Kalaturru, a sexless thing made by my father. Find that hand. You will get what you've come here for."

I put my nose in the dirt and smell it. It smells wonderful, like life.

"What did you come for?" I ask.

"I came for the love of my youth." She sounds amused. "But if you ask Ryan, he'll tell you what the others think, that of course it was to take over the realm of the underworld and cement my position as the most powerful goddess in Babylon."

"Don't you want to be the most powerful goddess?" I ask.

"What's more powerful than love?" she replies, and her voice is lighter now, her touch on my neck lighter.

"I don't know," I mumble into my forearms. "I don't even think I know what love is."

I wait for Ištar to answer me, but there's only silence, and then the smell of the deep earth is gone, and all I can smell is Ryan, rich and heady.

"Ryan?" I mumble, and he pulls me closer. "Ištar's weird," I slur.

"Shh," he says, and we move together to turn onto our sides, my head tucked into his neck.

When we wake up, Christian is where we left him, and Stan is rubbing his arms, and Roxie is humming as she looks across the waters.

We're lying down, Ryan and me, and I'm curled up next to him. On my other side is the lioness, keeping me warm. But I'm still stiff from sleeping mostly on the ground; Ryan and I must have separated during the night.

He's staring down at me with a weird look on his face. I grin up at him, because for a second, just a moment, it's like we're not in a Hell dimension at all. Just for a moment, staring into his eyes, it's just him and me and our bodies pressed together.

"You slept for a long time," he tells me. His breath smells like chocolate, which is unexpected. My breath probably smells like ass, but I open my mouth to talk to him anyway.

"I totally had a dream about Ištar," I announce.

Where she's sitting next to Ryan, Ištar smiles at me. Her breasts are so high and perky, I am totally jealous.

"What did she tell you?" asks Roxie. She looks almost excited, which, you know, might not be unwarranted.

I separate myself from Ryan and sit up, stretching. Ugh, yes, really sore from sleeping on the ground.

"She said that nothing is more—no, she asked me, 'What is more powerful than love?' and said that we are looking for the waters of life. In somebody's hand. Or something like that. The stars looked weird."

"There are no stars in the underworld, *chère*," says Roxie, but Ryan is shaking his head.

"Waters of life. From a hand? That could be a lot of things. A lot of dimensions. There's nothing in any of the tales giving the location of that kind of thing." Ryan sounds frustrated.

"The water of life is what Scots used to call Scotch," offers Roxie, brow furrowed. She really is super-gorgeous, even when she is angry at me and I am still sort of angry at her. The scars on her face only enhance her awesome mystery vibe.

Ryan thinks I'm pretty, though. He's been a real jerk, but he said so. I remember what his hands felt like on my body and shudder a little.

"Hey. Hey, Allie." Ryan snaps his fingers. "Did she say anything else?"

"Yeah, she said that you worry too much." I stick my tongue out at him and he rolls his eyes.

"Thanks, that's a real help."

I look over at Christian. "Christian? You have any ideas?" He clicks at me, and I scowl. "That is *unhelpful,*" I tell him, but he doesn't seem to care.

Ryan stands up and brushes his hands on his pants. "We have to get going," he says.

Roxie stands, and holds out her hands to me. I guess I am forgiven. When I take them, I feel her snakes slither over me and shudder again, this time in the bad way.

"Thanks," I force myself to say.

We stand by the edge of the water. I still have no idea how we're going to get across. I am not swimming, I am making that clear now. Not in these clothes. Or in that water—I do not trust Hell waterways.

Ryan has come up behind me. I can feel the heat of him through my coat, smell the sandalwood. He murmurs in my ear, "You've had a dream, Allie. Is that what the Door gave you?"

No. It's not the Door's voice—it's Ištar's, in my head. I can almost hear her frowning at the idea.

"No," I say. His mouth brushes my pulled-back hair. I can feel his lips touch my skin.

"What did you get, Allie?"

The Doors haven't given me anything here. I don't think. But now I send my thoughts out to that Door on the other island, the one we need to get to, and all I say is, *Help*.

Ryan exhales.

And a black boat rises from the waters.

If there is one thing I don't want to do, it's step into that boat. There is no way. It is rickety and old, and, I realize, it is not actually black. It's a deep, dark red. So red that it *looks* black. It's only slightly bigger than a row boat.

You know something? I don't approve of this Hell dimension stuff. I really don't. I don't approve of elemental demons, and I don't approve of rickety boats, and I just do not approve of any of this bullshit. I especially don't approve of being a blood bank. These damn hunters—Ryan included—might as well be vampires, because that's all they see when they look at me: blood.

"Come on, Allie," says Ryan. He has Stan leaning on him on one side, and with his other arm he takes my elbow. I *hate* that every time he touches me I *feel* it. I feel it. He touches me and I just want to melt all over him.

"I don't want to," I tell him mulishly.

"You have to, *chère*." Roxie on my other side. Christian is already clambering into the boat, his feet making

weird noises. Not the noise that boots make, but, I realize, the spider noises. He's making the spider noises,
but it's him making them, not the spider.

I look over at Ryan to see if he noticed it too. He's
watching Christian and his mouth is set in a grim line.
I guess that's a yes.

"Okay," I announce. "I will get in the damn boat.
But I don't like it."

"You don't have to like it." Roxie takes my other
arm. "Come on, *chère,* let's go." She takes a deep
breath before clambering into the boat. It rocks in the
water, and the water splashes a little. Where it hits the
lava rocks, it sizzles.

And I realize: Roxie doesn't want to do this either.
No one is happy about this. And I've been so caught
up in my own issues that I haven't realized it. As much
as this is an adventure, this also sucks for *everyone,*
not just me.

So now I feel like shit.

I climb into the boat, careful to make sure it doesn't
rock, and that I don't touch the water. I'm not sure if it
sizzled because it's cold and it hit something hot, or
for another reason. Whatever the reason, I don't want
to touch the water.

I help Roxie hoist Stan into the boat, and Ryan jumps
in, with, of course, a minimum of rocking and splash-
ing. Does he do everything perfectly on the first try? I
would hate him for that, except it's too impressive.

The boat moves quickly across the water.

"Do you think this is, like, the Egyptian Hell dimension and we have to put coins under our tongues or something?"

Roxie snickers. "Where you been learning this stuff?" she asks me. "That's not how it works at all."

"Greek?" I guess.

Roxie shakes her head. She's got her hat in her lap, so I can see her hair. Her hair is cropped close to her head, but where it's growing out, it's curly, really curly, the way I always wished my hair would be. But my hair is plain brown, not endless black like hers, and it's totally straight. It's got a little bit of body, but it's totally straight.

"I don't know where we are. I mean, I'm not sure." She looks over at Ryan. He shakes his head. Stan is leaning on him, sleeping again.

"He should be a werewolf by now, shouldn't he?" I ask.

"Yeah, he should." Ryan's back to grim again. "I don't know why he's not. Maybe something in the underworlds is keeping him from turning completely. Most likely it's just slowing it down."

I reach out my hand to touch Stan's werewolf bite. The glow is still there, and a bruise, like the way he looked when he was shooting up heroin. I tell Ryan and Roxie, and then I say, "That's why he stopped, you know? Did you know that?"

Roxie's got an arm around me now. I'm on my knees in the boat. "He stopped doing heroin because he hated the way his arm looked all the time." I sniff a little, and try to keep from crying. "He's such a vain fuck."

Roxie and Ryan don't say anything. I wish it was Ryan's arm around me. It's not fair that it's not.

I turn, and look over the side of the boat. I can see Ryan's women in the water, and Roxie's snakes sometimes. One of the snakes twists and hisses at me, and I jerk back.

Hey, if I can see them and their avatars, I bet I can see me and mine. I tilt myself further over the side, and I see—

Blue. Blue light, in dashing fires that sling around me. A pair of ghostly wings rise up behind my back. I suck in a breath, and, I am totally not kidding, one of the little blue fires comes zipping up and into my mouth. I open my mouth and stick out my tongue—it's right there, bobbing. I let out my breath—the fire goes zipping away again.

Roxie suddenly hauls me backwards toward the center of the boat. "Play dress-up later," she says.

I scowl at her. "I'm *blue*," I say loudly.

"Shh," she and Ryan chorus. They sure agree when they're chastising me, even if they don't agree on anything else. What a pain in the ass.

I sit down in a corner of the boat, opposite Christian, and stare at his spider. It's not an ugly spider, I guess, as spiders go. I don't know—I am not a spider expert. It's a black spider, with long legs, and beady eyes, and I swear it's staring back at me, and it's fucking creepy as these Hells. Christian's eyes are kind of melting into its eyes, and his legs are kind of melting into its legs, and I don't like what I'm seeing at all.

Because I think what I'm seeing is someone actually turning into a demon before my very eyes. Like, I think he is literally turning into a demon.

I put my head down on my knees so that I don't have to look at anything anymore. With my face this close to the boat, I have realized a new and horrible thing: The boat is made of blood. It is not some kind of varnish. It smells like human blood.

I lift my head, but I sniff a little deeper. I smell Stan. He smells different now. Like something stronger is crowding out the things that make him Stan. The stale makeup is gone entirely—there's a little bit of the stale sex left. Mostly what's left of Stan are those endless summer sunsets when I watched him practice the ollie over and over again on his skateboard until he got it right, talking shit and maybe wishing I wasn't too worried about chipping my nails to do something that looked so purely *fun*.

That's what's left of Stan.

The rest of him is . . . it chitters in my mind, and it smells like death. I am starting to think I am not doing this "smelling" thing entirely with my nose.

I don't think there's any saving him—but I'm not going to give up on him. If there's a way to save him in these stupid underworlds, I am going to find it.

Maybe when we sleep next, Ūsat will come visit me and tell me how to save Stan. Or what the blue stuff all around me is.

Wings are cool, though. I dig the wings.

The boat bumps up against the lava rocks. I stand up and turn around—I can't see where we came from anymore, but when I close my eyes, I can see the Door, glowing a little, but it's *really* far off in the distance. It makes me think of sitting on the roof of the diner, facing Manhattan. Amanda and Stan and I did that a few times together, stared out at the skyline. Without the Twin Towers there, Manhattan could be any city, except for the bridges. But from the diner, the bridges are blurry, fuzzy, and if you don't know what you're looking for you can't see them.

That's what it's like, looking at the Door across the water with my eyes shut.

"Come on, Allie," says Ryan. He's standing on the rocks, and he lifts his arms to help me down. I let him take all my weight, and he swings me over the side of the boat like I'm weightless, his hands tight under my arms. My duster flaps around me, and I hope it looks awesome.

I'm unsteady on the lava rocks when I land, and Ryan has to help Stan out of the boat too.

Stan rubs at his temples, where the kerchief touches. "I'm really hungry," he whines. "I am *really* hungry, Allie."

Roxie catches my eye and gives me a *look,* like the kind she gives Ryan, moving her eyebrows and everything. I completely understand what she's not saying: Stan is not human anymore, and we should kill him.

I shake my head a little, the slightest nod no. She lifts one shoulder and lets it drop, then turns away. She's saying: *It's your funeral.*

Christian is clicking away, standing by the Door. This one glows brown. It's an old, weathered door, like the way my Door was when it first opened. I miss my Door, kind of, but not really. But it was kind of pretty, in a disgusting, scary way. The high arch of the top, the wrought iron fence inside with nothing behind it, just darkness and, sometimes, demons.

I don't even have to look at him; Ryan hands me his obsidian knife, and I slice another finger, drip my blood at the bottom of the Door. "You know me," I say softly. "You know me."

Allie. The Door flares a brighter brown, turns almost yellow, or orange, and I have to squint. I look behind me at Ryan. His hands are in fists. He's not squinting. I pass him back the knife.

"Ooh, hello," says Stan. He's stumbled over to the Door and pressed his hand to the wooden frame. "Hello," he says again.

"What the fuck?" says Roxie. She pushes back her duster and puts a hand on her sword.

"Don't," I say. *"Don't."* I pull Stan away from the Door. He whimpers. I pat his hair around the bandanna. Somehow, even through all this, glitter gets on my hand.

I can still smell the summer.

"I can't just give up," I tell the others briskly, and slide away from Roxie's disgust and Ryan's disapproval and Christian's half-step toward us. "Come on, Stan, through the Door."

12

I would like to think that I accomplished something really important by my decisive actions. Point one: No one messes with my posse. Even with the semi-demonic ones. This is because I am determined, which is another word for stubborn, which is another word, sometimes, for stupid.

Here is the other point, the second thing I have accomplished by heading through the Door with Stan, my head held high: I have just marched, unprotected, into an unknown Hell.

Stan's ahead of me, and I don't realize my mistake at first. I mean, the other time I did it, it wasn't so bad—just a bunch of lava-filled craters to accidentally fall into. At least there was *light*. In this Hell, we're in the dark, and it's a small space, like a closet. I can hear my and Stan's breathing bouncing off walls, damp walls, that are really nearby. I can't see a thing, though—which now that I'm experiencing it, gives me a new appreciation for what Stan's going through, being blindfolded in Hell. I mean, I am in *Hell*. I can't *see*. There could be *anything* in the dark.

I'm breathing hard. The sound echoes. Stan says, almost normal, "So what's this one like?"

"Um," I say. I am hoping that the others come through quickly. I would really like to get some kind of light in here, even if it's the light of Doors showing up in my mind's eye.

For a second, I think that maybe I *thought* that, you know, in the *thinky Door voice* that makes things happen, because suddenly I do sense a light. I look up. It's green, the color of glowsticks. I am not sure whether this is a good development, but on the other hand, I am really grateful for the light.

Until it starts to move.

From the light I can see that the Door opened into a crevice, and the crevice has a chimney of rock leading in a diagonal up. And crawling down, closer and closer, is . . . Have you ever seen a pill bug up close? Cute name for something with no face, over a dozen stumpy, reticulated legs, wet-looking armor plating that slides in and out of itself as it crawls over rocks and feels forward with its long, twitching antennae.

Now imagine it big. And out of every chink in its plating comes a green glow.

It's close now. Directly above our heads. It's stopped moving.

And now, the light goes out.

The darkness closes in on me, darker than before because now I know what's out there. The bug suddenly lights again, and just as quickly goes out. And again. And again.

In the distance, high above us, I see another glow. And it's bringing friends.

I blink hard. My vision is shot. I don't need my eyes for this, though: I very carefully, very slowly, reach under my coat and unwrap the cold-iron chain from around my waist.

"Stan," I say quietly. The bug above us doesn't move to my voice, though I think it twitches when the air moves a little near it. "Stan, I need you to sit down, okay?" He doesn't answer. "Okay?"

"Is it bad, Allie?" he whispers.

"It's going to be," I say. I run my hand along the chain until I get to the end. The two ends feel solid in my palms, and I fold the chain together so I'm holding a solid loop of pain for any demon that gets near. Silver heals, salt binds, iron kills. Which is good, because there are now four bugs above us, and I count three more above them.

Stan sits. And I lift the chain up and wait for one of them to get too close.

The Door suddenly flares open, blinding me *again,* and Roxie comes through.

"You all right, *chère?*" she calls. She can't see a thing either.

"I am right here," I say quietly. "Please watch out for Stan on the floor, and the monsters up and to the right of us."

I hear Roxie shift abruptly, and someone's knife hitting the rocks—I see a spark—

I wish Roxie could use the sword, since it is big and impressive and I'm pretty sure magical, but I guess a small space is not the best place to use a long-reach weapon. The dark is back, and the bugs have gone black.

Roxie doesn't say a word. I am glad she believes me. I wish she'd say something about where Ryan and Christian are. Or just Ryan.

The first pill bug glows again. Then they all do— seven of them. They pulse, off-rhythm. Roxie inhales. The bugs start advancing, crawling down the walls, surrounding us.

The Door opens. "Goddammit," I say out loud, because I just want this *done.* I wish I was enough of a bitch to have snuck a crossbow into Hell, even if it would've screwed our chances with the Door-hounds *or whatever.* Then I could have pegged off the monsters with, I don't know, my sudden preternatural ability to aim stuff, and actually been *happy* about seeing Ryan and Christian alive.

Well, alive for the moment, anyway. We're all silent. The Door is dark. We're working blind. Ryan says, "What's—" before Roxie says, "Demons above us," and they all shift and pull out weapons and wait.

It stays dark for a long time. Long enough that I wonder if the Door scared them off. I hope.

The bugs flare in unison, like the flash-bang magics an old hunter once showed me, fire and sulphur and a bang you hear in your soul instead of your ears. I squint through the spots in my vision—the bugs are moving. And they're moving fast.

Their glow is fading—I don't think they want to show off their position. The first one to reach us rears up, clinging half on the wall for just long enough to take aim and launch itself at Roxie. Roxie grunts and I can hear her under her breath say "ew ew ew ew *ew*"— and I hear a crunching noise as she rips the bug off her and throws it at the wall. There's another crunching noise. I am impressed by her aim.

Something touches my hair.

I remember the nights at the diner when we were bored, and the Door was quiet, and Ryan would show me different ways to kill things. I remember this instead of screaming. I twist away from the bug and I swing my looped chain down on the wall where I felt the thing. I hit the top of something, but instead of the nice crunching like Roxie had, the bug just comes loose of the wall and hits the ground. By my feet. By Stan.

I lift my heel and *stomp*.

Now *there* is a crunching noise. I lift my foot, and there's a tiny glow beneath me: I hit the glowy goo bits.

I turn around to keep my back to the wall again, and wait. In the midst of shuffling footsteps and the quick turns of leather moving, I hear a sharp clang, someone's knife on stone, a hard brush against my hand, and then the crunch we're all waiting for. It's all quiet for a moment. And then Ryan saying, "How many?"

Roxie says, "Three."

Christian clicks. But he does it once, so I'm figuring that's his count.

"One," I say.

"Really?" Roxie says.

"Shut up, yes."

"And I got two," says Ryan. People were apparently busy while I was squishing things. "That all of them?"

"I think so," I say. I lift my foot. A tiny bit of glow. "But I have an idea," I say.

When you open demonic pill bugs, you get to their glow. When you dip something like, say, the tip of Ryan's obsidian knife before he's noticed what you're doing, you can get enough of a light to see about a foot. Though it rubs off really easily, which is the only reason why Ryan will talk to me ever again.

Roxie sticks her hand into the demon and then lifts her fist, dripping—she scans the walls. "Nothing," she says. "I think we've got them for now."

"That is really gross," I say.

"Grow up," she says, but she smiles at me, so I think I still win points for holding my own in the fight. She nods. "You should do the spell. Then we can get some rocks, light 'em up, get out of here."

I reach for Ryan's knife, then realize: It is covered in bug guts. He raises his eyebrows in the way that means *You are the one who put the knife in demon goo.* I scowl and stick my hand out for Roxie's. She laughs, and gives me the one that isn't dulled. Roxie was the one whose knife hit the wall.

I slice my finger—this is really starting to hurt a lot, maybe I should start using my arm instead?—and drop the blood, say the words. Doors light up.

And up. "Sorry, everybody," I say. "Everything's thataway." I point. At the very least, we're going to have to shimmy up the rock chimney to get anywhere near the next Door.

Christian's feeling around with his spider legs, and pushing rocks over near the open dead bug. He is helpful. I feel sorry he's turning into a demon.

I kneel and start dipping rocks into the goo, and as

Christian starts doing the same, that's when I see that I've got a cut on the back of my hand. It's small, just a chunk of skin torn away down to the blood. It could be from a flying chip of rock from where Roxie's knife cut into the side of the crevasse, or it could be from the bug.

I swallow. "I need silver, oh my god," I say, and Ryan looks over at me from where he's cleaning off the knife again on his shirt.

"I—" He stops and clears his throat. "We have nothing to melt it with, nothing to melt it in."

"Didn't anyone bring a *lighter*?" I demand, and Roxie shakes her head.

"Even if we had brought one, *chère,* it wouldn't get hot enough. And there's no place to start a fire and magic it hotter." She swings her arm out, indicating the crevasse we're in. The rock—now that there's more, steadier light, it looks like sandstone, maybe, or something else that's kind of soft and weird looking. What is it called? Sedimentary rock, right? That's the kind that builds on itself until it has so many layers and is really tall.

I take a deep breath and close my eyes. The demon goo stinks, and Christian's still dipping more and more. The light's getting brighter. And I've got a cut on my hand.

I can't tell if it's green from the light of the goo, or green from—

"Okay, I guess we just have to wait to see if I am infected with demon." I am nowhere near as calm as I sound.

Ryan takes my hand and stares down at it. His hat covers his whole face. I can't see what he's thinking.

"You could ask the Door," he finally says. What? Is he seriously suggesting I ask a Door for something? Who is this stranger?

On this side of the Door, it is a cave into rocks, and it glows a greyish silver. It looks sluggish, like it doesn't get a lot of use. Maybe it doesn't. Maybe it's lonely, like all the other Doors here. Like Owen's Door in the hospital. Maybe it just wants someone to love it.

Well, it has Stan. He's sitting propped up against the Door, bleeding. Oh, shit, Stan.

"Oh, shit." I move away from Ryan. "Stan." I drop to my knees, and it hurts, the stone under my knees is hard, but—*Stan*.

"It hurts, Allie, it hurts," he says dazedly. His blood is black and looks tacky, and it's dripping onto the rocks, between Stan's fingers. He has his hand pressed to his leg; there's a bite, a big one, and now I know what the pill bugs would've done to us if they'd gotten close enough.

"Do not touch him," says Ryan. He crouches down on one side, and Roxie on the other. Christian doesn't give a damn; he just keeps dipping rocks. We will run out soon.

"I bet it's painful," says Ryan finally. He's just staring at Stan, at the blood dripping through his fingers. A thick droplet forms and hits the rocks—around us, I see Doors abruptly break into light, like when I drop my blood. Except the colors are darker, and the Door that lights up for Stan isn't the one that lit up for me. It's green, and damp, and I don't like it. Ryan doesn't see it. Instead, he says, "Sorry, Stan."

Stan gives a shaky laugh. "Sure, boyfriend."

Ryan shrugs and looks at me. "We can't touch him. *You* can't touch him—you have an open wound. If any of his blood gets into you . . ."

Ryan doesn't have to finish that thought. If any of Stan's blood gets into me, that's it for me, isn't it? I'm definitely a werewolf after that. And if there isn't a way to fix Stan, there definitely isn't a way to fix me.

"Stan," Ryan says. "Can you move?"

"I don't even know if I can, like, breathe," he replies, but he starts struggling to his feet, his back moving up against the rocks of the Door slowly. He takes a deep breath and lets it out, and I smell death on him. Now the summer scent is fading. I don't know how long I'll still have him.

"Come on," says Roxie. "We've got a long climb." She resheaths her knives, and grabs my hand. One quick squeeze, and suddenly I feel a little better. I've got Roxie by my side, and she's got my back. She must like me a little bit, otherwise she'd have killed

Stan when she had the chance, in the middle of the battle.

Ryan jerks his head in Christian's direction. "You ready, Christian?" That's the first time I've ever heard him address Christian directly, I think, since even before this started.

Christian just clicks at him. I look at Roxie, and we have a conversation with our eyebrows. I am getting fluent in eyebrow-ese. If Christian doesn't die before this is over, we're going to have to kill him; he's almost entirely demon now.

"How can an avatar turn into a demon?" I ask softly.

"What is the sound of one hand clapping?" she replies, and I frown at her.

"I'm serious."

Ryan's carefully binding up Stan's leg with Christian's bandanna. I guess Christian doesn't really need it anymore. Ryan helps Stan up, then looks at us. "Everybody pick up a rock. Let's go."

"How the hell can we get up there?" I did not bring my spelunking gear, nor had I been informed it would be necessary before I started this trip.

"We climb," says Ryan unnecessarily. "With our *hands*." He shoots a small grin at me. I think he's *enjoying* this.

"This isn't *fun*," I snap.

"No, but it's interesting," he says, and I scowl at him.

"Jerk."

"Bitch."

"Lovebirds," says Roxie, and I can tell she's trying not to laugh. She's not exactly succeeding.

"Okay—let me—" I sigh, and close my eyes. There are Doors everywhere, mostly up, and as soon as I focus on them, they all pop brightly, and they all want to *talk* to me.

Allie!

Allie!

Allie!

The closest one glows blue, and is *huge,* like four or five times the size of my body, tall, wide. Up.

I point up and sigh again. "Up, about fifty feet," I tell them.

Christian chitters. I turn to look at him. "Listen, you still have hands. Remember how to use them." *Remember how to use them,* I order him.

Ryan sets the pace, something easy for Stan, but constant. He's talking, I think to distract me from stuff, but I stop listening after a while, because it's depressing, and I get annoyed when I get depressed. He lectures me on demons, giving me the history of a demon called *druj,* the Zoroastrian demon of lies. It doesn't sound too interesting. Blah blah, it lies and turns things into chaos, and can only be combated with the truth. What good is a demon that can't be *fought*?

Roxie climbs near Christian. He clicks and she

hisses, and I'm sure it has meaning to them, but it gives me a headache. Stan just feels around, and follows our avatars' voices, and he's more quiet than before, and I hear him suck in his breath every once in a while when he moves wrong.

Climbing the rocks is really difficult, and the further we get from the brown Door, the darker it gets in this dimension, and the louder the buzzing.

I interrupt Ryan's explanation of *lajabless,* a Caribbean demon with a cow foot who lures men to their deaths.

"What's with the buzzing?"

"That's the flies." He says it like it's not the grossest thing in the world. "You didn't wonder why there's not any light? The flies block it out."

"Now you're making stuff up." I slip on a rock, and have to grab it again. Pill bugs and flies and I am getting very disgusted by Hell dimensions in general, oh my god. My hands are sore and I am pretty sure they're going to start bleeding soon. My shoes, at least, are perfect for this. They have round toes that are strong and dig into the soft rock easily, but the bottoms are wearing off from all the walking, and are getting slippery.

"Seriously. They don't bite or anything, they just . . . exist."

"Great," I mutter. "I feel a lot better."

"Have you ever heard of the *dwen*?" he asks me.

"Nope, is that another Caribbean demon?"

"It's from Trinidad. When a child dies before it's baptized, its feet turn backwards, and it can't go anywhere."

I'm not a child, and I've never been baptized. My family is—was—about as far from religious as it comes.

"Well, I guess I'm screwed then," I say, and grab another piece of rock, haul myself up, grab a piece of rock, haul myself up.

13

I have never been so relieved to see a Door in my life. The soft blue glow is actually *comforting*. For a few moments, as we climbed, there was nothing but blackness and buzzing, the hissing and clicking from Roxie and Christian, and the noise of rocks breaking off and falling—except no noise of them hitting the ground.

I collapse in front of the Door, and take a deep breath. Everything smells and tastes blue, icy like wintergreen gum or spearmint tea. No—like toothpaste. The air is like toothpaste, and instead of being thinner so high up, it's thicker. The Door is on a cliff, facing a deep crevasse. Our glow rocks are starting to fade, but the light from the Door makes up for it.

"My stomach," I groan. Have you ever pulled yourself up anywhere? I just used muscles I swear I didn't even know I had.

"It doesn't really hurt," Ryan tells me. He's helping

Roxie haul Stan up over the edge. "None of this really *exists*. It's why you're not hungry."

"Yeah, then how come Stan got hurt? And Christian's avatar—"

"Because they're demons," hisses Roxie. "They really exist here. We don't."

"This looks like it exists to me," I say, pointing at the scrape on my hand from earlier. "And look!" I hold out my hands, palms up. "And if he's Mr. Existence, how did Stan climb the rocks with his leg ripped open?"

"He did it because he had to. The limits of human—demon—anyone's endurance . . ." Ryan trails off. "You have no idea what you're really capable of, Allie. None of us do."

"I'm capable of being cranky," I grouse, and lay on my back on the rock. It's pretty smooth, and there are no bugs or anything. Just the blue light from the Door, making everything around it glow. My skin looks almost translucent.

"Say hello to the Door, Allie." Roxie crouches beside me and offers up her knife. I shake my head.

"I don't need that," I tell her, and roll over until I'm on my stomach in front of the Door. It dwarfs everything I've ever seen before in my life. It is the skyscraper of Doors, for sure. It looks just like the Door at the bottom of the crevasse, though—all rock and stone, like something out of *The Lord of the Rings*.

Now Viggo Mortensen . . . He'd perk me right up.

(Who am I kidding? Ryan is way hotter than Viggo Mortensen, I swear.)

I pick the scab off one of my old wounds, and smear my finger right outside the Doorway. *You know me, you know me, you know me . . .*

You're so tired, Allie, says the Door. *I can fix that. I can help you.*

I don't want your help.

That's a lie. You're a liar, liar, liar liar, it chants. *Liar liar liar.*

Can you help Stan? I demand.

Nothing can help him now! I swear the Door even *cackles.*

Then shut up, I say, and push with my thoughts, and move the Door away from me, move it away. Its voice fades. Thank god.

"Allie, make the circle." Ryan holds out another crayon. I take it; it's brand new, and called "macaroni and cheese." I raise my eyebrows at him—I'm just saying, I'm getting better at communicating with my eyebrows, seriously!—and he shrugs. "It was as close to flesh as I could get."

So gross. I draw out the circle, and, for good measure, drip a little blood where it meets, and then I pull out my salt.

"Salt?" Roxie's sitting next to Stan, but not close

enough for him to touch her. Christian is on the other side of the circle, as far away from the Door as he can get, and Ryan is standing in the middle, watching me.

"This Door makes me nervous."

"Allie the Door Whisperer says this? That's . . . not good." Ryan shakes his head. "Salt."

"Salt," I agree, and shake some out of my leather flask. It fizzes when it hits my blood which, you know, is weird. For good measure, I shake some onto the scrape on the back of my hand. It doesn't fizz, it just burns. I hiss through my teeth, but don't say anything.

The limits of human endurance, and all that.

We all nap a little. Well, Ryan doesn't; he's got his back to all of us, staring over the edge of the cliff back down into the crevasse. It's hard to keep my eyes closed—the light of the Door burns really brightly, more brightly when my eyes are closed than when they are open.

I don't care what Ryan says—I'm exhausted and it's *real*.

I miss my diner. I miss it a lot. I left a note for Dawn, asking her to open and close, and I'm sure she will. It's not like I am worried about it—except I am totally worried about it.

I spent three years training with Sally to run the diner. She told me on my second day that as soon as I walked in, she knew I'd either be the one to take over running the diner when she retired, or I'd be a miserable flop.

Now that I know what I know about the Doors, and how they give you what you want . . . well, I wonder about what was really going on. I think about it a lot, sometimes. I can go for weeks without it ever crossing my mind, but every time I make a mistake, every time the cash register doesn't balance out, every time I cook an order and get it wrong, I wonder. I wonder if Sally really wanted to leave the diner to me. I wonder if she really wanted to retire to Florida. I don't *own* the diner—she still does. I guess I'm just kind of the caretaker, in case she ever comes back.

Or in case I can ever afford to buy it from her. Which I've been saving to do for four years at this point. And I have more money than I should, really, and I wonder if that's the Door too.

I feel a tap on my shoulder, and, "Hey." I roll over and put my back to the Door. It makes me uneasy, but I want to face Ryan, and I know that if anything comes though the Door, he'll be better than me at taking it down.

Not that anything's come through any of the Doors in the Hell dimensions, but it can't hurt to be careful.

Ryan is crouched next to me, his women just behind him. They smile creepy smiles. He flows down until he's sitting cross-legged. Ištar sits next to me, and the lioness curls up carefully so that part of her is touching me and part of her is touching Ryan.

He acts like he doesn't notice what they're doing, just takes off his hat and runs his hand through his hair; it sticks up a little, right at the nape of his neck, and if he was any closer I'd flatten it for him. Because I am not at all obvious.

Ūsat catches my eye, and smooths the hair at the nape of Ryan's neck, but she's not corporeal, so the hair is still sticking up. I appreciate the sentiment, though.

"I could hear you thinking from all the way over there," he says.

"You could *hear me?*" I ask incredulously. "It's getting stronger?"

"No—I meant—" He makes a face. "Sorry. Figure of speech. Might not be a good idea in these parts."

"Oh thank god," I say. And much as I hate to remind him that he probably has better things to do . . . "Shouldn't you be keeping an eye out for demons and stuff?"

He hooks a thumb over his shoulder. Behind him, Roxie's settled at the cliff edge. She's rubbing her knee. "She likes to do the watch," he explains quietly.

I prop my head up on my hand. "I was thinking about my diner," I confess. "I know I should be thinking about something important, but . . ."

Ryan nods. "It's important to keep your mind in the game," he says. "But it's also important to remember *why* we're doing this. What it's for. Keep yourself grounded in the real world."

"You guys don't." I wave my other hand over at Roxie and Christian. "You guys hate the world."

"We don't hate the world." He frowns; Ištar sighs. "We don't hate people. You said that before, too, that we disrespect the very people we're protecting. It's not true. You won't find people more focused on keeping a world of mundanes safe. But—the kind of people we are, that we have to be . . . it doesn't fit nine-to-five. We're security guards, and truckers, and the bluest collars you ever saw. And a lot of mundanes grew up thinking it was okay to treat working guys like—"

"Like shit," I say. It's what I would've done; it's what I did do, until I jumped the tracks six years back. "You've probably saved the lives of hundreds of people, and they have no idea, and they treat you like shit." I roll onto my back and stare up at the ceiling. We'd climbed a long way up to get here, and I can see where the tunnels keep going up. Or down.

I guess it depends on which way you're going. "Why do you do it?" I ask the ceiling.

He doesn't say anything. But the tips of his fingers touch the hair behind my left ear. Just a little bit. But. He's touching my hair.

"How can't I?" he says at last. His voice is deep, and he sounds sad, so sad. "I know what's out there," he says. "I know what goes bump in the night. How do you think I got started? I didn't have anyone crashing in to save *me* in the nick of time." His touch disappears. "I didn't have anyone to save the rest of them."

Them? "Them?" I ask.

Ryan's quiet for a long time, and I wonder if he's going to finish. I wonder if he would've, if I hadn't opened my mouth about it.

It's Ištar's voice I hear when he says, "When I was younger, in the winter, I used to catch seasonal work, cutting down Christmas trees to send south. A lot of us did it—it was a quick buck, just a couple of weekends' worth of work. The guys hiring would drive us most of the way, and then we'd hike through the snow up to the tree lot. Not far."

He pauses, then: "I was cutting down a tree when it happened. The guys with me all died. I didn't."

I'm almost afraid to say anything, but I've got to know. "What was it?"

"A hidebehind. One of the natural demons that shows up without a Door. They move fast and don't like to be seen; hence the name. But they watch, and they wait, and then they steal loggers away when no one's looking." He laughs a little, the kind of laugh people have when they're saying something sad or horrible, not the laugh of someone actually amused. "I was the last one, and the only reason I didn't get taken too was because I was the one working with the chainsaw. I was the one who had a giant mass of iron to spin around, and I was the one who cut the thing's head off before it could move behind me again."

He sighs. I can feel his breath touch my skin. "I hiked back to the checkpoint, and then I kept going. The rest of my crew missing, and me with a bloody chainsaw. Not good. So I left."

Snow, huh? I wonder about his "Southern" accent, and then realize: Lots of places have a South. "How old were you?" I ask.

"Nineteen."

"Do you have a family? I mean, do they wonder what's up with you?"

"Don't know," he says. "I'm always afraid to go back."

"But—don't you miss them? Don't you want to be with your family?" I can't imagine having family and *not* wanting to be with them. I can't—I miss having a family so much. Not that I ever really had a *family*; can you miss what you never had?

I can feel Ryan looking at me, so I turn my head and look up at him, and suddenly I can see just how tired he is, how alone, how much he hates being alone, but he feels like he has to, that the people around him always get killed.

Always except me.

"You would have saved those men if you could have. You were just a kid. You had no idea what you were up against." I stretch my hand out to pat his leg, and he flinches, so I let it drop.

"I killed the thing that got them, and the dead don't care much about anything anymore. So I'm not a hero. But I couldn't ever return to the world of the mundanes."

"I think you *are* a hero," I say, and this time I don't let him flinch away. Ūsat, standing behind Ryan like a protective mother bear or something, smiles approvingly. Ištar puts her hand over mine. I can feel it, a little bit, cool and damp. I practically don't even see them anymore, they are so much a part of him, but this feels weird. Then Ištar takes her hand away, and disappears. When I look for her, she's standing with Ūsat, standing over us.

The lioness purrs a little.

I look down at my hand; the scrape is gone, and there's not even a scar.

Add that to the list of crazy things that have been happening.

"Why do you do it?" he says challengingly, backing away, putting space between us literally and figuratively.

I repeat back to him what he said to me: "How can I not?"

"Stan and Amanda don't."

"Yeah, I know." I look down. "But I have to. It's my diner. It's my Door. It was my fault—at least partially.

I didn't stop Amanda from doing her stupid summoning spell. I didn't . . ." I stop myself. I'm a different person from when this all started, and that means that now, instead of just whining about all the things that I didn't do, I recognize that not all of this is my fault. Not all of it's my fault, and I don't have to take all the responsibility.

I still feel like shit, though.

"It's not all your fault," says Ryan, as though he read my mind. He smiles at me, a flash of blue-white in the Door light, and then stands up. "And you're . . . doing pretty good." He settles his hat on his head, and tugs the brim down so I can't see his eyes anymore. "Time to get going."

I stand up and take a deep breath of the thick minty air. "I'm ready." I'm not ready at all. I want a nap. I want a chocolate bar. I want my diner. Dawn probably thinks Ryan and I are in some love nest somewhere sexing it up. Close, but not close enough.

The blue Door leads us into a cave. Note: I do not go first into this Door, because while I can kick a lot of ass, I am also (mostly) not dumb, and my learning curve is pretty damn steep.

When I follow Roxie, though, there are no immediate demons. But . . . it's creepy—creepier than the rocks, creepier than anything, because it looks *human*. The floor is worn smooth, and the walls were carved out of the rock. There are torches in sconces on the walls, flickering with orange fire. I mean, it's regular-looking fire. It's orange and yellow like regular fire. It flickers slightly. It's normal, it's all normal, in an amusement-park set design kind of way. Normal.

It is kind of freaking me out.

I have a drama-free blood drop; the next Door is kind of far, but at least we won't have to climb to get to it. Christian's spider legs click on the stone floor of the cave as we walk through it. Ryan's boots thump, and Roxie's shitkickers don't make any noise at all. My shoes make clunking sounds.

Stan is still wearing tennis shoes. He's limping, but we're going to be lucky to get the hell out of these caves without having to fight him.

"Allie, I'm hungry," he says, and his voice is husky, too deep and scratchy. "I'm really really hungry."

"You can eat soon." I try to sound reassuring, but I'm pretty sure I just sound scared.

We pass by a room. When I look in, the firelight reflects off a crystal-encrusted wall, like a giant geode. Pretty. We pass by it, and another cave room appears. It seems to be empty, except for firelight and a short well all the way in the back. On the edge of the well is balanced a full tin cup of water, just asking to be picked up and drunk. I almost go into that one, but this is Hell. I think the odds are good that if I tried to drink from the cup, my face would be eaten off.

"Minos?" Ryan mutters, and Roxie punches his shoulder. He ignores her and keeps muttering, and I hear a whisper in my head that sounds like Ryan. I've been talking with my mental voice, but I haven't been doing a lot of listening lately, and I am super-curious. *I saw that movie once,* he's thinking, *what was it, hands holding up candles, monster at the end of the hall? Always monsters. Are these Hells my memories? Hell is what you bring with you. I brought—*

His voice stops, and then instead of words I see . . . I see me. From above, flush and naked and almost kind of pretty. Ryan's memory. I open my eyes—I didn't even notice I'd closed them, I am losing points on the secret psychic front—and everyone's stopped and looking at me.

Out loud, with Ūsat's voice, Ryan says, "Stay out of my head, Allie."

"Then talk to me," I request, and I hate how desperate I sound, but I'd like some human interaction that happens out loud and isn't filled with deep meaning or the end of the world or death. "Talk to me, please."

"You couldn't wait to get me to shut up on the rocks," he taunts.

"Please, Ryan," and I am so appalled to hear my voice break in the middle of his name. "Please."

"Ryan," says Roxie sharply.

"Come walk with me, Allie," he says, and I step around Christian to get to Ryan.

"Tell me about names," I request. I thread my arm through his. Ūsat and Ištar smile at me approvingly, and the lioness brushes against me with every step we take. I let my newly healed hand down. She's tall, so it rests on her back as we walk, and I feel more comfortable.

"Names are . . . magic." Ryan puts his other hand over mine. It's warm and dry and anchors me. "It's a part of you, like your blood. If a demon or a witch gets a part of you—"

I frown. "Is it contagion magic again? Like with salt?"

He nods. "It's related. Doing something to a part of you can be made the same as doing it to *you*. So names, true names . . . those are something you want to protect."

"So does that mean everyone has two names?"

"No, not everyone. Only people who know that they're supposed to. That's why hunters always say, 'You can call me,' instead of, 'My name is . . . '" He pauses but I don't let him start again.

"I said my name in front of our Door."

"Your *real* real name?" Ryan asks me sharply. I shake my head, and he lets out a breath. "Good," he says. "If your true name was spoken in front of the Door, it might be able to . . . do things. And not just *your* Door—what one Door knows, they all know."

I bite my lip. "What about Stan?"

"He has another name, doesn't he? The Door doesn't know his true name, just the one he's called by."

I look down at the floor. The light from the sconces casts strange shadows. There are more shadows than there are hunters; apparently Ūsat and Ištar and the lioness even cast shadows. There's not a lioness shadow, actually—where hers would be is just another woman.

I shudder.

"What about—Amanda. She doesn't have a second name." I look up at Ryan, and I can see his eyes under the brim of his hat. I wish I had a hat. All I have are my stupid sunglasses, and all they're really good for is holding my bangs away from my face.

"If she doesn't have a second name, it could go either way. It might be how she conjured up the Door so easily. A true name is a powerful thing. We don't really understand the mechanism for the creation of Doors—I'm quoting Narnia here, by the way—but there might be *something* out there that was drawn to that kind of bait . . ." I can *hear* Ryan shrugging. In my head it feels like a rolling of the shoulders, or maybe like I just rolled my head around on my neck and something popped a little. "It never made sense, how the Door came to you three so quickly, so easily. Just popped right into existence."

"Spontaneous vivification," I say wisely, and he chuckles.

"I wish I'd never taught you that phrase." He squeezes my hand before he drops his. "You overuse it."

"It's a great phrase. I love it." I squeeze his arm once and then take it back. I plunge my hand into the pocket of my coat. My bandanna is in there. It's the same pink one I was wearing days ago—it feels like weeks already. Maybe time really does move differently in the Hell dimensions. "Do you think time moves differently in the Hell dimensions?"

"Maybe." Ryan shrugs again, mentally. "Maybe not. I guess we'll find out if we ever get the Hell out of here. Just need to find some damn—" I can kind of hear his mind grinding to a halt, and readjusting, and a sort of flurry of thoughts that end with him saying, "Damn. I *knew* I knew something about a hand and the waters of life." He's excited. "Do you know the story of the Hand of Franklin?" he asks me.

I shake my head.

"It's this Canadian thing. This guy named Franklin was looking for a passage through the Northwest Territories, and his expedition got lost. I don't remember all the details, but there's a song about it, about how Franklin's hand is still reaching toward the Beaufort Sea."

"Maybe we're looking for the Hand of Franklin, then," I say, teasingly. "Might as well call it something."

"Might as well," he agrees.

"Do you think that the Hand of Franklin literally is what we're looking for? I mean, I bet it's called something completely different, but what if it's the same kind of thing?"

"What if we're looking for a hand that's reaching toward a sea?" Ryan asks.

I roll my eyes. "Well, I don't *know*. But doesn't it stand to reason that most stories about water and hands and life would be about the same things?"

"No, not at all," he replies, but he grins.

"So are you Canadian?" I ask, knowing even as I did that he wasn't going to answer me.

He grins down at me. "I'm not telling you my name," he says. "Especially not in Hell."

I grin back at him. "That's okay, I'm not telling you mine either." I would if he asked, but he wouldn't ever ask. Maybe he doesn't care to know.

I finger my bandanna. Maybe he doesn't *want* to know, maybe it would put me in danger, maybe maybe maybe—

Maybe, whispers something. *Maybe*—

Shit, Ryan's going to kill me if I'm in his head again—but he's stopping, and so is Roxie. And the whispering doesn't resolve into words again, it's just a quiet shushing noise, like a river flowing.

Roxie holds up her hand, and in the firelight her face is covered in flickering shadows. The shadows can't hide that she looks scared.

This is the woman who jumped on a *dragon*. I do not want to see what scares her. Her snakes are silent and unmoving.

The shushing is coming from the dark spot in the tunnel ahead of us; by the shape, it's either another cave room or a new path. A new gross path. There's no way we can take a route around it, though, unless we turn around, and that's not an option.

"Listen," Christian's spider says softly. It's the first thing he's said in a while. He ignores Roxie's hand and moves around her, heading toward the noise. Ryan starts to follow, guiding Stan—then Stan stops, and cocks his head to the side.

"It's okay," Stan says. His voice is even deeper than before. Stan, my Stan, is barely there anymore. My guilt is a knot in my stomach. I made him forget. I did this. I can't ever take it back, or I would.

Stan, I am so sorry, I think, and I hope that he can hear me, if he's anywhere at all that he can hear.

"It's just some mom singing," Stan continues. "It's kind of nice, actually—"

Ryan twists around Stan just in time to catch Roxie as she makes a run for the shushing, and he wraps his arms around her from behind, making a bear hug she can't break from. She's trying like hell, though, and I am seriously impressed with both of their efforts here, even while I am freaking the hell out.

"Allie," Ryan—Usat—grinds out, "blindfold her—"

ow." Roxie fights dirty. And he wants me to help. Great.

I pull my bandanna out of my pocket, and try to slide sideways toward Roxie. She's keening now, inhuman, and her snakes . . . they're dying, and limp on her body. The shushing is getting louder, and Christian is wavering back and forth between going on and turning back to help us with whatever's going on with Roxie—and Stan's started walking, hands out, toward Christian and the new cave.

Roxie flings her head back to break Ryan's nose, and thank god they've sparred together or whatever hunters do to socialize, because his nose isn't there—my kerchief is. It's not a great blindfold, but it's enough—she's suddenly limp in Ryan's arms, and breathing shallowly.

"What the hell is it?" I ask. Ryan gingerly lets Roxie go—she stands on her own, but she's not steady on her feet.

"I have a suspicion," Ūsat says. She's practically corporeal. So is Ištar. Ryan carefully takes Roxie's hand and starts moving toward the cave. I grab Stan's sleeve and follow.

14

The cave is wide enough that we can all stand shoulder to shoulder at the entrance, even Christian's giant spider. I think of that line from *Mary Poppins*: "Shoulder to shoulder into the fray." Okay, we're not suffragettes, but the sentiment stands. There are no sconces on the walls in this cave, just a giant fire in a chasm through the middle. The fire isn't orange—it's black. It's black fire, and it's so hot, I can feel it from where we're standing, so many feet away from it.

Along the far wall, across the chasm, is a giant snake. Except it isn't a snake—it's half-snake, half-woman. The snake half has dark, thick skin rather than scales. The woman half has long dark hair that falls in thick curls down its back and pooling around it like a blanket. It—she—the thing's making that shushing noise that Christian and Stan, our resident part-demons, recognize as actually meaning something.

Stan said it was a mom singing. Roxie's Door likes to hum at her—I am starting to wonder if maybe Ryan's thought before wasn't wrong: Hell is what you bring with you.

I am starting to wonder what kind of monster Roxie brought with her that drove her to that kind of madness.

The thing, still shushing, reaches down into its mass of beautiful hair and lifts a bundle out of the curl of its tail. It cradles it for a moment, whispering and rocking, and then brings it up to its face.

The thing's mouth cracks open like a snake's, and it . . .

"What's it eating, Ryan?" I ask quietly. I know what it's eating. I know. But I have to ask.

"A baby," says Ištar, and she starts to cry.

Roxie, beneath the blindfold, is shaking. I want to turn away—it's not a real baby, real babies don't go to Hell, just tell me it isn't a real baby, Ryan.

Ūsat says softly, "That's a lamia."

I look down at my coat. I am wearing the skin of a monster that eats babies.

I want to throw up.

"They live in caves," Ryan says. He's carefully moving Roxie past the doorway, getting her farther down the corridor and away from this abomination. "They come out in hospitals a lot. And parks. And—"

"Shut up," I say. I grab hold of Stan's arm and I'm following Ryan like there's nothing horrible happening just a few feet away.

And then, just like that, like it was nothing, we're past the cave with the fire and the chasm, and we're back in a corridor with sconces and regular orange fire.

Except I can still hear the shushing, I can still hear whispers of Roxie's nightmare.

And I wonder what I brought with me into Hell.

I take us through the corridors, closing my eyes every few feet to make sure we're going in the right direction. We turn left at one fork in the cave, right at another. I feel like we're going in circles, but we can't be, because we're getting closer and closer to a black Door.

"It's black," I murmur to Ryan as soon as I know. He's put Stan on Christian's back, and they're talking to each other. Stan is singing in his head, a song about Little Red Riding Hood, and the wolf who eats her. At the end of the song, the wolf eats her, and she dies. He eats her intestines first, and then her eyeballs.

It's fucking gruesome. When the song ends, Stan starts over. That's what he's doing. He's not talking— he's singing.

"I wish we knew what the colors meant." Ryan sounds more frustrated than I feel.

"I fucking hate this," Roxie chimes in. She's left the

blindfold on, and she's moving slowly. Her boots still don't make noise, but the snakes look sick, sick like they're still dying from being so close to the lamia.

"Is the lamia an elemental?" I ask. "There's no way it can be, right, if it makes Roxie sick?"

"No, it's just a regular demon."

I kick at the floor. If there was a pebble, I would kick it, but there's nothing here. Just empty corridors of stone. "Why do we wear their skin? Why do we wear the skin of things that, that—"

"Because it works," Ryan says quietly. "It's a demon, it's a really bad demon, but wearing its skin means we can get out of some fights alive. We do what we have to."

Ryan trails a hand along the wall, but is careful not to touch the sconce he's near. It looks like it would be painful to touch, since it's kind of on fire and everything. "Sometimes we think something is only folklore, but it turns out to be real. That's what Narnia says happened with the lamia skin. Some hunter got one to come through her Door, and suddenly a whole new world of protection opens up for us. Then again, sometimes we think something is real, but it turns out to be folklore."

"Like zombies, right?" I made that mistake some time in the first month that I knew Ryan. I asked him to teach me how to shoot a gun, in case there was a zombie attack. He laughed at me, and explained that zombies only existed in B-movies and crappy horror novels.

I *like* zombies. Mostly because of that. In fact, I watch all the zombie movies I can get my hands on. Okay, that's not a lot because Blockbuster doesn't exactly stock a regular supply, but I've seen *all* the *Resident Evil* movies, and that British movie about the virus, and that really weird Italian one with Rupert Everett that Ryan had me rent one night so we could deconstruct the action.

Okay, so I've seen a couple of zombie movies. They're still my favorite.

"Kind of like that, yeah," says Ryan.

"But a golem," says Roxie tiredly. "Every once in a while, we've got to kill a golem."

"Golems?"

"It's not really a zombie." Ryan shakes his head. "It's a man, made out of mud, and in its mouth it has a piece of paper with the Hebrew name of God on it. Or sometimes it works with a piece of paper that says 'life'."

"So if I built a golem, it could go on a rampage and, like, destroy the city and eat everyone's brains?"

"They don't eat brains." Ryan pauses. "They can be violent, though."

"Now that the Kabbala is everywhere, more people are building golem," Roxie says. "They're considered elementals because they're made of the earth." She stumbles, but catches herself before I can catch her. Not like I'd be a lot of help; we'd probably both fall down. But it's the thought that counts, right? "Williamsburg had an infestation a couple of years ago, back when it was mostly a Jewish neighborhood. A lot of Hasidic Jews study the Kabbala, and it's always some obnoxious teenager looking to prove that he doesn't have to be over forty to study it."

"Is that, like, a law? Because I can really see Amanda making some golems and setting them loose. Honestly, an army doing her every bidding? Maybe that's why she's not answering the phone."

Ryan frowns at me. "Amanda isn't smart enough to build an army of golem."

"Amanda," I counter, "was smart enough to open a Door."

"Amanda wouldn't get her hands dirty enough to build men out of mud," Ryan amends. "And it's just a guideline." Ryan quietly, unobtrusively, pushes me toward the wall so he can walk next to Roxie. There's no way she could knock him down, so I'm definitely in support of this plan. "Like people who are over forty never do stupid shit like make golem and set them loose."

But I'm not really listening anymore, because I hear something: the shushing again. There's a corner in front of us, a sharp turn to the left.

If it is another lamia, I am going to kill it.

We round the corner, and it's not a lamia, thank god.

It is a corridor with a thousand glowing Doors, marching on either side to infinity, or something equally poetic. Whatever. I am unimpressed.

Really? one of them says.

What would impress you, Allie? another one says.

We could give it to you, says another.

Oh shit.

"We've got problems," I say.

"Figures," Ryan grinds out. He's staring at something I can't see, and his nails are digging into his palms. "Is the Door we need nearby?"

We could bring you to it, says the Door to my right, ever so helpfully.

I roll my eyes. Doors unleash horrible, scary demons, and I guess they can manipulate your emotions and trap you in them, but really?

I am realizing that when they're just talking to you, a lot of Doors are kind of whiny.

I turn to say as much to everybody else, kind of re-assure them that everything's going to be okay, but— um, maybe everything is not going to be okay. Ryan is swaying in place, muttering "Not real," over and over. Christian has taken off his baseball cap and is holding it out toward the Door on the left. Roxie is playing with her knives, and not in a reassuring way. Stan is actually about to touch a Door.

I yell "Stop!" and because I am an idiot, I think it too.

Everything pauses, everybody stuck in place. Only the avatars are moving still, and they are looking at me with weird expressions. The Door next to me says, *We are glad we could do that for you.*

Oh my god, I am tired of this bullshit. I look around. Up ahead is a Door that looks a bit off. I march up to it. It looks the same as the others—almost—but it smells really different. "Hi," I say.

Hello, Allie.

I go back to the group, and one by one drag them over to the Door. When I've got them lined up as close as I can, I think to the Doors, *Go.*

Everyone gets unstuck, like a wax museum come to life. And I shove them all as hard as I can through the Door—it doesn't even want my blood, it just wanted *me*—and follow immediately after.

15

My knees go out from under me, and I'm face down. At first I think I've fallen off a ledge.

All I can hear is crying and screaming. Under me is garbage, trash, it's disgusting, and I can smell it because my face is in it. The whole dimension smells of it.

Under the garbage are people, and they are *people,* and they are screaming, and in front of me is a *semyazza*, and I start screaming, just like the people under the garbage.

The people are naked and writhing, and I crawl as fast as I can backwards, backwards right into Ryan, screaming.

I will never say "if I'm lucky" ever *fucking* again.

The lioness leaps in front of me, and, frankly, I'm sick of the symbolism of everything, and I'd like *something* to be straightforward, just for once, please, Christ.

I know he's moving, and I know I'm probably hampering him, but I don't look above the hem of Ryan's coat. I hear a thunking noise.

"Oh, honey—" Roxie is kneeling next to me, her hat pulled down, bandanna in hand, and she pushes my sunglasses down over my eyes, and everything dims, the screaming, the smell of garbage, everything.

"'Oh, honey' what?" I ask. My voice is hoarse from screaming, and my body won't work, I can't stand up.

"This is *the* Hell," she tells me, and puts her arms around me, and the snakes cover me. "The one you know."

The one I know?

Oh. The one I *know*. The one I kind of believe in. Belief makes things real sometimes. You learn that from the hunters too. "Shouldn't the snakes be evil here?"

"*And Moses made a serpent of brass,*" says Ryan. He squats next to me. Roxie pulls Stan over, and now Stan and everyone is coiled around me. Unlike all the other hells we've been through, this one is filled with creatures, surrounding us and watching us and coming too close. I am fucking petrified of *semyazzas* after what one did to me when it came out of my Door five years back. I touch my hand to my stomach, over the scar. There could be another *semyazza* out there. There could be lots. They could be hiding; they could be waiting.

"And Moses made a serpent of brass," Ryan repeats, Ištar and Ūsat's voices high behind him, reverberating in my ears over the screaming from below us, and then Christian joins him, the clicking soft, *"and put it upon a pole,"* and now Roxie too, *"and it came to pass, that if a serpent had bitten any man, when he beheld the serpent of brass, he lived. And the children of Israel set forward."*

"Come on," Stan whispers to me, "who's my tough girl?" and I feel better, and when they help me stand, the *semyazza* is in pieces all over the place. Ryan's knife, the big obsidian one, is gleaming, clean, on the ground. He picks it up.

"Let's go," he says. This dimension is harder for me, and there are dragons that look like dead worms, worse than the Kur dragon, flying above us, screaming with the humans, and the snakes on Roxie hiss and slither, and Christian's spider clicks as we walk forward. Ištar and Ūsat and the lioness pad in front of us, even in front of Ryan.

Stan stumbles next to me. Now that I'm really looking at him, even through the werewolf he looks sick. He must believe in this Hell a little bit too.

I wonder what it's like to be gay and believe in this Hell. Believe that maybe this is where you're going to end up. Except Stan is already dead, and this is a werewolf in his body.

"I'm hungry," he groans. His hand is on his stomach, and I close my eyes and look away. Everything is dim through the sunglasses; I can barely see the Doors.

"I can't see a Door," I say.

"What?" yells Roxie, looking over her shoulder at me.

"I can't see a Door!" I call back. It hurts to yell. I just want to lie down. I want to lie down and give up.

Then Ryan is at my side. "Allie. Allie. Come on. Keep walking."

"I don't want to, I want to lie down, I can't do this, Ryan, I can't do this, I can't keep going—"

I slump to the floor. The screaming is fucking deafening. Everything hurts, everyone hurts. It's so lonely here, it's so scary, everyone is so scared—

The next thing I know, there's a sharp pain. Ryan's got his obsidian knife in his hand, and a grim look on his face, and my battered and bruised hands are bleeding. The smell of blood brings me back to myself, and I sniff, let out a long breath. Ryan holds my bleeding hands—he cut my palms—over the circle he drew in "macaroni and cheese"-colored crayon. The blood hisses and spits where it hits the ground.

"Talk to the Door," he says firmly. "Find the Door."

I press my palms to the circle, pressing the blood in, and close my eyes. The screaming dies down—just a little, but enough to let me *see*.

"It's through. It's through—it's maybe—maybe another hour?" I guess.

"We're going to stay here for a while, then, Allie."
Ryan is crouched next to me, but he's careful to keep
his duster from breaking the circle. His duster made of
lamia skin. Lamias eat babies. I'm wearing lamia skin
and they eat babies, and—

I feel vomit rise in my throat and I clap my hands to
my face. There's blood all over my mouth and teeth
and tongue, and I can taste it, metallic like the smell of
a wet penny.

"Oh, god," I groan, and fall over. "Do we have to
stay here? I can't, Ryan, I can't—"

"You can, and you will," he says firmly. He gets
down on the ground next to me, and pulls me so we're
heart to heart. The lioness settles down next to us. Ryan
doesn't just wrap me in his coat this time; he pulls his
hat so it shades me, and the screaming goes quiet.

I can feel everyone else curl around us. I guess
we're all secretly afraid of this Hell dimension. I guess
none of us ever wants to believe this part is real. It's
easy to ignore crazy Norse demons and weird Sumerian demons and stupid vampires—it's all so old, it's
all so meaningless to our everyday lives.

But we're saturated with Christianity, and even Ju-
daism to some extent, I guess, and the more I think
about it, the more I realize how *immediate* it all is.
There are things here that I've never seen before, but I
still sort of recognize them, you know? Things with

sneering human faces, long horns, parts of animals all mixed together. Demons, the way we've been taught.

One of the things comes close and sits just outside the circle. It looks like a man on a snake-necked lion, except the man has the head of a bull and a sheep growing out of the back of his neck. As the heads breathe, they exhale steam. The steam smells like sulphur. That's brimstone. That, kids, is tradition.

I fall asleep to the sound of Roxie, Christian, and Ryan murmuring to each other; I fall asleep in a cloud of steam to "*Be gracious to me, O God, be gracious to me . . . Be merciful unto me, O God, my soul is among lions . . .*"

I don't dream, which is kind of disappointing. When I open my eyes, though, I do feel really rested, and—

And I'm naked. And I'm on a grassy hill. And there is a rock under my ass.

"Uh, Ryan?" I blink, and he's next to me, sprawled on his back. Also naked—except for his hat. Which, let me just say, is incredibly sexy. I don't see any avatars around. Am I dreaming? Best dream *ever*. My hair is loose, and when I crawl on top of him and tuck my face into his neck, my hair is just long enough to touch his chest. He smells delicious. I want to eat him up.

Uh, not literally.

"Ryan," I murmur into his neck.

"Allie," he gasps, and sits up. I'm on his lap again, and, oh, god, does he feel good.

"Please—" I feel like I'm always begging him for things, and this time he gives me what I want, just lifts me up and sets me down, inches sliding in, and then he's inside me, burning hot, and I'm moving on him, and it's the best thing I've ever felt in my entire life. I never want to feel anything else but Ryan inside me.

He bites down on my neck and I shudder over him, coming hard; he's barely even touched me, and I'm coming.

Then he flips us over, and I'm on my back, my legs wrapped around his waist, heels digging into thick muscle, and I'm coming again as he lifts me up and slams into me, over and over again. My arms are stretched out to the side and my head is turned to the side, and I'm gasping, I can't catch my breath, it's just waves of pleasure crashing over me, pulling me under.

All I can feel is Ryan.

When I open my eyes again, I'm sore all over. I look down at my body. Still naked. Still on a grassy knoll somewhere. Covered in red marks that will blossom into bruises, and bite marks. He bit me hard enough on my left breast that I can still see the imprint of his teeth.

I let my head fall back to the ground, and there's that damn rock again.

I roll over, and look over at Ryan from under my eyelashes. At some point in our crazy sexual fury, his hat got knocked off, and his hair is sticking up everywhere. It's getting long, and it's almost curly. I want to run my hands through it. I want to bite him, and chew on his lips, and suck on his nipples, and touch him everywhere—but it's not the furor of before. It's just what I want, not what I have to do.

"Uh . . ." I turn away from him and put my head in my arms. The grass smells like grass, and it's so wonderful, such an amazing change from the smells of blood and death. The sun shining on me is warm, and I feel comfortable for the first time since I found out the Door was gone.

"Allie," he says, and touches my shoulder gently. "Allie."

"Yeaaaah," I say.

I can feel him moving against me as he sits up. "Fuck."

"Mmmm," I say agreeably.

"Ashmedai," he tells me.

"Bless you," I say, as if he had sneezed. That's what it sounded like, anyway. I mean, I am used to the weird languages, and all that crap, but Ashmedai is a new one to me.

"Ashmedai. Trickster demon. Shit. And we saw it, too. It was outside the circle when we went to sleep."

"The weird lion-snake thing?" He nods. I am getting a sneaking suspicion. "What does this demon do, exactly?"

Ryan sighs, and rubs his face with his hand. "It gets people to have sex."

"What?" I sit up too and my hair falls everywhere. I can still feel Ryan's hand in it, pulling my head back so he could suck on my neck. I shiver a little. I want him again. Except . . . "We were just raped by a demon?"

"No," Ryan says. "He wouldn't have made us. He . . . represents what's already there. The Christian demons are all like that. All sin exists within man, so—"

"So this guy shows up, gets us naked, and all he's doing is just telling us that we want to do it anyway?" Ryan looks away. I blink hard. "Okay, or that *I* want to do it. Not you, evidently. Sorry that the demon clue-mobile ran you down. He's not coming back, right?"

Ryan shakes his head but he's looking at me again. "It's not just you, Allie," he says. "You know I feel—"

"Shut up," I say. "I don't need you to be a hunter or a hero or whatever and save me with the power of flirting. I've seen you do that with other people. I've seen you do that with Dawn, with Amanda, with stupid blonde girls on the street—hell, I've seen you do that with *Stan*. So what if I have a demon airing my dirty laundry? I don't need you to make it better."

The calluses of his hand—gun calluses, knife, all hard work and magic—they feel rough on my face when he turns my head toward him, and his mouth comes down hard on mine. He tastes like grass, and salt, and heat, and *now*. He breaks the kiss suddenly. I'm afraid, but he's just staring at me, and—he hasn't looked that way since the first time we kissed, like I was killing him just by existing. Like he was killing me.

"No," I say. I pull my hands up; I cup his jaw so he can't turn from me again. "I am real. I am here. And you aren't the death of me."

I say this out loud, and then I say it with the brush of my lips against his forehead, against that hot skin and lines of worry. I kiss his cheek, and his nose, and him. I kiss him, and his mouth opens under mine and I'm falling into him, into the feel and the taste and his hands wrap around my waist, pulling me up and tight against him.

We can get closer. I know we can. I draw him back to the ground, my arms around him. He sighs, and lays his head against my collarbone.

"I need to tell you, Allie. I want you to know," he whispers on my skin. It's so quiet, so light, that the breath runs across my skin and my nipple peaks up high and hard just from the sensation. His hand moves, slowly, up to my breast. His palm touches my nipple, making it trace circles on his hand, a single pinprick touch that drives me wild. He pauses, and moves his hand away again, like that's a candy he's not allowed to taste.

"My avatars," he says. "They're not goddesses. They're every woman I've ever been with. Ever cared about. Three women, all dead. They've followed me. They're warning me. Warning you." His voice is empty, and alone. "It's a bad idea, Allie. It's always been a bad idea."

"You idiot," I say, because he is, and I want to cry. "So Ūsat, Ištar, the tabby cat—were they hunters?"

He takes a ragged breath. "No, they were normal girls, just like—"

I pull his head up, and he's shocked enough to stop talking. "*Not* like me," I say fiercely. "Look at where we are. No offense to your ghosts or anything, but I bet they'd be shitting themselves if they went through a Door to Hell. I bet they didn't kill demons. I bet they didn't fight. I'm not them, Ryan. I was never them. You get to *keep* me."

He is staring at me, lost and uncertain and for a moment I swear I hear the lioness purr, and in that moment his eyes fill with something I've never seen before, ever, not from him or from anybody, and when he kisses me, it's like we're kissing for the first time, except this time it's gentle, and a little awkward.

I can speak his eyebrow-ese now, but I have no idea what he's saying with his mouth.

When he pulls away, I am seriously turned on— again—and expecting sex, but he really pulls away and stands up. I frown up at him. What's going on inside his stupid moody head? "Where's my hat?" he asks, and I pick it up off the ground and hand it to him.

There he is again, naked with his hat on. I want to bone him so hard, I swear to fucking god, but he's turned around. The view is just as nice from the back, all muscle and round ass, and heavy thighs. I have never considered myself an ass girl, but Ryan has made me re-evaluate everything else about myself—why not that too?

"I hate to ask this," he says, still turned away from me, "but I need you to find a Door."

"Are we actually—I mean, this isn't a vision or something?" I ask uncertainly. Because it could totally be a shared vision, weirder things have happened to me every single day before breakfast.

"Not a vision," he confirms. "But it is a . . . look, there are Hell dimensions, right? Some of them are big enough to fill a world. And some of them are really, really small." He gestures around, almost helplessly. "If this was Ashmedai, then he probably just borrowed whatever was closest to our ideal."

"My ideal is . . . grass?"

"Um?" This is the first time I've ever heard *him* sound uncertain about anything, I think. Jeez.

"So grass and water and sunshine. Got it." I push my hair behind my ears even though it looks terrible, and I kind of wish that Ištar was around so that I'm not the only naked chick.

"Can you find the Door here? You don't have to—I mean, you don't have to talk to it. Don't ask it for anything. Just find it." He doesn't turn around. I know he's got to be feeling really awkward, but *I* am feeling a little rejected.

Like, just because I understand his feelings? Does not really make it okay for him to treat me weirdly.

But whatever.

I close my eyes, and I whisper, *Where are you?,* and then when I open them, next to Ryan is the Door.

Hi, it says, and I swear it sounds cheerful. *Come walk through me, Allie.*

What do you want? I ask it suspiciously.

I want nothing of you, it tells me.

"It doesn't want anything from me," I tell Ryan, and he nods sharply, turns around, and strides through the Door.

I take my time. It's nice here, and I don't exactly want to go back to the Christian Hell dimension full of screaming and death. The Door is . . . it's pretty. It stands about half again as tall as me, and inside it is another Door, and then another, and then another, each one getting slightly smaller. It's wider on top than it is on the bottom, and it has hieroglyphs carved into it. I bet Ryan or Roxie—or, heck, Narnia—could read them, but to me they're just decoration.

It glows coppery in the sunlight.

I stroke the outside of it, and it *purrs* at me. *You're pretty,* I tell it, and step through.

16

I'm in my disgusting lamia gear again, and my hair is gross and still in a ponytail, and everything smells like death again, and it's gross, and there's screaming—but this time I'm ready for it. It can't beat me.

I pull my sunglasses down, and the screaming dims a notch. *Fuck you,* I think defiantly.

I hear all the Doors everywhere laugh at me.

"Ashmedai, huh?" says Roxie, and winks at me. I laugh, and I'm kind of surprised to find out that I *can* laugh. "You'll have to tell me all about it."

"Uh-uh," I tell her. "It's all mine."

"We were pretty worried when you disappeared—"

"We've been gone for *hours*, I'm surprised you're still *here*," I say, and she shakes her head.

"Under five minutes."

"So time *does* work differently. Hmm."

Roxie hands me my bandanna. "Thanks for this,"

she says, "but I don't need it anymore. If we're close to the Door—"

"About an hour's walk," I tell her.

"Let's go then." She pats me on the shoulder, and one of her snakes hisses at me. I hiss back, and giggle.

Ryan can freak out all he wants. I think he might actually like me, and that's why he's freaking out. He likes me, just a little, and doesn't want to—or is afraid to. I'm not stupid, I can figure this shit out.

And I had *fun*. Fuck this hell dimension and all its demons and death. Ashmedai is totally going on my Christmas card list.

Except make that another couple of times that I've had sex without a condom. I'm starting to feel downright irresponsible. Just because Ryan makes all my thoughts fly out of my head . . . I am going to have to stop at a drugstore when we get out of the Hell dimensions and get myself the morning-after pill. Just in case. I don't know how much time has passed in our dimension, but I haven't taken a birth control pill in a couple of Hell dimension–days.

I am *almost* worried. But it's hard to be worried about missing a few doses of Ortho Tri-Cyclin. Particularly when faced with, you know, being eviscerated by the legions of the damned.

We trudge through slowly, and hit the Door, and it

opens right up, no blood required. *You know me,* I say as we walk through its pink glow, and it laughs at me.

The Hell we step into is beautiful. I guess they can't all be disgusting and ugly. It's full of rivers and lush grass, just like the Ashmedai underworld. At the horizon, a sun is setting. It sets the whole time, never quite leaving. Everything has a beautiful pink glow. Even Christian isn't clicking anymore.

Roxie strides ahead of us, her coat flapping in a very sexy way. If I were the kind of girl who liked other girls, I would like Roxie for sure.

She walks until she finds a patch of grass in the sunlight. I know I was just in a wonderful, lush, grass-filled Hell dimension, but I don't think it's something I'll ever get tired of. I hand Stan off to Christian and then settle down next to Roxie.

Roxie shrugs out of her coat and pulls off her hat. "I am taking a *nap,*" she murmurs, and drops right to sleep.

This is the first dimension where Christian is totally okay; I guess arachnids like sunlight and grass? Don't people turn into arachnids in some Egyptian myth?

I say this to Christian, who's sitting on the other side of Roxie, stretched out on his back, his baseball cap over his face. He lifts up the baseball cap and gives me a disdainful glare. He's gotten good at those. "That's *Greece* and arachnids *hate* it," he says in his clicking.

"*Sorry*, god." I roll my eyes. "Whatever, okay?"

"The Greeks thought they invented everything." Ryan's voice when he interrupts is almost totally Ūsat's. "They even stole Ursiris and made him Dionysus." He/she snorts. The lioness knocks her head under my hand for a scritch, so I decide I won't bitchsmack Ūsat just yet.

True confession: If these avatars really are the ghosts of Ryan's past, whoever Ūsat was was really *annoying*. I am kind of disappointed in Ryan's taste, which does not speak well for me.

"We don't make circles here," says Ūsat through Ryan. "We don't need to." Ūsat stretches out too. "This is my domain. You've never seen one of *my* demons."

The lioness is falling asleep, and so is Ištar.

"Ursiris isn't Hades, he's not some vengeful, hideous, deformed creature trying to make everyone as miserable as he is." She pets the land beside her. "He likes it here." Now she's bitter. "Without me."

The land ripples up. A hand forms, and it stretches up to stroke her throat. Creepy-tastic.

"With me only sometimes," she amends.

Ryan rubs his chin and grimaces—maybe he has noticed the sandpaper covering his face? "I am tired," he says quietly in his own voice, "of not knowing what the Hell is going on." He shakes his head. "I feel like a newbie again. Do you know how long it's been since I really had no clue what to do?"

I can't tell if he's actually talking to me, but I answer anyway. "Five years ago. You wanted to kiss me, you knew I wanted to kiss you, and then when you didn't, and I didn't, and you ran out of the room, a *semyazza* burned my stomach off and you didn't know how to fix it."

Ryan doesn't say anything for a minute. He turns to look at me, and his eyes are hooded, dark. "I knew what to do," he says. "It was just harder to do with you."

"I do not even know how to interpret that," I say. He just stares at me. "Is this . . . about your women?" I guess.

"No," he says. "This is about me and you."

"Well, that has to be a lie, because everything you do is to keep people from getting close to you," I snap. Oh, he is pissing me off. "Why did you walk away from me in Ashmedai's Hell?"

"Allie—"

"Everything you do is about walking away from anyone caring about you—your family. Me. Anyone—"

"Allie—"

"Your logic is *wrong,* it's not being around you that hurts people, Ryan. It's your *attitude*. Because you could have lots of people who care about you, to make this easier—"

"Allie!" he roars. Roxie looks over at us, a weird look on her face. I shake my head a little, my hair swishing, and she looks away again.

"You can't scare me by yelling," I say to him.

"You *should* be scared. People who are near me *die,* okay? I am not making this up. This isn't a game. This isn't—"

"Yeah? Well I've been near you for *years,* and I'm still alive!"

"But you won't always be." He's not yelling now, just looking down at his hands. The lioness shimmers under them; she's not really there, though.

"Nobody will always be anywhere. If there's one single thing that I learned from being poor and having everyone abandon me . . ." I take a deep breath. "You just have to take what you can get." You just have to take what's there and appreciate it while you have it. I never knew that before, but I know it now, and I know it's *hard*. It's hard to appreciate that I once had a closet full of Manolos and Gucci, and don't anymore. It's hard to appreciate that Stan and I once had a pretty good relationship, but that he's going to die because of me.

"Maybe I want more than that," he says, and I can't tell if he's angry or sad when he says it. He rubs his face again, and settles his Stetson on his head. He goes back to sit with Stan without looking at me again.

Well, most of him goes, anyway. Ištar and Ūsat follow after, like the ghosts in a long-exposure photograph. The lioness stays behind, shimmers back into being.

She is *staring* at me.

"Shut up," I tell her, and she shakes her head and yawns. She settles on her haunches like an overgrown tea cozy, and I can tell she's in for the long staring haul.

Fine. Fine. I shove my sunglasses on and try to go to sleep. It's hard, though, because I keep thinking about Ryan shoving everyone away so that he can die alone, without hurting anyone.

He's not going to shove me away. I will not allow it.

I wake up when Ryan touches my shoulder.

"Time for walking again?" I ask tiredly, and sit up.

"I'm sorry," he says, but he's not looking at me. I don't think he's apologizing for waking me up. He looks so sad. I move over to sit next to him and put my hand on his knee.

"Thanks for doing this," I say softly. "I know it's not easy. I know I'm a pain in the ass. I know Amanda is totally shirking and Stan is . . . there's nothing here for Stan."

"He's going to die." Ryan looks at me, and I think he's sorry.

"Yeah," I admit, and I hate it.

He notices. "I should've done more. I could've gone out earlier to get him. But I didn't, because I was too busy arguing about bringing you to Hell at all," he says. His eyes have tiny lines crinkling the corners. He lets me close enough that I can *see* his tiny lines.

"I'm glad you tried," I say. "I mean, it would be kind of gross if you were the kind of person who could just—Look, you said I didn't have to come. Remember? You said."

Behind us, Roxie murmurs in her sleep, and I hear her move, her leather swishing against itself.

"If you'd said yes . . ." Ryan looks rueful. "I would've taken you to Long Island to hide from everyone else, would've actually gone to Amanda's house instead of just wandering Battery Park and thinking stupid things. You'd be safe."

I snort. "And that would clearly be some kind of coffee-making demon pretending to be me. I'd never agree—I *didn't* agree. And even if it really was me, and I had agreed, it would all be an elaborate ruse." I nod decidedly. "I'd just find myself a Door out on Long Island and chase after you."

He laughs quietly. He stretches his legs out in front of him. They go on forever, encased in black lamia skin. "I think that's why I like you so much," he says. "You don't put up with me trying to be a white knight."

"Oh, I totally do. Just not the times when your white knight stuff leaves me out of the game." I pause, and I know my voice sounds different. "You like me?" This is so embarrassing. This is junior high social drama all over again.

Two high spots of color, one on either cheek. Ryan's blushing again. "Yeah," he says. "I—yeah."

Maybe not so embarrassing. I touch his chin and turn him to me. I lean forward and brush my lips against his. "Thank you," I whisper.

"You're welcome," he whispers back, and he hesitates, he stops, and for a second, a split second, I think he's going to push me away again, even after all this, but instead his hand comes up to my face, and we're *kissing,* really kissing, and god, how could I have missed this already?

His mouth is warm and doesn't taste like anything except *him.* I breathe in the air he exhales. I feel shaky all over, like I'm going to fly apart at any second.

"We shouldn't," he says against my mouth, but doesn't pull away.

"We shouldn't," I agree, "but—I want to."

"I want to, too."

"I am still here," says Roxie in a cold voice, and I giggle.

"Me too," says Christian.

"Me three," says Stan, and snickers. "But feel free to keep going."

"Sorry, sorry, I'm sorry." I move away from Ryan—a little bit. He drops his hand from my face, and I want to think it's reluctantly. His mouth is wet, shiny. I wonder what I look like to him. I'm not the beautiful one— Amanda is the beautiful one. I'm passably pretty, pleasingly plump. I have round thighs.

But he said he liked me. And he blushed. And now

he's pushing me down, and his coat is around both of us, and before I go back to sleep I think to myself: Ryan is secretly a romantic.

When we wake up, Christian is gone. We didn't hear him leave and none of us saw him go. All we can see is the river and nothing else forever and ever, and the Door to the next dimension doesn't say anything at all.

17

"**B**e careful here," warns Ryan when I step through the Door.

"Why?" Something crunches under my foot, and my first thought is that it's more bugs, but then I look around. We're just in some woods. Tall trees with leafy canopies that block out most of the light from above, and a forest floor with pine needles and rocks and just a little dampness. I look around. It's exactly the same in every direction. Flat land and trees. Boring.

The trees look kind of weird, though. I squint. There are big scratch marks ringing a lot of them, all the way up. Cats? Bears?

Except I think I recognize the scratches. This wide, and this deep, and . . .

And I once cautered an entire ingot of silver onto Ryan's back to heal a set of scratch marks just like those.

"I know this Hell," Ryan says. He looks at me and

Roxie, and then looks pointedly at Stan. "I think we *all* know this one. Allie, after you've got the location for the next Door, take a minute, okay? But keep your eyes open."

I think I know what Ryan's saying. And I hate it.

Stan's standing a few feet away, hands curled loosely into fists. He still looks like Stan, but I can't smell summertime on him anymore.

I drop the blood. The Door obligingly pops up before I can even identify myself. Good for it. I point for Ryan and Roxie's benefit, but instead of marching forward I walk over to Stan.

"Hey," I say quietly, and take him by the hand. He's warm. So warm. "Come on," I say. "I've got some gossip I never told you . . ."

As we walk through the trees, I keep up a good low-level talk about Ryan, and me, and the diner, and the Doors, and how sorry I am. I talk about Amanda, and how I wish she was with us, even though she'd be no help. She'd complain the whole time. She probably would have snuck something forbidden with her through the Door, like a pack of cigarettes and a flask. She would have brought Scotch, because it is what gets her drunk the fastest. Even after years of drinking, she only needs a few sips of Scotch to be pretty wasted.

But she always buys the good stuff to do it, the kind of Scotch that costs at least a hundred dollars for the bottle. And it wouldn't matter to her if any of it got spilled somehow, because she could just buy another bottle.

I remember being that casual with money. And I remember, right after my mother left, when it was still all just like a dream, like these bad things were happening to someone else, Amanda got me really drunk on a bottle of vodka that cost hundreds of dollars, because it was filtered through crushed diamonds instead of being filtered through charcoal.

Amanda knew all about it, and told me all about it, and all I could think, while she was talking, was that all of my money was gone—gone with my mother to Rio with Rio—and I would never be able to afford to buy anything like that ever again, unless I married well. And who would I marry?

"You could marry Stan!" suggested Amanda brightly, and I almost punched her.

"Why would I want to marry Stan?" I had sneered. "What the hell would I do with him?"

Amanda hadn't even blinked at my snide tone. She just said, "Spend his money, of course," and poured me some more vodka.

Later that night, I cried all over her, and she rocked me until I fell asleep. The next day, she brought me coffee. Not that she made it or anything—that would have been going a step too far, even for someone who prided herself on going to extremes. No, making the coffee was for the help. But she brought it to me, and knelt by the bed in the pool house, and woke me up gently.

She's always been there for me. It's just easiest for her to be there when money and alcohol are involved. She even gave my dad the money he needed to go find himself on a commune in Arizona. He's still there, for all I know. I got a few postcards the first month, and then nothing.

Amanda and Stan are the only people who have never abandoned me, not even at my worst.

Except for now. Why hadn't Amanda answered her phone when I called her? It wasn't like I'd just called once—I'd called a bunch of times, and each time I'd left a message. Each message was more urgent-sounding than the last. I mean, the Door disappeared! We went hunting Doors! I touched one! We decided to go *through* a Door! Stan got bit by a werewolf! Everything had been escalating, and I couldn't get Amanda on the phone, or find her anywhere.

I shouldn't have left her in our dimension. What if something had actually happened to her? But Ryan and I had both figured that she was just on an epic bender. Which she probably was, right? Maybe still is.

I miss Christian's clicking. I wonder where he's gone. Maybe what I said about arachnids hit him hard or something. Maybe he went full demon at last. Maybe it's my fault. Maybe everything is my fault. Maybe he's gone on to Hades's underworld, where he can be with a bunch of other arachnids. Maybe he's gone back to Jackson. Maybe . . .

One at a time, I say all these things to Stan. He doesn't say anything at all.

Stan. Stan. Stan. Please, wherever you are, *remember*.

The worst thing about this Hell dimension is that it is fucking boring. The worst thing about this Hell dimension is that it is quiet, except for the crunching of our feet on dead pine needles and sticks.

The worst thing about this Hell dimension is when Stan rips his kerchief off and bares his teeth at me and snarls, and I slam Betsy into his chest without even thinking. I've had her palmed for the last hour. Just waiting. And now he stares down at the nail sticking out of his heart with a totally surprised look on his face. His eyes are black, and faceted.

"Allie—" he says, *Stan* says, before he falls, and Ryan and Roxie just stand there.

I drop to my knees. "I love you," I tell him, and I try to put everything into those words. I think about pulling Betsy out of his chest, but I couldn't if I tried; it'd be covered with his blood, and then the werewolf might get me. I don't care about the *werewolf* dying. I've killed those. I've killed lots of those.

Stan's gasping for air.

Iron will slow a werewolf down, but for the kill, you

need silver. Silver heals. It heals the body that used to be human, and kills the werewolf in the process. I don't have a gun here, and I don't have a cauter. I pull out the silver ankh I'd strung around his chest before we left our dimension and slam the end of it right on top of Betsy and deep into his chest.

The werewolf screams. And then it dies.

I pull off my Seal of Solomon, the pretty pendant one, and wrap it around Stan's wrist. I tuck the pendant into his hand. He'll need protection, in Hell. I hope he finds his way back to the Egyptian underworld. Or Ashmedai's—I told him where it was, what it looked like. Maybe he'll find it, and be happy there.

It's all I can give him. It's all I can give him and I hate it.

Ryan touches my arm, very lightly; I can barely feel it through the disgusting lamia leather of my duster.

"Allie . . ." he starts.

"Don't," I say. I pull away, and stand up. I start walking toward the Door again.

I can kill vampires without getting hurt. They're not hard at all. They just crumple. I can kill werewolves. I can kill one of my best friends.

I wasn't going to, but I do; I look back. And I see werewolves climbing down from the trees, gathering up Stan's body, and carrying him back to the canopy above us. Ryan was right about the bandanna after all;

the werewolf in Stan saw Hell, and Hell's werewolves found him.

The Door in this dimension is green, of course, and it glows brighter when I touch it. I go to cut my hand again, my mind tiredly reaching out to it; the knife's barely hit skin before the Door is suddenly warm against me, happy to see me, pleased to give me anything I want. But it can't give me Stan back, or my parents. It can't actually give me anything I *want*.

The green Door is covered in leaves and branches that we have to push out of the way as we walk through.

I look around, and despite myself: "Are we seriously back in the caves?" I am totally appalled.

"I don't know." Roxie looks around and squints into the darkness. Again with the sconces attached somehow—magically?—to the smooth cave walls. Again with the sort-of-damp air, the wind that isn't really blowing.

"I am sick of this shit." I slump against the wall, and slide down until I'm sitting on the floor of the cave. The Door here is just a mouth of another cave. It hardly glows at all.

Hello? I push at it.

Hello, it says, but it sounds reluctant.

Don't you want to give me anything? Or whine at me about how hard it is to be a Door in this age of people not appreciating how great Hell dimensions are? I pick at some mud crusted on my shoes. They are not pristine and white anymore. Not that they were exactly pristine when we started, since they're my kitchen shoes. They get grease on them, and barbeque sauce, and all kinds of crap. Now they've also got, like, demon guts, and other terrible things. Maybe even some of Stan's blood.

No, it replies. *I just want to be left alone.*

Yeah, I know how that feels. I stop talking to it, and leave it alone.

When I look up, Roxie and Ryan are whispering furiously. Roxie is gesturing at me. Ryan's got his hat pulled down pretty far over his eyes. Ūsat and Ištar and the lioness look bored. The snakes look bored. Even in the middle of all of this, I'm starting to be totally bored too. This whole thing is boring the crap out of me. I bet—I bet all the avatars, and whatever's protecting me, know there's nothing going on here, so they don't have to protect us. Nothing going on, nothing dangerous . . . which, in Hell? Unusual.

"There's no way this is the same dimension," I announce. "For one thing, this Door doesn't want to talk to me. For another, if we were in another lamia dimension, the snakes would be freaking out, wouldn't they?"

"Yeah, we already figured that out while you were communing with evil," says Roxie.

"No need to be nasty." I slide back up the wall until I am standing up. "I was just *saying.*"

"So where are we?" Ryan asks tiredly.

"This is—" I shut my eyes and *look* for a Door. The whole world is dark. I can see even darker shapes where the avatars are, shadows, greenish-blue. The Doors are bright, colors swirling around, beckoning me to come to them.

But I'm being pulled somewhere else—to the shape the Doors make. They are small in comparison to the shadow inside them. They surround it.

It's a hand.

Gotcha. "This is where the Hand of Franklin is."

When I open my eyes, Roxie looks confused. I roll my eyes. "It's just what Ryan and I have been calling the hand that we're looking for. The waters of life. This is where we'll find it," I say. "I can see it. It's here."

"Where?" Roxie looks at me from under the brim of her hat, totally skeptical.

Where? I ask. And a voice, made of many voices, says, *Here.*

Um. Weird. But let's run with it. I point toward the other end of the cave, where the tunnel curves out of sight.

Ryan is looking at me strangely. "How do you know?" he asks, and it's almost cute how bewildered he sounds.

"Well . . . I haven't really wanted to say anything," I

tell him, "but I'm kind of getting more and more psychic. Like, the psychic dreams, you know? And the Doors."

"I thought you only had one psychic dream."

"Yeah, but that's one more than I've ever had before," I point out. I turn to Roxie. "And the Doors—they talk a lot. It's not even feelings anymore. They want to have actual conversations with me. They want to do what I tell them. That's not exactly normal."

Roxie snorts. "*Chère,* we've been traipsing through the underworld. What part of normal is *that*?"

I almost smile. "Good point."

"What the hell are we standing around for?" demands Ryan. "If the hand is here, the waters of life, whatever Ištar wants us to find—if that's here, let's just go get it."

We walk quickly to the tunnel, and make the first turn. Nothing jumps out at us, nothing tries to kill us. The silence is eerie; not even Ryan's boots make noise.

The tunnel turns one more time, and then abruptly opens into an enormous cavern, like the size of three diners laid end to end, lit with fires set in giant braziers. Except can you call a room made totally of gold a cavern? I think there must a different word. Like, *holy shit*.

I am instantly aware that I have not forgotten the

approximate value of gold on the open market. Maybe this is the Hell of temptation. Gorgeous golden temptation.

Ryan says, without even looking at me, "You don't need it."

So says him. He doesn't have to count out every night, or think about the quality of food to buy, or where to get the money for some new signage, or how long I'll have to save up to buy out Sally. Gold would be a *great* idea.

It takes me a second to realize that instead of thinking about expensive clothes and big houses and getting my old life back, the first thing I thought of to do with the money is put it back into the diner. That the life I have now is more worth keeping than the one taken from me, and not just because Ryan's in it.

I do not even know what to do with this realization.

Roxie touches my shoulder, and points toward the end of the cavern. In the middle of all this shiny gold, almost in shadow, is a tall-backed chair—no, wait, a throne?—made of some dull rock. And there's something sitting in it.

We walk closer, since there's not a lot of other options, and the thing in the throne becomes clearer. It's—look, you've seen *Psycho,* right? Everyone's seen *Psycho.* The thing on the throne? It's Norman Bates's mother, minus the dress and wig. A dead thing with mouth open wide, tilted sideways against the throne with its hands palm-up in its lap. Its feet don't quite touch the floor—like they shriveled up as the mummy dried.

I sniff the air. I smell metal and stale air. And I smell, somehow, *time*.

Because I may possibly be dumb, I send my thoughts out with a careful *Hello?*

Something speaks. It's the same thing I heard before, a voice made of many voices. *I am the Kalaturru,* it says, while, simultaneously, it also says, *I am the Kurgarru.*

I swallow. "Everybody hear that?"

I look over at Roxie, standing next to me. Her snakes are absolutely still, and her eyes are wide. "Yeah," she says. "I hear that."

On my other side, Ryan's women are arrayed behind him, a train of ghosts pretending to be goddesses. Ryan's looking at me. He just nods and steps in front of me.

"We seek the waters of life to close the Doors." He sounds weirdly formal. Like when he was thanking Owen way back in the hospital, saying something because that's what you have to do, not because you mean it.

Why do you bother doing something like that? Why make up a formality that no one cares about? Unless maybe it used to mean something. Maybe it used to be important, and we've just all forgotten why—which, you know, just leads to little accidents like the dragon back in Kur trying to eat us because we didn't perform some stupid rites we didn't even know about. "There are rites to be performed in the netherworld"—why didn't Narnia mention *that* before we left our dimension?

The mummy says, with its layered voices, *I look for companionship. Do you wish to partake of my hospitality?*

Avatars, I have noticed, are useful things to keep an eye on in times of trial. For instance: Roxie's snakes are hissing, all of them, in one long sound that is getting more and more quiet, like air from a tire. Ryan's women are wavering in place, looking less real and more like projections on smoke.

And then there's my avatar, whatever it is. Blue, that's what. Blue, and glowing, and there are tiny pinpoints of blue around me, and wings, I can suddenly *feel* them, a weight that isn't a weight. I let out a breath, and a sudden breeze swirls around me, lifting my ponytail, coming under my wings, lifting *me*.

All the avatars are getting weaker by being around this mummy. Except mine. The mummy wants companionship, it wants, god, what, an equal? Someone worthy of the hospitality? Whatever my avatar is, it thinks it's up for the challenge, and nobody else's does.

What happens if you ask for hospitality and are unworthy of it?

Shit.

I dive my mind into Ryan's, I see the thought that will become the word, I see *We wish to partake of your hospitality,* and I'm already running when I hear him say "We—"

I bum rush Ryan and plow square into his back. It startles him enough that he stumbles to the side and glares at me. "Allie, what the hell?"

"Shut up," I say, and before he can stop me I step forward and say, "*I* wish to partake of your hospitality."

I don't know what the mummy shoots at me, but it feels like a sudden punch to the gut; I'm flying backwards through the air, high up, with a long fall. I'm going to puke, if I don't die from a thousand broken bones when I land.

The ground rushes up, and I can hear Ryan yelling, and I let out a breath—

Caterpillars of blue light crawl over my skin and across my vision. A wind swirls around me; my wings catch it. I float. I fly. I land without squishing.

I can feel a bruise, but it's not nearly as bad as it could be. Actually, I kind of feel like dancing. I walk back to Ryan and Roxie and step between the two of them. Roxie's swearing, but in an awed way instead of a pissed-off one. Ryan's just staring at my wings like he wishes he could touch them. Maybe later.

I throw the mummy a look. "That wasn't very nice,"

I say chidingly. The voice of the Kalaturru/Kurgarru laughs. It's hollow and echoes through the cave.

The elemental spirits protect you. You may have my hospitality.

Slowly the mummy's hands lift from its lap. The sound is unbelievably gross, if only because it sounds so mundane, paper shuffling or leather whispering and not at all someone's dead and dried skin *moving*. The mummy breaks its left hand off, holds it out to us with its right.

I blow a little breeze around myself and float to the mummy. It looks less creepy close up. More sad. I wish there was companionship to give it. I take its hand.

"Thank you, K—Kalaturru and Kur—Kurgurru." I have totally slaughtered that, but the thing is lonely *and* it broke off its own hand for us, the least I can do is make the attempt.

There are rites to be performed in the netherworld, it tells me, and I nod soberly. The hand's dry and cracking in mine, like it's going to fall apart at any second.

My blue glow surrounds it. The fingers curl, making disgusting cracking noises, until only the pointer finger is sticking out. It's pointing at one of the cavern walls, still decorated in a gold-on-gold-on-gold motif, but when I look closer I can see a twist in the metal, an odd line that forms—oh yes, I see me a Door.

"I guess that's the way home," I call over my shoulder. I turn around, and Roxie and Ryan just stare at me. I stick my tongue out at them.

Ištar laughs, and that breaks the tension.

"I wasn't expecting you to have *wings*," says Ryan.

"I told you I wasn't like other girls." I grin at him, and walk toward the wall. It shimmers a little, until it looks like gold water. I hold the mummy hand tighter, and step through.

18

I've stepped through into a house, I think. It's all a little blurry and blue-gold still. I blink a couple of times and hold the hand against my chest. I'm totally alone, and I'm not back in my diner, or in the movie theater, or anywhere else it would make sense for a Door to let me out. I'm—

It's *my* house. I'm in my old bedroom. It used to be one of my favorite places in the world, it really was— it's as big as the entire diner, kitchen included, and the walls are a deep purple-blue. My bed was one of those giant four posters, with a canopy, because when I was a little girl, I wanted to be a princess, and that's the kind of bed princesses had.

Looking back on it, I *was* a princess. I lived in a huge house that in any other time period would have been considered a castle. I had everything I ever wanted, and just didn't know it.

Except now I have my diner, and I have my friends, and I have Ryan, and I know this sounds terrible, but I don't know that I'd trade it all, not even to have my parents back.

They were shitty parents, but they were *my* parents.

But—would they even recognize me now?

I step further into the room. There are my bookshelves, with all the books I never read on them. I must be the only girl in the whole world who's never read *Black Beauty*—but I had a first edition, in perfect condition. I remember it because it brought the highest price of all the books when it was sold at auction.

My parents had a lot of debt, it turned out. My mother took all the cash when she left, liquidated all their stocks and bonds and did whatever people do when they're planning to not come back and deal with the fallout, the aftermath.

The house was sold at auction, too.

This can't be my house. But there are all the stuffed animals that I gave to Goodwill, and there's my collection of shot glasses from all over the world, and—

I jerk open the bottom drawer of the dresser. There are my sex toys, and the strawberry-flavored lube that I'd never even had a chance to try. There's even my worn copy of Colette's biography and *Lady Chatterley's Lover* and the trilogy of books about how Sleeping Beauty became a sex slave. I hadn't needed to hide them, but that was what normal girls did, and I was nothing if not completely normal, right up until the moment I met Ryan.

"Allie!" calls my mother. I walk over to the doorway of the room and look out into the hallway. She's standing right there. I thought I didn't remember what she looks like, but I was wrong. I remember her exactly. This is her. Her dark curly hair, her dark brown eyes, her pale skin stretched tightly across her bones.

"Plastic surgery is for people who don't have our bone structure," she used to say.

"Allie, darling." She holds my face in her hands, and I hear the Kalaturru's hand crack as I squeeze it tighter. "Where have you been? It's almost suppertime. We're eating with the Standishes tonight. That child of theirs is running amuck, do you know anything about that?"

Stan. She's talking about Stan. I shake my head. She presses a kiss to my forehead, and my heart twists in my chest. She's offering me everything—she's offering me family, and friends, no blood and no death.

But that's not the most important thing to me anymore, is it? Because it's all going to be kind of boring without my diner. Without *Ryan*.

And she never called me Allie. She always used my full name.

I look around. Everything looks wrong.

She's calling me Allie because she doesn't know

my real name. She's calling me Allie because this is one of the Hells, and the Doors don't *know* my real name. No one's called me by my real name since my mother left, how could the Doors know it?

They couldn't.

I'm still in Hell.

"I'll be down in a minute, Mom," I say, and she smiles at me. Perfect teeth. Mine have always been a bit crooked, even with the application of painful braces.

"Okay, don't take too long. And, please, darling, change into something presentable."

A totally inappropriate laugh bursts out of me. I'm wearing a leather vest and leather pants and a leather duster. And I'm holding a mummy hand. Yes, if we're having supper with Stan and his parents, I should definitely change into something more presentable. Preferably—I mean, I know my mother. Preferably something Chanel.

She turns and walks down the stairs, the front stairs that curve around. They get wider at the bottom, like something out of a crazy movie. This was my mother's dream house. She designed it and my father had it built for her.

She always thought we were a class above everyone else, even the Standishes, even Amanda's family. We had the nicest house, the nicest pool, the nicest pool house.

I flop down onto the bed and stare at the canopy. It's

purple with black ruffles, and, if I remember correctly, it's made out of raw Nepalese silk, or something else decadent and unnecessary.

It all seems unnecessary now. It all seems ridiculous.

I close my eyes and search for Doors, but can't find any. I'm stuck here, I guess.

Are you there? I call. *I need you.*

But there's no answer.

I feel the bed dip a little, and surge up, and when I open my eyes, the lioness is sitting at the foot of the bed, staring at me with wide unblinking eyes. Except she doesn't look quite like Ryan's lioness. Which makes sense, I suppose. This one's the real goddess, whereas the other's just one of Ryan's nightmares.

"This is your Hell, huh?" I ask. "You the ghost of what might have been?"

She looks reproachful.

"I've totally figured it out. This is what my future would have been like if my mother hadn't left. What do I have to do to get out of here?" I look down at the hand in my hand. It just looks like a desiccated old grey hand. The flesh of it is crinkly, like the casing of a sausage.

The lioness doesn't say anything, just sits there. Outside the huge picture window, the sun is setting. As it sets, the room gets darker and darker, until I'm lying in pitch blackness, the blackness of the dimension with the crevasse.

And I talk to the lioness. I've been doing a lot of talking lately, except this time, instead of talking to Stan about all the things in the past, I talk to the lioness about *now*.

Like: I love Ryan. I think I've been skirting around it, but—she's a lion, I think I can tell her of all people. I love him, and I don't even know what he thinks of me.

I figure I've told her one home truth, so I follow it up with telling her that I don't miss my parents. And then how badly I feel about what happened to Stan, and how worried I am about Amanda. Saying it all out loud makes it all feel a bit more *real.* Like I am creating reality out of my words, except I know I'm not, because that's all real, and *this,* this room, this dimension, this is what's a lie.

The bed underneath me gets harder and harder, and I cry while I talk about Stan. I can't see the lioness anymore, but I can feel her at my feet, the warmth of her. It's freezing in the room, and my body is chilled. My hand is cramped where it's wrapped around the hand of the Kalaturru, but I refuse to let it go. If I put it down, I'm not sure I'll ever be able to pick it up again.

I don't know when I closed my eyes, but when I open them again, I'm in a dark place, and there are stars. Roxie said there were no stars in the underworld, but what does she know?

The lioness rubs her face against my shoulder, and then lies down in front of me.

I'm sorry that you could not fix Stan, the lioness finally offers.

"Yeah, well, life's a bitch," I tell her.

If it is any consolation, she starts, and I cut her off.

"It's not. Nothing is a consolation. I killed one of my best friends."

He was not your friend anymore. He was dead the moment the werewolf bit him. You know that. She puts her head on her front paws and stares at me. I stare back.

"You know that doesn't make it any better." I stare back at her, and she changes the subject.

You found what you came for. Well done.

"The hand? Thanks. Will that stop the end of the world?" Oh Hell. I am apparently taking lessons in tactful questioning from Ryan.

She laughs. *Few can see my Hell for what it is, and I appreciate those who can know themselves. I came to give you a gift: I will answer three questions for you, and do so with as much truth as I can. To answer your first question: The hand can pause the earth and air, but it can't stop it.*

"Wow, and thank you for springing that on me *after* I'd asked a question. Not very helpful," I snap at her. "Fine. Second question: What *will* stop the end of the world?"

Salt and silver, girl, the lioness says, sounding almost annoyed. *You know this.*

I feel like I'm failing some kind of test here, with answers I couldn't possibly know. That is what is called passive-aggressive argument, lioness, and I do not appreciate it.

"Let's skip the bullshit," I say. "What answer should I be trying to cleverly wrangle from you?"

Ah, says the lioness. If lions could grin, I think she would. *The Door-hounds are not aspects of the Doors themselves, nor are they strictly demons,* she says, and I swear for a second she sounds like Narnia. *They are merely creatures that occupy the interstitials. They kill those who cross their space not out of hate, but because the Doors ask it of them. They are lonely creatures, and Doors are the only company they've found.* The lioness stands, and stretches. I can feel the stretch in my body as she cracks her spine in three places. The warmth of the stretching flows through me.

You've met a Door-hound, she says. In the darkness, a purple creature, tentacles with light dustings of fur at the end, swims around her. It's a tiny version of the monster from the hospital. It's a monster like this that killed Jackson.

For a moment, I hate them.

Oh yes, I imagine you do, the lioness says. *But you have experience with loving those who do wrong without realizing it. You might want to remember that later.* And she turns and walks into the darkness.

A Door pops up where she disappears, and the

tentacle monster—the Door-hound—swims into it, growing larger as it goes. The Door turns purple-green for a second, like a bruise, and then—*Hello, Allie,* the Door says.

Yo, I say to it. *I've been missing you.* And it's actually true.

We missed you too, it says. *What can we do for you?*

Wishes. I make too many wishes. But I figure it can't really get *much* worse at this point. So I ask: *Take me back to Ryan and Roxie. We've got shit to do.*

It would be silly if we helped you destroy us.

I don't really care about destroying you. I'm kind of surprised to realize that I mean it. Today is a day of re-evaluated self-image. *I just want to fix the balance. You know it's all screwed up.*

We understand, but—

Oh, just shut up and do what I tell you. I sound about as exasperated with the Doors as Ryan always sounds when he's talking to *me.* Ha ha.

I step through the Door.

Time slows as I go through the Door, and for a moment I hear the lioness say *interstitials*—that means the space between places. In the interstitial of the lioness's Hell—the Hell of truth, I guess, and isn't that Hell for enough people?—and a place that smells an awful lot like *home,* I can feel Ryan and Roxie, paused midstep in the Kalaturru/Kurgarru's Door. And there's something else, too. The thing that lives in the interstitials. The Door-hound.

It smells purple. And lonely.

And then the moment ends, and Ryan is Ryan, Roxie is Roxie, and I'm me.

Except, maybe for first time ever, I am *all* of me.

19

When I turn around, the first thing I see is that some-one's pulled down Roxie's BUTTER FLAVORING box wall. The theater's dark, and on the screen is something animated, with a lot of animals wearing col-ored hats. Roxie and Ryan are right behind me. There are people actually sitting near us, but they're not, you know, jumping up and screaming about these people who mysteriously appeared out of nowhere covered in blood and goo and carrying a mummy's hand.

"This is weird," I whisper.

"*This* is the part you think is weird?" teases Roxie. She resettles her Stetson on her head. Ryan does the same thing. I pull my sunglasses down from my hair onto my nose.

"It looks like we're home," says Ryan unnecessarily.

"What if this is another Hell dimension?" Roxie challenges.

"Hell dimensions don't have Disney," I say. "Smells too human."

Ryan looks around. "So, what now?"

"Got to get the van, *cher*," Roxie says.

"Sounds good to me," I say. We head out of the theater and into the lobby, where teenagers look at us suspiciously. I see a bank of pay phones on the wall. "Hey, guys, give me a second?"

Ryan looks like he wants to argue, or even ask why I need to make a phone call *right now,* but instead he gestures to the hand that I'm still holding. "You might want to put that away first," he says mildly.

Hmm. "Good point." I tuck it into the pocket of my duster, and wow, that is an awkward lump. I hope it is a lot more solid than it looks, because it will be very embarrassing if we have to go all the way back into Hell to get the mummy's other hand.

I lope over to the block of pay phones and punch in my credit card number. It's going to cost about a million dollars, even though it's a local call, but I don't care. Especially after those special moments in my old bedroom, I want to know about my life *here,* and now. Irrational? Probably. But it feels necessary. It *smells* necessary.

Dawn picks up on the third ring. "Sally's Diner," she says, and when I say "It's Allie," she squeals.

"Oh my god, Allie! You've been gone for almost a week! Where did you go? Were you with Ryan?"

It can't hurt to let her think the best of the situation. "Yeah, Ryan took me away for a while." I let the force of Ashmedai's Hell dimension come out in my voice, so that I sound kind of seductive. I also, I am sure, sound exhausted. And I'm *starving*. I wonder if I can convince Roxie and Ryan that before we do anything else, we need to get some pizza.

"You have no idea," Dawn is saying. "The shit that is going down in the city, Allie. The shit that's going down! It is fucked up, I swear to you. It is like gang fights or something, I don't know. I've been having everybody stay at the diner, just so we can keep tabs, you know? The radio's saying the mayor's going to call a state of emergency and declare martial law, and all sorts of wild things have been reported roaming the streets, like wild dogs and, I am not even kidding, walking *trees*. And—"

I cut her off. "Any word from Amanda?"

"Nothing. But—well, the phone is ringing off the fucking hook, but whenever I pick up, it's just someone crying. Could that be—?" She sounds really distressed.

"Dawn, I'll be back soon. In fact, I think we might be there very soon to pick up some stuff. Okay? But right now I've got to go."

She cheers up enough to ask if Ryan is kissing my neck, and I giggle.

"Not yet," I say, and hang up the phone.

Then I lean against it. Damn it, Amanda, *where are you*?

I don't bother to call her. For a second, I forget I'm not in Hell anymore, and I just *reach* for her. And—Jesus, it *works*. There she is, a pinpoint of sick light, and I'm following—

Into a solid fucking brick wall. *Ow.*

I open my eyes. I'm gasping. The theater lobby wavers in front of me for a second. I lever myself away from the phone bank and stumble back to Ryan and Roxie.

"Anything?" Ryan asks, touching my elbow, holding me up.

I shake my head. He doesn't need to know I tried to use my Hell powers in the real world. I'll stick with what Dawn told me.

"It's bad," I say. "We'll have to drive carefully."

We actually blend in pretty easily with the denizens of Sheepshead Bay—they're all wearing bizarre outfits, and taking advantage of the warm spring afternoon to sit outside and sip cappuccinos while they wait for their movies to start, like my only living best friend isn't somewhere I can't find and my only dead best friend is off being mourned in Hell by the very monsters he was becoming.

These people have no sense of perspective.

When we reach the parking lot of the movie theater,

sitting on the hood of Roxie's van is Narnia. She looks super-pissed, and I am ready to fight her. Just let me at her. I took down one of those giant pill bugs, and I took down the fucking Hell dimension of truth—I can take on one annoying psychic witch.

"You're late," she says, and holds out a bag. Ryan takes it, and pulls out bagels. Maybe she can live to see another day. Maybe.

"I'll let you live if one of those has cream cheese and tomatoes and onion," I tell her.

She sniffs at me. She's wearing Balenciaga today, a neat brown suit with a subtle blue and cream plaid pattern, and brown knee-high leather boots. I wonder if it's lamia leather, or if she just wears cow leather like everyone else.

"It's even on an everything bagel," she says, and Ryan tosses me a bagel wrapped in butcher's paper. I rip into the paper. Nothing compares to New York bagels, nothing, not even the best organic chocolate can compare to a bagel from New York. And with cream cheese, tomatoes, and onion? It's like Heaven.

Which is appropriate.

Roxie's got what looks like cream cheese and lox on hers, and Ryan's cream cheese is a funny color. I lean over his arm and sniff it.

"Walnut raisin cream cheese?" I ask, eyebrows up. That's so . . . *girly*.

"With maple syrup," he says and takes a big bite.

My heart sinks a little. I've known Ryan for six years, and in all that time, I never knew that he likes girly cream cheese. I always just buy regular.

Narnia smirks at me like she knows what I'm thinking.

"I just got back from Hell," I say to her. "Don't fuck with me, bitch."

"I'm here to help," she snaps. "Don't be an idiot." She waves a hand at me and her eyes flash with the sparks.

"Don't you wave at me!" The effect is slightly diminished because my mouth is full of bagel.

"Give me the hand," she orders. Ryan snickers.

"No."

"Give me the hand."

"What's the magic word?" I sneer.

"Right. Now." Narnia's voice is like ice, and I swear the temperature drops ten degrees.

"You don't have to be a bitch about it," I grumble, juggling the bagel to get the hand out of my pocket again. "How'd you know we came back with a hand, anyway?"

"Need I remind you that I am a psychic witch?" She smirks at me again, and gently caresses the hand. Okay, that's more than a little creepy. "I knew the moment you entered the realm of the Kalaturru." She looks up at me, and her eyes flare a little, but the sparks stay inside. "How did you escape the Hell of lies?"

Because the point wasn't the lie. The point was the truths I had to tell. How do I even explain that? Answer: Probably by not trying. "Well, it was clearly a bunch of lies, so I just . . ." I wave the hand holding the bagel, and part of a piece of tomato falls out with a squelch. Oops. "It was just a bunch of lies," I finish lamely.

"Hmm."

"Allie's a lot stronger than we gave her credit for," says Roxie loyally. And it's true. I *am* a lot stronger than they gave me credit for. So there.

"And my avatar is an elemental spirit." It's my turn to smirk at Narnia's stupid face.

"I knew that," she says absently, still stroking the hand. "It's clear just by looking at you. Air, right? It comes off you in waves. That's why you're so . . ." She trails off and snorts a little. "Arrogant."

"I'm arrogant? Me?" I feel more than a little affronted. "Seriously?" I turn to Ryan. "Me?"

"Okay, Allie, settle down—"

"Everyone shut up," says Narnia. She sounds a little grim. I wish wistfully for some coffee or a bottle of water, and also to not have to look at her perfectly coiffed head or listen to her perfectly modulated voice.

I can't stop myself. I sneer at Narnia. "I want you to understand that I have about the same level of excitement at this point about seeing the bagels as stopping the end of the world," I tell her.

"Just stand there," she snarls back, and whips a

Zippo out of a tiny little pocket. I bet it's engraved. I bet it's custom. She seems like the kind of person to have a custom lighter, even if she doesn't smoke.

Next to me, Ryan's pulled a pouch of tobacco out of the bag that held bagels, and is rolling a cigarette.

"Give me some silver," says Narnia, impatiently, like she'd asked three or four times and had been ignored, except she *hadn't*. What gave her the right to act like the queen of the world? *We* were the ones who had done everything.

Roxie pulls her medallion over her head and hands it over. It's like nothing I've ever seen before but it's big and it's silver. Ryan gives his—a big Star of David. Mine's gone, still with Stan. Narnia puts them both in the palm of the hand, sets the hand on the ground, and motions to me.

I stay where I am.

"Come here," she orders.

"What's the magic word?" Ugh, I am a bitch. And repetitive. Narnia brings out the worst in me.

Her eyes flash gold sparks. Uck—I am so *tired* of that. I bet it's just a stupid trick, too. I bet I could—

I think about the little blue lights I breathed in Hell, and I inhale, thinking, *If I could pull this in, pull it up, flash it out*—

And flash! I see blue. I didn't think that would work.

"I didn't think that would work!" I say to everyone's surprised faces.

"Of course it did," says Narnia. Whatever, witch, you are startled, and I win.

Narnia gestures me over again. She pulls a small pouch out of the top of one of her boots. I can see a little knife settled next to it. Maybe her boots are like our lamia-skin coats.

I shudder at the memory of lamias.

"Ready?"

"For what?" I stare skeptically at the bag.

"Put your hand out and think about your avatar, like you did just now," she instructs, her voice a little softer. "We need it." She pours some of whatever's in the bag into my hand. It's salt.

Then she lights it on fire.

I shriek really loudly, but don't drop the salt. It doesn't even hurt. The fire is golden, and gorgeous.

"Think about your avatar," she says again. I take a deep breath and think about the gorgeous blue waves that come off me, the way my eyes sparked with blue fire when Narnia pissed me off. I think about my wings. I can smell the smoke from Ryan's cigarette, and the dry crackling of Roxie's snakes, and sweat, and—

Narnia grabs my hand and overturns the fire onto the mummy's hand and the silver medallions, and there's a giant noise.

When I open my eyes, I'm floating about a foot off the ground, and surrounded by blue light. I blink, and crash to the asphalt.

"Oww," I whine, because, really, I could have at least landed on my feet.

Water is gushing out of the hand, spreading faster than water should, going in every direction. The water is also ice cold, ocean cold, and I know this because I have landed in it.

Narnia's smirking, and Ryan's still smoking, and Roxie's eyes are wide.

"I really didn't think that would actually work," says Narnia. She sounds pretty satisfied with herself.

The hand is lying on the ground, melted silver all over it. As fast as it came, the water stops gushing out, and the water surrounding me and edging into the distance disappears.

The asphalt abruptly cracks apart, and the hand falls into the ground. My mouth drops open as the asphalt seals itself up again.

"That was fucked up," I announce, and scramble to my feet. My bagel is *not* sitting well in my stomach, and I am super-glad that I didn't drink any coffee, because I'd probably puke it all back up.

"Allie, try to find the Doors," says Narnia. She leans back against the truck, smirking.

I blink at her and try to think fast. "I don't know what you're—"

Narnia snorts. "Don't be coy. I know you did it in Hell, and I know you've tried to do it here too. Try it again."

Well. Okay, fine. But if my brain splats against a big mental brick wall, I am going to cut someone.

I think, in my Door voice, *Where are you?* and the sound bounces out through the city, looking for spontaneous Doors. Nothing stops me, and I realize: It feels *really good* to be able to do this.

Only three Doors I don't recognize answer. That's pretty good, particularly out of all the hundreds of spontaneously vivified Doors I know existed five minutes back.

I kind of wonder what Hell looks like now.

Narnia sighs.

"I'm a little sorry that it's over," she says. Roxie's glaring at her. I guess it takes more than a bagel to keep Roxie from wanting to kill her. "It felt really interesting. I'll have to record it all . . ." She trails off and looks around at us. "What? It's over, it's done. I could really use a coffee."

"So is my Door back where it was before?" I finish the bagel by cramming an entire quarter of it into my mouth. There is a delicate look of disgust on Narnia's face. I will smack that bitch up if she says one word about my eating habits.

But instead she says, "Of course not." She's talking to me like I'm an idiot, and only Ryan's hand on my shoulder is holding me back from punching her. Ryan's hand and the knowledge that it would probably hurt a lot. "This was just stopping the end of the world. Temporarily."

Narnia stands up straight, teeters a little on the stiletto heels of her boots, and rights herself. No one moves to help her. "But the pieces are all still in play to start it right back up again, and soon."

"So we went through a pile of Hells for . . . no good reason at all?" I am displeased.

"You went through nine. Every Door leads to nine underworlds one way or another. And I wouldn't call saving the world, even temporarily, nothing." Narnia grins, a real actual smile, and I'm taken aback by how *pretty* she is when she's not sneering or smirking or making that generally annoyed face she has.

"Narnia. What next." Ryan's clearly losing *his* patience too.

Narnia taps a perfectly manicured finger—French, of course—against her mouth. "You came back through the Door with what we needed—time. With the extra Doors gone for the moment, we have a chance at correcting whatever's the central issue. I just don't know what the central issue *is* here. Something—it's not very strong, but it's there—is blocking me from feeling where Allie's Door has gone. I'm supposed to feel them." Narnia's mouth turns down in an attractive pout.

What? I know I don't like her, but she is cute. That's part of why I don't like her. I'm sticky and sweaty, and one of my hands still has salt on it. I try wiping it off on my coat, but it's sticking to me, kind of gold-tinged.

"Because it all comes back to your Door," Narnia continues. "It's the only anomaly in this scenario. How did it move? *Why* did it move? And how is it related to the world ending in earth and air?"

She looks at all of us and when we don't say anything, begins tapping her foot. I think she must have seen the three AM PBS how-to-brainstorm series. And then decided it took too long.

Ryan looks speculatively into the distance. "I can't answer the third one, but I bet I can answer the first. Allie, remember when you did that stupid thing in the first Hell?"

"First Hell?" asks Narnia. "And *Allie* did something stupid. Oh, do go on."

I shoot a nasty look at her. "You mean when I moved the Door so that it was right by us?"

"Yeah." He looks at Narnia. "She wished for it to move, and it moved. Could someone have wished it away from the diner?"

"That sounds . . . eerily plausible." Narnia nods.

"I thought you knew everything already," I say to Narnia. Maybe I sound a little nasty. I'm trying not to. After all, I am the one Ryan *likes*—likes enough to shove away at every opportunity. He doesn't seem to ever be shoving away Narnia. That either means he doesn't care enough about her, or he thinks she can take care of herself without his participation.

I don't know if that's comforting or not. I feel a little annoyed.

"No, I don't," Narnia snaps. "If I knew everything, you wouldn't have had to go into the Hells to help me figure it out."

"So . . ." Roxie's voice is a jolt; she's been quiet this whole time. "That leaves the question of why it moved, and how it's ending the world."

Narnia nods. "Yes. With Allie's little discovery, I think I can answer the 'why'—the Door will do what it thinks is in its best interest. Or rather, will grant the wishes that fit best with getting more wishes. So if someone wished it to move, and the Door knew there'd be more wishes to come, it would go."

"Why does it care about getting more wishes?" I cross my arms and glare. "This is crazy Door history that no one's bothered to tell me, isn't it?"

Narnia smirks. "Might be." Ryan rolls his eyes and goes to stand next to Roxie. I glare at Narnia. Narnia glares at me. She lets out a huffed breath. "Doors are . . . they're symbols. Mostly. Or allegories. Or morality tales. They're metaphysical manifestations of the choice between following the gods' path for you and making your own fate." She waves her hand. "Or they're not."

"This," I say, with what I feel is supreme good temper, "is not helpful."

"Doors gain power through wishes," Narnia bites out. "Because . . . Look, the Doors, so far as we know, are a test for humanity. That's why we have Doors. Something, or someone, out there wants to gather data on us, and see how we deal with these little magical darlings. So the Doors grant wishes because it draws us to them, and the wishes feed the Doors, so they want to stay near us. It's a balance, a very carefully created balance."

I frown. "With some puppet master in the background."

Narnia nods reluctantly. "That's what we think. But maybe that's not the case at all. Maybe there's no reason for Doors to exist. Maybe we're just unlucky enough to have that kind of temptation in our lives. It's not something we can really test."

I remember that Door in the mummy's Hell, that just wanted to be left alone. "Maybe," I say, "the Doors don't have much choice in the matter either."

Her eyes flash, except I think she's just thinking something, not deliberately trying to intimidate. She looks down, smiles slightly to herself. "Well," she says. "That's a theory. But if there's one thing I've learned, it's that everything about Doors involves a choice. Do you or don't you? What sort of person are you? What's more important: your heart's desire, or your desire's heart?"

I blink. Ryan snorts, and Roxie says, "Dammit, she's gonna start rhyming soon."

Narnia gives herself a little shake, and the glare is back. "Your Door moved, which means someone wished it away, and the Door thought it was a good enough deal to allow it. We need someone who knows about your Door; someone who knows about wishes; and someone who has the potential to create enough trouble to be worth a Door's time." She sniffs. "You and your stupid friends fit the bill. You're the only mundanes who've ever opened a Door and lasted longer than a week."

"What, and it couldn't have been a hunter?" I just— I can't even. Yes, we were dumb, but—

"Can't have been a hunter," Narnia says. "Their thoughts are mine." Roxie squawks behind us, but we both ignore her. "Really, Allie," Narnia says. "*Think.*"

I don't *want* to think. And I don't like the answers I'm coming up with anyway.

I know it's not me, because I had too much going for me by having the Door in the basement. (For the record, I hate that. Hate hate hate.) And it's not Stan— Stan's dead, he can't still be wishing things, making all this garbage necessary. I test it anyway, sending my mind to his house, his clubs, his favorite booth to nap in in the diner—and no Doors pop up. He didn't have it.

Which only leaves—

Ryan puts his hand on my shoulder. I hardly feel the weight of it. "Amanda," Ryan says.

I let out a breath. "Amanda."

"Who's Amanda?" asks Roxie. "The other one who summoned the Door with you?"

I'm so tired. "It was her idea in the first place. We thought it was a joke . . ." I stare at the ground. "Shit. This is just like her. If she realized she could move the Door, get 24/7 time with it—"

"Allie," Roxie says. "Check it first. You found the Doors before, yeah? Look for your Door now."

I blink at her. And then I close my eyes, and say, *Door? Where are you?*

Allie! It sounds really happy to hear me. I get a picture of a big house on a rolling lawn that tapers into a beach with sparkling blue water, tiny waves lapping at the shore. I see a pool behind the house and a pool house with brown and cream towels and matching bed linens.

And the Door, sitting in the middle of all of it. I know that house. I know that beach. And I know that pool house.

The Door is huge. The Door is at least three times the size it was when it was in the basement of the diner, swollen with wishes, gurgling with its own happiness.

"Oh, shit." I open my eyes. They're tearing a little, so I rub at them—bad move with the salt still on my hand. Now my eyes sting, too. "Fuck."

"So, we're talking bad?" Ryan says.

I nod. "The Door's with Amanda, out on Long Island." I giggle a little. I don't mean to. "Guess it really was the Hand of Franklin, huh? It pointed toward the ocean."

"Allie," Roxie says, and I swallow my laughter and try again.

"It's badder than the three of us," I say, and then nod at Narnia. "Four if you count Tolkien over here."

Narnia looks ready to breathe fire. Can she do that, though, like, for real? That would be equally cool and terrifying. I will ask Ryan later.

Ryan takes off his hat and swipes a hand through his hair, and some grass falls out of it. I am reminded very vividly of what we did in the grass.

I close my eyes for a moment.

"Here's what I'm thinking," Ryan says. He puts his hat back on his head. "Narnia. Can you get us backup?"

She sighs. "I know where you're going with this. And it's going to be exhausting," says Narnia. She turns her hands palms up, stands with her legs slightly spread, and her eyes flash. I *hear* her sparking, feel her magic reach out around us, touching each hunter. It doesn't touch me, though, which I call unfair—I form a little hook out of my inner blue and toss it after her magic.

Look. I hate to be ignored. This must be really clear by now.

Except instead of paying attention to me, I end up

following behind her everywhere she goes, and "meet" all the hunters. Narnia knows them all by name—not true names, but hunter names. There's Fagey—who wants to be called Fagey?—and Moshe, Theresa, Smith, Curlique, and Starr (that's more like it). They keep going and going, Fedoras and Stetsons and Baseball Caps, at work, at home, having sex, eating supper.

Come, says Narnia. It's like my Door voice, but it doesn't smell like "Door" at all. It's powerful, though, and it's directed at me. I grab her hand tightly, and show her a picture of the house, the roads that lead out to Noyack Bay and Sag Harbor, the trees and beaches and endless blue ocean. Then, because she's never been there, I show her my diner, everything I can remember about it. The red vinyl booths, and the green vinyl chairs, and the blue sparkly vinyl padding on the stools that sit up at the counter. The tables decoupaged with old articles about hippie protests that Sally had gone to back in her hey-day. I show her Williamsburg, the part that I live in, it's all concrete and subways and old row tenements.

Tell them to meet there, I say in my Door voice. And—Narnia shudders. She wrenches her hand from mine, and cuts her magic from my blue. Everything goes dark.

When I open my eyes, I'm being held up off the ground by Ryan, and Narnia is in Roxie's arms, her head hanging back.

"I want a cup of coffee," I slur, and my eyes slide shut again.

When I open them again, I'm in the van, lying down. On one side of me are the crossbows. On the other side is Narnia. She looks terrible—her face is ashen, her lips are pale under their perfect application of Elizabeth Arden, and there are dark circles under her eyes.

While I'm staring at her, she opens her eyes and stares back at me. "Thanks for the creepy help," she says hoarsely. "I couldn't have done that without you."

"I just followed you," I tell her.

She corrects me: "You loaned me your power. And you have a lot of it. You never use it."

Whatever. "I told everybody to go to the diner."

Narnia makes a tiny moue of distaste. "I know. Not the best idea, but there wasn't much I could do to stop you." She doesn't say anything for a second, and then: "I'm sorry your friend died. Stan, right?" She doesn't wait for me to answer. "Amanda might die too. I think the Door knows her true name." Narnia's eyes flutter shut, and I keep my mouth closed.

The Door does know Amanda's name. Amanda's never had a nickname; she's never wanted one. But I always hated my real name, and made everyone call me Allie starting when I was just a kid. And Stan was always Stan because his father was Charles, and it was just easier, so that we didn't get Charles Standish III mixed up with Charles Standish IV. Charles Standish II was Grandpa Charlie. I never met Charles Standish I.

My mother always said that their fetish for naming the first son was tacky, but she invited them over for supper every month anyway.

Of the three of us who opened a Door—three mundanes who lived longer than a week—Stan's dead from a werewolf bite, Amanda's in the thrall of a Door to Hell that knows her true name, and I . . . I don't even know what I am.

As we drive, I can see the skylines and buildings give way to trees. The sun is setting, and the sky is pink and orange.

Before we get to the diner, Narnia wakes up enough to explain a little about what she's going to do when we get to Amanda's. It has to do with magic, and hunters holding off demons so that we can get inside, and somehow we can make the Door move back to the diner, try to get it to spit out the wishes, or just get smaller, or take away its power—

I spend most of her speechifying trying to nap, sunglasses perched precariously on my nose. I know I should be listening, because what she's going to do is important to what I have to do, but . . . I don't think there's really any way to prepare for this.

Before the van is even parked, I am jumping out. I

have never been so happy to see my tiny storefront diner in my life. There are vamps standing outside it, and it's full dark, but I snarl at them, and they don't even bother me. I don't bother them either; there's enough time for hunting them down and killing them with all the iron I can find later.

I stop when I get inside. The diner is full of hunters. The smell of lamia clothes makes me gag a little. I push my way through them, and let Ryan and Roxie and Narnia do the talking.

Dawn is in the back. It's nice to see her too. She has orange streaks in her hair today, and her eyeliner is mixed with glitter and smeared all around her eyes. She looks a little like a crazy raccoon, and I feel a pang in my heart. I like her a lot, and she's awesome, and I am glad she's not dead.

"Shit, Allie, do you *see* those . . ." She trails off when she sees my clothes, my sweat-matted hair, my crooked sunglasses.

"I can't talk now, Dawn. I really can't," I tell her. My voice is hoarse. I don't bother taking off the sunglasses.

"O-okay," she says, but stares at me expectantly.

"I'm not even going to promise to explain this to you later, because I probably won't," I tell her. "I have to go."

I jog up the stairs into my apartment, without waiting

for her to answer me. It's stuffy and smells stale. I just take a deep breath and get what I need: my Seal of Solomon, and a new nail.

Amanda was the one who gave me Betsy. After we met Ryan, she went online and bought me "coffin nails" off a Wiccan website. She laughed and laughed when they came, but Ryan said it only mattered that they were actual iron. I've wounded a lot of bad things with Betsy since then, even if she is a gimmick.

But now Betsy's gone, still stuck in Stan somewhere in a Hell dimension, and I need a new nail.

"I'm going to call you Dan," I tell the nail. "Steely Dan." I giggle a little. I might be getting hysterical. I can't tell. I tuck Steely Dan into one of my pockets, and reach under my pillow for the Seal of Solomon that Ryan gave me so long ago. I string it onto an old stainless steel chain necklace that I have, taking off its charm as I do it. It's from when Amanda and I were really young, before we met Stan, when we promised to be best friends forever, and used our allowances to buy matching BFF necklaces. It's not a coincidence that I picked that chain. It's the oldest steel that I have, and the Seal of Solomon is my most important piece of silver.

I don't know if stuff like that really matters, but just in case it does, I want to be prepared.

The Seal of Solomon hangs too heavy around my neck, and it's going to give me a really bad headache.

But not yet. Maybe not 'til this is over. I keep my hand on the talisman for an extra second, and then take another deep breath and head back downstairs. It's too bad I don't have more weapons, like a sword or—

I have a knife. That's what I have. I run into the kitchen and grab my really good knife off the magnetic strip that runs across the wall. It's full of knives—bread knives, chopping knives, slicing knives, sushi knives, every kind of knife you can think of. I am a collector. I am a connoisseur. But the knife I take is the one I love, the too-expensive one that Sally gave me before she left.

I wrap it in a dishcloth, and tuck it into one of the inside pockets of the coat, under Dawn's watchful and curious eyes.

"Seriously, I am *never* going to tell you what's going on," I tell her. "If I don't come back, though, I want you to run the diner."

"I have *no clue* how to run a diner, Allie. That is, like, way above my pay grade."

"You'll learn. I did." I kiss her cheek, and head back out into the dining area, where the hunters have thinned out. They're all clutching pieces of paper.

"We gave them directions; yours were a little muddy," says Ryan. He looks at me a long moment, like he's going to say something else, but then he walks right out again.

Roxie catches my arm. "Come on. We're taking the van."

I look around the room one last time, the weird art on the walls that Dawn convinced me looked good. It was some local artist who painted trees, like Bob Ross. Happy little trees. The paintings don't really go with the '50s-style décor that Sally rocked, but they made people happy. They made me happy.

This diner made me happy. I really hope that I get to see it again, that Amanda's crazy hasn't ruined my life, that it won't kill me.

I really really *really* do not want to die today.

20

Two hours later, and I can tell we're getting close. I can smell the Atlantic, salt and fish and rot.

Amanda's driveway is long and winding, even though her family's house isn't set very far back off the road. It's a classic McMansion, built for flash, not substance. They have to put in new windows and carpets every time there's a hurricane and the house floods.

Ryan pulls open the back doors of the van and the scent of chlorine pours in. A pool next to the ocean. It's so damn decadent. And I am totally not the same person I was six years ago, because six years ago I thought the ocean was tacky, and pools were for rich people. Now I'd rather go in the ocean, touch the sand, than be in a giant tub of concrete and chlorine.

Everything is quiet. I really do not want to say "too quiet," but it is, it really is. I should hear the ocean. I should hear planes flying overhead. I should hear gulls, and a TV playing too loudly in the pool house, and stupid rich people's boats skipping across the dark water, out of sight behind the pretty white fence surrounding us and the pool.

There's nothing.

I've been through Hells today, and *now* I'm terrified.

I don't know what Ryan's thinking. I guess I mean literally—I haven't heard anything since I followed Narnia to call the hunters. Maybe I burnt myself out.

Ryan's not looking at me, and I bet he isn't thinking about Amanda—Amanda who he's known for six years and probably never slept with, Amanda I've known since I was *two*. I'm clutching my weapons and wondering if I'm ever going to see Amanda alive again.

The pool house windows are kind of staring at me.

A Baseball Cap carrying something under one arm holds up his hand, and we all stop. It's Owen. He's still in uniform. He points half of us toward the other side of the pool to make the approach; his group is apparently going to do something complicated that looks like waving their arms like propellers. I do not understand this crazy military gesturing. Everyone else does, though, because about half the hunters nod, and the rest are already moving.

Behind me, I hear clicky clicky heels. For a moment I think it's Amanda—but it's only Narnia. Ryan hears her heels and winces. Narnia makes a face at me when she sees me watching; I can't believe she's still wearing Balenciaga.

But she just pulls off her boots—she really is *tiny* when she's not in the stilettos—and, of course, she's wearing thigh-high stockings that she rolls down and tucks into the boots. Then she unbuttons her jacket, strips off her camisole, unzips her skirt, and she's naked. Her body is gorgeous. She's got none of the scars that I do.

Some of the hunters are staring at her. Roxie is. Ryan isn't. Ryan's looking at the house, ignoring us all.

I look back at Narnia, and watch as she lowers herself naked into the pool, and I have to say, that takes balls. I know what's happened in that pool; I took the blackmail photos at those parties.

I don't care about the people who are staring at her. Ryan so clearly doesn't care that I feel kind of petty. Jesus. Narnia's naked in a pool filled with god-knows-what, here to do something weird and witchy to save *my* friend (and maybe the world, okay, whatever), and all I can think is *Suck it, bitch, I got him and you didn't.*

Maybe I am meaner than I ought to be.

While Narnia's dog-paddling to the center of the pool, half of Owen's group has inched itself along the right-side fencing; the other half has already scaled the fence and is probably heading around the front of the house. I think about the front of the house, think like poking the roof of your mouth with your tongue to see if you're ticklish there, and I get nothing. It's not . . . bad, like the pool house. But it could be, I guess. It could become so.

Ryan's group heads along the left-side fencing, closer to the pool. We're all positioning ourselves. I hang back near Narnia; I watch what's happening.

Ryan and Owen, leading their groups, look at each other for a long moment. They nod, and both move to open the front door of the beach house. On the ride over there was a lot of talk about magical protections, entrances that are traps, stuff like that. Everybody brought a little something to aid their way, but nothing as big as Ryan with his salt and iron–packed shotgun shells and Owen with, I kid you not, a bleached white horse's skull with colored ribbons tied on. That is what he is carrying. How did he get that on the train? Maybe one of the other Baseball Caps said it was for a modern interpretation of *A Midsummer Night's Dream*. Maybe one of the Fedoras said it was because Owen was foreign. Maybe they all turned and whispered loudly, "You think that's weird? *That guy* thinks he has a magic *gun*."

I wish Stan was still alive so I could tell him my theory, and hear him snicker about hunters and their bones and/or guns. I wish Amanda was safe somewhere on the other end of the cell phone, bitching and constant. I even wish Dawn was here, except not really, because she's not really involved in this, and she would probably die.

I wish my daydreams weren't filled with death. It gives me cause to worry about my future state of sanity.

I can't hear anything from Ryan's head, but from Owen I hear a whisper. He's rocking the horse's head in time to it. *Agorwch y drysau, gadewch i ni chwarae, mae'n oer yn yr eira . . .*

That's not British.

Roxie's humming lullabies in her mind. A sixteen-year-old punk hunter with metal caps on her teeth is wondering if she should have taken the time to write that fan letter to Neil Gaiman. An older guy, somewhere behind me, is wishing he'd called his mother. I guess everyone's got a story.

For my part, I shut it out, quiet my head. I slide my sunglasses down onto my nose. I've got Steely Dan in one hand, the Seal of Solomon talisman around my neck, and the iron chain around my waist. I've been to Hell. I've got silver in me. I am ready to roll.

The front of the house explodes.

Ryan and Owen, closest to the front door, are thrown the farthest—Owen's horsie goes flying into the pool, and Ryan's shotgun hits the ground and cracks a shot into the air, because, you know, walking into the presence of a Door means that maybe you should be able to fire things immediately and not worry about flipping the safety first. If we both survive this, I am going to make so much fucking fun of him. If.

All the rest of us are either on the ground or on one knee—it wasn't a fire explosion, but it was *something*. I reach out.

You know me, I say to the Door.

I know you, agrees the Door, its voice odd. *Don't come any closer.*

"Don't go any closer!" I yell, but everybody's a little deaf from the explosion, and all the hunters are talking, they can't hear me.

What do you want? I ask it desperately, but there's no answer.

Roxie recovers first, and, swearing, pulls out her knives and makes a run for the giant hole where the stucco used to be.

A wave of blackness pours out of the hole, fog and bees and malevolence. Roxie jumps, and slides right through it—she screams, and I can't see anything of her but the flash of her knives, slicing.

Things start moving fast.

Hunters run toward the house, some shouting things, some bleeding from self-inflicted wounds. I think there's a berserker in there. I'm standing still, watching. The only other person not moving is Narnia. This is because she is sitting on a three-foot plume of water in the center of the pool. Her eye sockets are sunken, totally empty. When the black bee thing rears up, and a wisp of it swings out over the top of the fence, Narnia's pool water snaps out and there's a burning smell. I cannot remember if burning chlorine is actually healthy to inhale. If I live through this, then I'll worry about it.

I look for Ryan. He's pulled himself up and gone to snatch his shotgun. His nose is bleeding. He doesn't look at me. He hasn't looked at me since we got here. I get the impression he thinks I'm going to die.

I might die. There are more things coming out of the house now. A group of vampires, wings spread, meet the oncoming hunters in a tumbling mess—they die easy, though, since all the hunters are carrying iron. Behind them come the werewolves. Tall and mangy, with long claws between their fingers and black eyes with a thousand facets. They're harder to kill, and I start seeing some of my hunters, *my* hunters, go down. The hunters need silver, not iron, for the werewolves; it takes a moment for them to switch pockets, pull out different weapons to match what's going on. But they do, and—

The Door, or whatever is inside, tries something different.

Allie! I hear a sweet, almost girlish voice say. It's the Door. *Allie!*

That's all it's doing, saying my name. Whatever. But I look around, and some of the hunters . . . they're not just looking puzzled and then going back to kicking ass. They're stopping. I brush across the hunters' minds, checking in, because this is not normal. And in every head, I hear a different name.

Tommy!

Reynard!

Nox!

Jessica!

Most of the names are dumb sounding or just, you know, not quite right. They *smell* off. But not all. Like Jessica. She's about thirty feet away, the length of the diner, and she was fighting a pair of vampires that had made it through the first rush. Now she's standing still, looking in the direction of the house, and the vampires are pushed up against her, their mouth proboscis in her neck and their wings curled all around her.

Jessica must be her true name. She said it in front of a Door once, and what one Door knows, they all know. My Door's using all the names it has to try and take just one more of us out.

It's doing everything it can to keep us from getting inside.

The fight's about equal now, if *equal* means hunters are outnumbered five to one, but they're at least holding their ground. I'm still standing back, parallel to Narnia in the pool. Her water whips are still flying around, keeping most of the malevolence in our tiny area. I don't know what would happen if she couldn't do it—I think the world really would die. But at least she's doing something. I'm just standing here.

It's not that I'm a coward. And it's not that I don't think this is my fight. But here is a true thing: I am extremely pragmatic. I need to survive for as long as possible, because I am the only person still alive who knows anything about Amanda. And that's what this is going to take. Hell is what you bring with you—the Door is what you need it to be.

I bet I know the things Amanda needs.

The black fog abruptly rears back and shrinks back into the pool house. I can't see Roxie. It looks almost normal, the house I mean, except for the part where it has an explosion tearing the living room up from the inside out and blood drips from the walls. The werewolves and vampires keep fighting, but they're dying, and now some hunters are binding up their wounds and looking at the house. We all know we have to go in. It's just a matter of how many of us are going to die to get in there.

One of the older hunters—not Ryan, thank god not Ryan—swears abruptly and makes a run for the house.

No no no no—I realize I'm chanting it, but not in his head, not with the voice that might save him. He pulls out a giant two-headed ax as he runs and ducks around hunters and demons and bodies, so many bodies. He runs until he hits the living room.

The walls of the pool house aren't real.

I thought we were looking at the house, all blown up, but we weren't. I'm not sure it's even a house anymore. The roof abruptly drops down to accommodate the slicing bite the house takes out of the hunter. His body is split into half a dozen pieces, and when those fall, they start to rot on the ground.

I am thinking that maybe getting into the house is going to be harder than it appears. Everyone else is having the same thought, because the survivors are getting together in small groups, still faction-based like idiots, but they are getting together. I can tell some stuff is happening, but I'm not a part of it.

Hey, I think in Narnia's direction. *You in there?*

New party trick? her voice says in my head.

You're one to talk about party tricks, blindey, I say. *Got anything I can do?*

Yes, she says. But then she doesn't say anything, and I get impatient.

And that would be . . . ?

I can hear her chuckle in my head, and it's almost not too bad. Kind of mellow, which is surprising. *Are you a hunter, or aren't you? Ride to the hounds, little hunter,* she says. *Hell is what you bring with you. Remember.* I can almost hear her turn off her internal radio and go back to bitch-slapping the situation from her little plume of water.

I wish I had Ryan here to bounce ideas off of and make sense of Narnia's crazy witch advice. Then again, I remember when Amanda and Stan and I were all caught smoking by the freshman English teacher in the school bathroom and tried to weasel our way out of detentions, and he said, "If wishes were horses, then beggars would ride." I thought about that a lot. The wishes I would wish if I could get horses out of the deal, never mind my complete lack of knowledge.

If wishes were horses . . . I'm not going to wish for a horse, particularly from a Door like that. But I bet . . . I bet I could find something to ride on.

I remember Ryan telling me that the big purple tentacle demon came because it felt some kind of affinity for me—or because something in me called to it. I remember him on the subway, saying we smelled like a demon already, the other demons wouldn't harass us.

I remember the lioness telling me I had experience loving things that do wrong without realizing it.

And I remember how one time, when we were seventeen, Amanda locked herself in the bathroom and cried and cried and I never found out why. She sounded so lonely, even though I was right there. And all I wanted to do was to just reach through the bathroom door and hold her.

Are you lonely? I call out to the house. *I want to help all lonely things.*

I see something move in the house.

Pretty soon, so does everybody else.

A giant, rolling, bruise-colored monster oozes out of the house. It's the size of two couches, one on top of the other. It has tentacles, dustings of fur at the tips, and it's using them to drag itself on the ground toward me.

This is a really, really big Door-hound. And I really, really hope I thought this out right.

The imaginary rabbit I had when I was six? Its name was Turtle. It looked absolutely nothing like this globular mess. I reach out with my mind and say, *Hi, Turtle. I'm so glad to see you.*

The tentacles move faster, the body swings closer. I will consider this a good sign, because the alternative is certain death. I stuff most of what I'm carrying by hand back into my pockets, and when the tentacle monster is within jumping-into-the-pool-to-escape distance, I say, *Take me inside.*

It doesn't even stop to think—I'm not sure it *can* think, really—just stops in front of me and lies down. If I don't mind walking on something squishy, I could walk right up on top of it.

Since that's the general idea, I do. And it *is* gross, I cannot even stress that enough. My shoes sink, and the whole demon smells like rotting fish.

Once I'm on, though, I'm golden. *Go into the house,* I think, and it gets up and starts to slither its way back. I sit down when the swaying gets too bad, and my butt sinks a little bit into Turtle's skin. Everybody's watching me make this attempt, but I can't see Ryan, even though I look. Maybe he's off getting killed, and is too busy to watch me make my move.

I guess I could die in a really nasty way in about a

minute, but by this point, so could anybody—if it's good enough for them, it's good enough for me.

Turtle slides over the patio, and we're at the explosion. *What a good boy. Go into the house,* I say again, and then I squinch my eyes as tightly shut as possible, because if I die, I would like to die without having to see any of my mangled corpse bits first, okay? I have very few desires in life, and that is officially one of them.

Turtle wasn't planning on stopping. He just steamrolls right in. And the house doesn't snap shut on me.

I'm in.

21

The inside of the house looks totally different from what we're seeing on the outside, and it is not an improvement. My Door's here, all right. It's different to see how big the Door is in person; it dwarfs everything. I bet Turtle could walk right through with me standing up and neither of us would touch the sides of my Door.

And we *could* just walk through, too, no trouble with this opening and closing bullshit. The iron gate is swung wide open, and the Door smells . . . okay, this is weird, but it smells *bloated*. It smells like it's been eating for hours, and it's stuffed to bursting but doesn't want to stop.

When I finally look away from my Door, I can see why.

Everything's a jumble, but I can see how it went down. There are some little things; sort of little, anyway. The kind of stuff I can see Amanda asking for just to test the Door out. Stacked on glass tabletops and strewn across the carpet are expensive shoes, expensive bags—really big cheesecakes, half-eaten, and heaps of boutique clothing. There's jewelry too, knuckle-sized diamonds and thick ropes of gold tennis bracelets, and a really astonishing array of drugs.

I recognize some of the clothes, some of the bags, from at least three weeks before the Door left the diner. I remember her jostling me into Ryan in the kitchen, giggling, saying she'd get the napkins for the holders, stepping over the line of salt and heading into the basement . . .

It happened right in front of us. We—I—

Shit.

I can't see Amanda anywhere in here. After the obvious stuff, things get even more out of control. Demons have been living here with her, I think, and they are not very tidy houseguests. I wonder what her parents think about that, and—then I can see it, I can just tell what she did next, I just *know* she started to wish for things to happen to people.

Amanda's always bitching about her parents. I can see them coming into the house just after she wished for the Door to come with her, away from the diner and the hunters. She'd sit there, right there in front, wishing anything that came into her head just because she could. Her parents would come in, and she'd turn toward them, and she'd say, *I wish—*

They were dicks, but I'm not sure they deserved whatever she might have wished on them. And it probably wasn't just them, after she took that plunge. I will bet good money that there are some names in the news in the next couple of weeks that I am way too familiar with.

And then after that . . . anything seems possible, doesn't it? With a Door granting you anything you want, and nothing to stop you, no stupid rules, no consequences, no regrets.

Except you asked her for things back, didn't you? I ask the Door.

Don't come close, the Door says thickly. It still sounds like a little girl, which it's never done before. I wonder if Amanda asked it to change, or if it's changed because it's been so close to Amanda. It does sound like her, a little bit.

Gonna blow up something again? I am a taunter. Shocking. I climb down off Turtle and send him to block the hole in the building. Don't want any hunters outside to get ideas about following me and getting their bodies torn into pieces. If anyone's making a grand exit, it's going to be me—and I'm not going anywhere.

I straighten my coat and then cross my arms. *So where's Amanda, big guy?* I ask. *Did you finally get her to walk in? One last big sacrifice and then you can call your own Apocalypse in?*

The Door doesn't say anything. But the iron gate, it starts to bleed. The blood smells like innocence. I don't want to know what Amanda's been feeding it, except I think I know anyway. She's never really liked animals.

Tell me where she is, Door, I say.

The gate swings, just the slightest bit. It says, *Behind you.*

"Hey, baby." It sounds like Amanda, if Amanda was dead. Amanda probably is dead. I turn around. I see her.

I carefully take off my sunglasses and hold them folded in my hand. It gives me a second to keep myself from throwing up. I'm not sure when it occurred to her to do it, before or after she killed her parents, before or after she splashed animal blood across the entrance to Hell, but at some point she decided that she could wish herself away. *Perfect plastic surgery,* that's what she said once. Hair any color, any length, any type. Skin any tone. Tall or tiny, curves or athletic skinniness. And then why bother with just the simple stuff? Turn on the TV, and there are celebrities marching across the screen; let's try them on too. And, Hell, get some of the men as well; I wonder how much sex she's having. Or had, anyway. Before it all started to break down.

Here is what I have learned about wishing things from Doors. After a while, it stops being a conscious decision. Me, I went one way with that. I stopped taking their garbage. I don't wish things anymore; I demand them. Roxie said the Doors were like animals; well, I'm the pack leader now. Queen of the Hats, indeed.

The other way you can go with wishing, I guess, is that if you can have everything, anything, any time, without even thinking . . . then maybe instead of one thing at a time, you get them all. At once. Forever.

Amanda is a monster.

Her skin bubbles as fat and bone twist, shrink, grow, and patches of color bloom across her like mold. Her hair is thick and writhing, twining around her as she steps closer. Limps closer, anyway; her legs are short, long, male, female, melting in and out of shape as she comes closer. She smiles at me; I think it's supposed to be a smile.

"Look what I did," she says. Her voice is getting all screwed up by all the shapes her throat is trying to be. "Isn't it wild?"

I nod. "Yeah. Yeah, it is."

"I'm telling you, those hunters are all lying shits," she says. " 'Don't talk to the Door, don't ask the Door for things.' 'It'll be your worst nightmare.' *What*ever. Oh my god, Allie, I have done the most *amazing* things."

Tears sting my eyes. "Yeah?"

The thing that was Amanda nods. "Totally." She giggles. "I tried to call you at the diner for some of the best stuff, but you were never around."

"I tried to call you, too. You never answered your phone."

Amanda frowns, and lifts her hand. A cell phone bubbles out of her skin. She looks at the phone for a moment, not even freaking out about the *cell phone growing out of her hand,* then she waves it in the air. "Huh," she says. "Bad reception. I'm sorry," she says, and she's *sorry,* she's actually fucking *sorry*. I could always tell when she was faking something. This . . . in the middle of all this, she's sorry she didn't check her fucking messages.

I swallow. "It's okay. It wasn't—it wasn't really important."

She brightens. "I'm really glad you came, actually. I think you should do this too. And, Stan, obviously. Could you call him? We should do something together, something really big."

"I can't call Stan." I settle for something like the truth. "He's roaming."

"Figures," Amanda says. "That's okay, though. You're here. Come on."

Come on, Allie, says the Door.

I was right. It *is* mimicking her voice.

Hurray for me.

"No," I say. "I think that'd be a bad idea."

Amanda's eyes narrow. Her mood turns on a dime. "God, Allie, what the hell? You listen to Ryan too fucking much," she spits out. She looks me up and down, actually seeing what I'm wearing, and her voice fills with disgust. "And you're *dressed* like them."

I rock slightly on my feet, settling my hips, squaring my shoulders. My hands clench, and the rhinestones on my sunglasses bite—I forgot I was holding them. "It's been a really busy couple of days," I say.

Come on, the Door says. It is sounding less bloated, more antsy.

I am busy here, please wait your turn, I say back.

Amanda flinches, and there's the tiniest whimper. She could hear my Door voice. And whatever she says about it, somewhere in her—some part that's still Amanda— she's frightened.

"Amanda," I say quietly. "We can fix this. If we go outside, together, we can get you help. You don't have to stay here with it. It can't make you."

She wavers. Literally. For a moment, Amanda, the real Amanda, forms out of the mess, and she's staring at me. Her eyes are the prettiest blue, I swear. I wanted eyes like hers when I was younger. And that soft mouth that she never appreciated, she's biting it now, and I can see blood welling up.

"I have to fix it first," she whispers. "I can do it, I can totally do it, I just have to—"

"No!" The sound tears itself from me, breaking out, and I reach for her, for my Amanda, but it's too late. She melts into a dozen shapes, and I can hear her, in my head I hear *I wish I wish one more thing*—

My Door laughs, and its gate swings out into the room, and when it swings back it has pulled Amanda against it, and through the Door, and then she's gone, whatever she's turned into, she's gone.

And that leaves me alone, in a house of dead wishes, with a suddenly very powerful and crowing Door.

Allie, the Door laughs, *I feel so good!* And it starts to grow. And it's not stopping. Could it grow big enough to eat the world? It's starting to look it.

I can't win against something like that. Not me alone, not me with all the hunters we could ever get together. And it's not listening to me anymore. Guess it thinks it's the queen now.

So . . . since I can't win, I might as well cheat.

Turtle, I say, *go fetch.*

The purple tentacle monster squirms out the blown-out side of the house and comes back a minute later with Ryan crouching on its back. Half of Ryan's face is covered in dried blood, and his lamia leather is shredded. The fun must have gotten more so after I came inside. Turtle dumps him down next to me and squirms back to the hole.

"Hi," I say to Ryan. "Do you hear anything weird?"

He's staring at me like I'm a ghost. I cough. "Yes," he says.

"Good," I say. "Wish for something."

He stops looking like I'm from beyond the grave, and starts heading toward annoyed. Thank god.

I finger my sunglasses; I suddenly remember that Amanda gave them to me. I put them on.

"Trust me," I say. "Ask *me* a wish."

Ryan says, "I trust you," and then I can feel the heat of his wish roll over me. I can't hear it, not precisely, but I can feel the power needed to fulfill it.

Listen: I have opened Doors. As of five minutes ago, I am the only person in hunter history—and Narnia *knows* the history—to open a Door, and survive the experience, and then *learn* from it. I've learned a lot of things in the last six years. Salt magic, contagion magic. I've got salt in my hand, now, and that salt touched all the Doors of the city, at least, when the Hand spread the waters of life. Add that to my blood, and whatever affects my blood in one place affects my blood in another.

I take out my good knife and slice my palm. Blood freely given is powerful. Ryan told me that.

My blood opened and closed nine Doors in Hell, and I created a tenth one.

My blood is in Doors. Ergo, the Doors are in me. And I want to grant Ryan's wish.

In this way, in this moment, for this man, for this reason: I *am* a Door.

I flare up, and I can feel Hells within me. I am bigger than this fucking wannabe Door in front of me. *You,* I say, and my voice is booming, *were made by a couplet that didn't even rhyme.*

Allie! it cries. It's shaking, shrinking. *I gave you so much, so much—don't you remember all the things you asked for? I gave them all to you! I gave you Ryan!*

Low blow, Door. I open my gates. *Sure,* I say, and my voice is rock hard. *But what have you done for me* lately?

My gates are iron. Iron kills. I learned that too. I learned it from Ryan. I learned everything from Ryan.

I wonder what he wished for.

Good-bye, I whisper, just for him, and I slam my gate against the Door.

The world ends. Some world, anyway. Really.

Good thing I'm just a girl who runs a diner, deep down. I may be a Door too, but I've got silver in me. Silver heals. Amanda couldn't do it; she never fought, she never earned the scars. I did.

Maybe it's just an allegory, but I take the last of the power from Ryan's wish, and I fix the world.

22

The kid guarding the Door is just that—a kid. He sleeps on the cot, eats the food I bring him, and reads a lot of comic books. When he fights the demons that come through the Door, he fights them quietly, without a lot of fuss. So he can't be that young, or he's been doing this for longer than I expect, because he's technically better than I am.

But he's not Ryan. He's not Ryan, and he's not sarcastic or snide, and he doesn't look at me with heat in his eyes. He doesn't wear a Stetson—he's a Baseball Cap. But he doesn't even bother trying to flirt. I'm sure he's heard the stories about me—how I opened the Door he guards. How I walked through a Door and came out the other side, how I rode a demon into a gutted house, how I used salt and silver to bring balance back into the world and keep more Doors from opening.

But my heart is dead. Stan is dead, Amanda is dead—all I had left were the diner and Ryan, and

Ryan's gone. I never even found out his real name. And I got my period the second day back, so it's not like there's going to be a mini-Ryan running around. Which I am pretty happy about, don't get me wrong; this isn't a life for babies. But . . .

I feel like all of it was for nothing—my life is emptier now, and saving the world, saving all those people . . . it wasn't as fulfilling as I thought it would be. I've walked through blood and fire, literally, and it wasn't enough— nothing I did was enough to keep Stan, to keep Amanda, to keep Ryan.

The Door gave me a booming business, and it gave me Ryan. The Door's quiet now, almost well-behaved— it opens like clockwork, like a normal Door, and it hardly talks at all.

And Ryan's gone.

I don't want to believe it was the Door, but the alternative is that I scared the living bejeezus out of him with my little "I'm a Door, FYI" revelation, and that's almost worse. Whatever it was, he left. He left me. He didn't even kiss me one last time; when I went back to just being Allie, when it was all over . . . the Door was back where it belonged, in the basement of the diner, and I was standing in front of it, and Ryan was gone.

The next morning, I was freshly showered, no longer smelling of brimstone and blood and silver. I was chopping peppers and onions for homefries, expecting Ryan to stroll through at any moment with a complaint about the Fedoras, a pile of questions, and a bitching-out for leaving without helping clean up . . . But what I got was this kid, this kid who said, "You can call me California," and I almost burst into tears right there.

"You can call me Allie," I replied. "Door's in the basement. Breakfast and lunch are free, but you've gotta sing for your supper and wash the dishes."

"I've never worked in a diner before," said California. "You'll have to show me."

"No problemo," I told him. "You'll love it. It will satisfy a need in you that you never knew you had." I was only half joking.

Now that it's been almost a month, I call him Cal and sometimes we sing along to the same bad pop music on the radio while we clean the kitchen at night. Say what you want about Fall Out Boy and Britney Spears, but there's no balm for the soul like a good slug of pop music.

But Cal's no Ryan. He doesn't steal my soap or make bad decisions about his emotional life or get angry with me when I accidentally use my psychic Door powers to make customers buy things they don't really want, like that skinny girl who bought the slice of key lime pie. I'm pretty sure she puked it up later, but I didn't make her *want* it, I only made her want to buy it. Once she bought it, eating it was automatic.

It's weird, the way my powers work. I'm still learning about them. There's no one to teach me, though, so

I figure that pretty soon I am going to fuck it up beyond all repair, and I'm going to have to post a notice
in *The Village Voice* for a psychic witch to come help
me. Anyone but Narnia, that's all I ask.

And I'm all set to learn to live my life without Ryan.
I've got it all planned out: I will be a badass older
hunter, fighting elementals like Roxie, telling stories of
my wayward youth, sung about in songs about the
Hells, a legend among my generation, a myth for gener-
ations to come.

Except then I turn around, belting out the sugary
lyrics to the Hillary Duff song on the radio as I put
more slices of pie in the dessert refrigerator, and there's
Narnia.

Dammit, I said anyone *but* her.

She's wearing Anne Taylor, which I can only assume
she's doing because that's what she considers slumming. She takes a seat in one of the window booths,
facing me, and she shoves the menu aside in favor of
staring at me. Her eyes are flashing again. Great.

I pick up two slices of that key lime pie and a couple rolls of silverware and head over to her table. She
makes a face when I put the dessert in front of her. I
carefully do not use the Door voice to suggest that she
should totally eat it, since that is probably bad eti-
quette with psychics.

"Cal does a good job here," I say, and take a bite of
pie. Delicious. Notice how I am not asking about Ryan,

by the way. I am many things, and I hope pathetic isn't one of them anymore.

"Really?" Narnia drawls. "How does he . . . compare?"

Pathetic, no. Vengeful, yes. If I find out by the end of this conversation that Narnia has Ryan in her bedroom and has for the last month, she is going to eat an entire *pie* before I let her leave.

I shrug casually. "He fights well. Nothing escapes. Then again, nothing big is really trying to get out these days."

She snorts. "Not surprising. I was not pleased when I realized I was going to have to write a study about you for the records."

I blink. "Really?"

"Don't get your hopes up, I'm going to avoid as much actual contact with you as possible." She shakes her head. "That's not why I'm here, though."

"Oh?" I say. I am the queen of gentle inquiry. Watch me eat pie with casual aplomb.

Narnia unrolls the silverware and pulls the fork out. She pokes at the plate. "What *is* this?"

"It is key lime pie, shut up, and if you don't tell me what is going on I am going to—"

"Do what?" Narnia stares at me, and, *rude,* I can feel her in my *head*.

Kick you out of my diner, bitch, I yell in her head. She flinches. I win.

Sort of. She looks at me again, though keeps out of my head. "So you're not going to, I don't know, become a Door again? Try to cure poverty and world hunger and hangnails with the power of your Hell magic? Make me eat pie whether I want to or not? Thank you, I *did* hear that one."

Oh. Um. "Um," I say. "I don't think so."

She sits back, and after a moment looks around. "Not that busy for lunchtime."

"It's doing better," I say. A little bit at a time, I'm finding ways to make the diner better without a Door doing it for me. I'm letting Dawn do more of the menu writing again, for one thing, and paying for her to get cooking classes. Little things like that. It'll work, eventually. And it'll be *real*.

Narnia abruptly nods. "Good," she says. She sticks her fork into the pie and cuts a huge bite. Before she puts it in her mouth, she says, "I'm sure everybody will be glad to come back here."

Wait. What?

She swallows and gets another bite. "Roxie's been chomping at the bit, for one thing. I mean, I've had to keep you in quarantine for a *month*. And, of course, I was worried *he* was going to go rogue on me just to see you through the window."

Wait. *What?*

"One semi-rogue and one mundane Door. No wonder you're both trouble," she says this time. "I should just reassign him back here and get both of you out of my hair."

I swallow and push my plate away. "Quarantine?"

Narnia nods, and picks up the last bite on her plate. "All hunters out, except California—he's going to end up being psychic, the *proper* way, and he's got protections laid on him to combat any Hell magic you might've leveled at him. Except you haven't. Cal's had nothing but good to say of you, which makes me doubt his abilities, but he's young yet." She chews, and swallows, and picks up my plate and sets it on hers. "You were a *Door*, Allie," she says as she cuts into my pie, hey, *my* pie. "You still are, or can be. Doors aren't good. I needed to know how far you fell."

I clear my throat, and—"The Door said it gave me Ryan," I say abruptly, and that was *not* planned, oh my god.

Narnia rolls her eyes. "Doors lie, don't you learn anything? *I* gave you Ryan. Idiot."

I'm grinning. Ear to ear. I poke Narnia's stack of plates. "So you eat, huh?"

"Are you kidding?" she says. "I eat like a horse. I was just staying away from your food because I'm not sure the health inspector's ever actually been on the *premises*."

"Bitch."

We actually smile at one another. Go figure. She

snaps her fingers, which I'm pretty sure is for dramatic effect, and the diner door slams open.

Ryan's standing in the doorway of the diner, Stetson in hand, half-smoked hand-rolled cigarette in the other, and he's staring at me.

"Holy . . ." I gasp a little. "Ryan." I glare at Narnia. "You did not tell me he was *here*," I mutter.

She smirks, and finishes my pie.

"Allie," Ryan says. He drops the cigarette and hurries toward me.

"Holy shit," comes a voice from the back. "This is Ryan?" Cal comes through the swinging door, where he's been washing pots. "Ryan?"

"Who're you?" demands Ryan, looking from Cal to me. Dawn pops out of the pass-through and is watching avidly. I think I can hear her cheering.

"Cool it, you jerk. He's the new hunter guarding the Door. Since my old hunter fucking *disappeared*!" I yell.

"I had to go!" he yells back.

"Oh yeah?" We sound like little kids.

"Yeah!"

We're toe to toe now, and I'm not backing down. "What was so important that you left me covered in the blood of my friends?"

"*I* didn't leave. *You* left," he says.

"Well it's not as if I went to *Newark*, I have been here this entire time and you *knew* it!"

That sets him back. And, okay, if Narnia had some magical thing set up where he couldn't get to me, it wasn't really fair either. We're both a little taken aback, and that seems to reset him to whatever he meant to say when he came into the diner.

"Allie, you're one of the strongest mundanes I've ever met," he tries, and I stop him right there.

"I've walked through Hell, I have an air elemental as my avatar, and I am a *Door to Hell*—"

"I was *there*," says Ryan, and he shoves his Stetson on his head like some kind of weird battle gear.

"Then you'd know that if there's anything I am, it's not *mundane*. Try again," I order.

"Allie, you're so damn powerful, I just—"

"Had to go hide behind your pet witch?" I hear Narnia mutter behind me, but I am beyond that. I put a hand on my hip and cock it out. That's right, bitch, I am so happy to see you I want to die, but fuck if you're getting off the hook.

"I was *scared*!" he bellows. "Not about the Door thing, fuck the Door thing. Do you want to know what I wished, when you asked me to wish something? When you asked me if I trusted you, and I fucking do, I trust you more than I've trusted anyone, and— Look, every other woman—I told you this, they all *died*. I killed them, with the demons and the Doors and the hunting. None of them could do what you did and live. None of them—"

"None of them were me." I fold my arms across my chest. "And I don't know what you wished, because no one's been around here to *tell* me."

He backs up and leans against a booth. His lamia leather gleams in the sunlight, and his mouth looks really kissable. I wouldn't mind kissing it, if kissing happened to be on the menu.

"Allie, you're the first woman I haven't had to protect. You're the first woman I've loved who's survived what I do. You're the first woman who could stand beside me—hell, you could take me out if you really wanted to." His gaze is clear and direct. He's not bullshitting. My heart is exploding.

I skip right to the important stuff: "You love me, huh?"

And he says it, just says it, like I haven't been waiting for this moment for six years—almost seven, at this point. Seven years, and he just says it. "I love you, Allie."

I move closer to him, arms still crossed.

"And?" I say grimly. As grimly as I can, considering I want to dance around the stupid kitchen.

"And when you asked me to, I wished that you would kick the ass of every fucking demon in the world. I wished that you knew you could do it even without my wishing it. I wished—"

I reach for him and he's there, in my arms.

"You are such a jerk," I say into his neck. I wrap my

arms around his waist; he's lost some weight. A few meals of Sally's Diner's special beef stew will take care of that.

"I'm sorry," he mutters into my hair. "I told Narnia that if she didn't pull you out of quarantine I was going to go open a Door and find you myself."

I am clearly a bad influence. "I . . ."

He pulls back. He looks worried. "I mean, if that's what you want. I—we—it doesn't have to change, if—"

Oh, so insecure. Gotta fix that. "I love you too, you know. I don't want you to protect me, I just—I just want you to stand beside me." It's the right thing to say. When I tilt my head up, he looks a little relieved; I want to kiss him. But: "If I wasn't a Door, I'd be a Fedora," I say stupidly.

"That's all right; I'm a jackass either way." His hand is in my hair, deep in it, cradling my head.

"At least we both know our flaws." I'm breathless, leaning into him, on my tiptoes so that our faces are even.

"I—I—" he stutters.

"You'd better be sorry."

"I'm sorry."

"You'd better be so much more than sorry."

"I'm so much more than sorry, you don't even know. Mostly because I've spent the last month thinking of all the right things to say and—" He stops and laughs, a real, genuine laugh. "I'm sorry, Allie."

"My name—" He shakes his head, but I put my fingers over his mouth. I'm barely speaking, my voice is just a breath, just a hint in his mind. "My name is Autumn. You can call me Allie."

"My name is Rian," he says, and there's that hint of his accent rolling through. I can't wait to learn where it's from, where *he's* from, what he's all about. I can't wait for all the fights we're going to have; I can't wait for the future. "You can call me Ryan."

And then our mouths are touching. Our mouths are finally touching, and he's finally back, and everything in the universe feels like it's slotting into place. I have my diner back, I have my Door with its disgusting demons that need to be killed, and I have Ryan.

I pull back just enough to say: "Don't tell Narnia, but I still have the purple tentacle monster. I got it a really big dog bed."

His arms come around me and hold me tightly to him. He laughs, and I can't resist: I knock the Stetson off his head, and it falls to the floor while we just kiss and kiss and kiss.

TOR
ROMANCE

Believe that love is magic

P lease join us at the website below
for more information about this
author and other great romance
selections, and to sign up for our
monthly newsletter!

www.tor-forge.com